U0010287

動物農莊

Animal Farm

政治諷刺小說最高傑作

喬治‧歐威爾 ——— 著

李立瑋 ——— 譯

晨星出版

愛藏本086

動物農莊【中英雙語版】
Animal Farm

掃描填寫線上回函，
立即享有晨星網路書店
50元購書金。

作　　者｜喬治‧歐威爾（George Orwell）
譯　　者｜李立瑋
繪　　者｜楊宛靜

責任編輯｜林儀涵
封面設計｜柯俊仰
封面繪圖｜曾銘祥
美術編輯｜黃偵瑜

創 辦 人｜陳銘民
發 行 所｜晨星出版有限公司
　　　　　台中市407工業區30路1號
　　　　　TEL：04-23595820　FAX：04-23550581
　　　　　E-mail：service@morningstar.com.tw
　　　　　http://www.morningstar.com.tw
　　　　　行政院新聞局版版台業字第2500號
法律顧問｜陳思成律師
讀者專線｜TEL：02-23672044 / 04-23595819#212
　　　　　FAX：02-23635741 / 04-23595493
　　　　　E-mail：service@morningstar.com.tw
網路書店｜http://www.morningstar.com.tw
郵政劃撥｜15060393（知己圖書股份有限公司）
印　　刷｜上好印刷股份有限公司

出版日期｜2016年03月15日
再版五刷｜2023年12月15日
定　　價｜新台幣300元‧特價199元
ISBN 978-986-443-104-5
Printed in Taiwan
All Right Reserved
版權所有‧翻印必究
如有缺頁或破損，請寄回更換

國家圖書館出版品預行編目資料
動物農莊 / 喬治‧歐威爾（George Orwell）著；李立瑋譯
臺中市：晨星，2016.03
愛藏本；86
譯自：Animal Farm
ISBN 978-986-443-104-5（平裝）
CIP 873.57　104028417

動物農莊・導讀

ANIMAL FARM

文字工作者／伊象菁

通往動物農莊的路不是單一的。如果按著前人的定論對號入座，在對照了作者歐威爾的企圖之後，或許會有原來如此的感受，但那肯定會少了寓言原有的興味。若是按圖索驥地將歷史事件一一明列，只能說是閱讀小說時天馬行空的想像力，恐怕會因而被勒緊韁繩。不過作為通往動物農莊的路徑之一，回過頭來說，動物農莊果真是一個充滿想像力的地方。

在由動物農莊的內容去談一些被延伸出來的問題之前，我們還是先回過頭來了解歐威爾當初創作的初衷，亦不失為另一種閱讀的方向，也是許多書評認為動物農莊的最大寓意，針對一九一七年俄國的二月革命到一九四三年底德黑蘭會議的蘇聯歷史，即史達林虛假的社會主義體制以及當時與蘇聯同一陣營的英美等國作出的嚴厲諷刺，希望可以以尖銳的筆觸提醒世人，蘇聯的社會主義不過是披著羊皮的狼，政客們為一己之私，無謂於百姓絲毫沒有減少的痛苦。

我們也幾乎可以將小說中的人物與事件與現實作一對照。老少校為列寧，拿破崙為史達林，雪球為托洛斯基。拿破崙手下的九隻惡犬正是俄國國家祕密警察，盲從的羊群為青年共產主義同盟，仲斯先生被影射為俄國沙皇，狐木農莊的皮爾金頓先生為英國，平徹菲爾德農莊的弗雷德里克先生為德國。小說中最重要的風車為產業五年計畫，還有其它的事件都可以找到對應的現實情況來一一呼應。不過歐威爾雖然是以俄國的社會主義作為諷刺的對象，但事實上最重要的還是要洞悉在整個事件背後被操控的權力問題。這也是以下所延伸出來的切入點。

權力，在此書裡以各種形式呈現。但即使權力改了各種樣貌，由誰來行使，都有著使人著魔與腐化的魔力。不管一開始動物們因為無法忍受權力而鬥爭，或者為了反抗人類剝削而鬥爭，到動物們成功地推翻人類的宰制而得著所謂的自由來說；權力，在鬥爭的過程裡，在鬥爭結束之後，都確實地被所謂的領導者以各種名義行使著，因此在鬥爭之前的私人資本的擁有或者領導者對動物們的控制，在結束鬥爭之後仍舊是存在著。

在這裡我們可以由小說中的情節導出一個食物鏈。權力是抽象的，唯有在被利用時成為具體可陳的事實，而利用者必須藉由私人資本的擁有以及對其他人生活的宰制，以成就他成為領導者，此一唯一獨有的階級。階級的產生必須以暴力形式呈現並維持，透過暴力的行使建立了階級的制度，而知識在本書裡，更是階級的體現，擁有知識者便是領導者，知識象徵權力，因此在本書裡的領導者無不獨攬知識與教育的權力，並以規訓與懲罰替代了原有的溝通與教育。

我們以本書的微言大義來體認這個世界的脈動，將會發現不管是在實行社會主義的國家或者資本主義國家，這個食物鏈緊緊地扣住甚至制約了每個人的生活。但我們必須深刻地思考果真是權力使人腐化嗎？權力是否真如小說之中所陳述，罪惡是本質的存在；或者是擁有權力者使權力腐化了？權力的本質究竟是什麼，或許才是歐威爾最想讓讀者們去思考的問題吧！

以權力的角度閱讀動物農莊或許是很嚴肅的，而且在歐威爾如此明顯的隱喻下，讀者的確也很容易地對號入座。我們或許可以再開啟另一個視窗，再從語言的角度來閱讀這部小說。當我們既定成俗地將豬指涉為貪婪、骯髒的對象時，歐威爾卻將豬打破慣例地另外樹立了一個聰明甚至狡滑的角色時，在閱讀上是否產生了另類的想像空間，這樣的例子在本書中俯拾皆是，很值得用心以自身的經歷去體會小說裡的寓意。

其實最有趣的閱讀方式是根本不要對本書有任何先入為主的想法，就只是去閱讀，看歐威爾如何將每個角色活靈活現地塑造出來。也不要再去想他要諷刺些什麼，歐威爾並沒有要告訴讀者什麼偉大的歷史，而是人性的本質，權力的本質，他們體現在每個人的人生之中，並因之不同。動物農莊其實真的要花點時間，好好地繞繞幾圈的。

第一章

入夜了，瓊斯先生鎖上了雞舍，在提燈光亮的搖曳中醉醺醺地穿過院子。到了後門，他啪啪兩聲甩掉了靴子，逕直進了儲藏室，又為自己滿上了最後的一杯啤酒，一飲而盡。接著，便循著瓊斯夫人的酣聲搖搖晃晃地摸上了床。

臥室的燈光剛一熄滅，整個農莊裡便泛起了一陣喧鬧。因為一種言論已經在日間傳遍，說是大豬梅傑——就是曾得過「美麗鬃毛獎」的那頭雄豬——在前一天晚上作了一個怪夢，他急於把夢的內容告知其他動物們。全體動物於是約定，一旦確定瓊斯先生不在後，他們就要在大穀倉裡聚會。因為大豬梅傑（他在動物圈裡一直有著這個稱號，儘管他曾以「威靈頓美神」的

008

名字在「肥豬展覽會」上獨領風騷）在農莊中的無上威望，每位動物無不情願犧牲一個小時的睡眠時間來聽聽他到底要說些什麼。

大穀倉一頭的平臺上，大豬梅傑安坐在他的草墊上，頭上的橫梁懸著吊燈。大豬梅傑已經十二歲了，近來已有些發福，但仍不失為一頭有著威嚴外表的豬。很快地，動物們漸漸聚齊，各按各的習性坐定位。最先到的是三隻狗：藍鈴、傑西和小鉗。然後是一群豬，坐在最靠近平臺的位置上。母雞們棲在窗臺，鴿子們則在椽子上撲楞著翅膀，綿羊和母牛臥在豬群的後面不停地反芻。一同進來的兩匹馬是拳師和克羅薇，他們的腳步很輕，多毛的蹄子仔細地尋找落點，惟恐傷到躲在乾草下的小動物。克羅薇是一匹已近中年的母馬，自從生了第四匹小駒之後就再也恢復不了往日的身材。拳師則是一匹高頭大馬，魁梧而強壯，雖然並不具備一流的智慧，卻有著眾所公認的堅韌與勤勞。隨後進來的是山羊穆勒和驢子本傑明。本傑明是農莊裡最老的動物，也是脾氣最壞的動物。他很少說話，縱使開了口，也脫不了尖刻與憤世

嫉俗的口吻。比如，他會說，上帝給了他一條驅趕蒼蠅的尾巴，但他寧願上帝既沒有創造蒼蠅也沒有創造尾巴。他從來都一臉嚴肅，他說沒有什麼事情值得他發笑。值得一提的是，儘管他自己從不承認，但他確實是和拳師非常投合，他們兩個經常一起在果園裡消磨時間，肩並肩地吃著草，卻從不說一句話。

一群找不到媽媽的小鴨子隨後湧了進來，尋找合適的落腳處以防被大動物們踩到。克羅薇把前腿圍成了圈，給了這些小鴨子一片可以安睡的棲息之地。她是一匹為瓊斯先生拉座車的母馬，扭扭捏捏地晃了進來。她擠到前方一個顯眼的地方，瀟灑地抖了抖鬃毛，想把大家的注意力吸引到她那紮在鬃毛上的漂亮紅絲帶上。最後進來的是貓，像往常一樣四下張望著找尋最暖和的地方，最後擠在拳師和克羅薇之間。

白馬莫莉照例是要遲到的。

除了睡在後門外的烏鴉摩西，所有的動物都已到齊了。大豬梅傑見到大家都已安然落座並且全神貫注，便清了清嗓子開始講話：「同志們，你們一定都已聽說我昨晚的怪夢了。但是，我想過一會兒再講我的夢。有些事情我想先說。同志們，我的大限將至，但在我死前，我覺得有義務將自己的一些心得和大家分享。我已走過了漫漫長路，我已費盡了無窮的思索，我想我已明白了生命的真諦，我想這就是我要對你們說的。

「同志們，我們活著究竟是為了什麼？看看吧，我們的生命悲慘、勞苦而短暫。我們吃飽飯不過是為了讓身體還能夠繼續工作，直到用盡最後的一點力氣；當我們不再有用的時候，就會被殘忍地送進屠宰場。在整個英格蘭，只有那些一歲以下的幼獸才懂得什麼是快樂，什麼是休閒。在整個英格蘭，沒有一隻動物是自由的。在動物的生命裡，只有悲慘和奴役：這就是赤裸裸的現實。

「但這就是命運嗎？這只是因為我們的土地貧瘠得不能讓他的子民過上體面的生活？不是的，同志們，絕對不是！我們的英格蘭土地肥沃、氣候宜人，即使我們的數量再多上幾倍也吃不完它所提供的食物。單是我們的這個小農莊就足夠養活十二匹馬、二十頭牛和上百隻綿羊——而且，都能過上比我們現在更舒適、更體面的生活。為什麼我們還要再繼續這種悲慘處境呢？因為人類，人類從我們的手裡偷走了我們幾乎全部的產出。同志們，這就是問題的答案。歸結成一個詞——人類。人類是我們唯一的敵人。除掉人類，就永遠除掉了勞苦和飢餓。「人類是這世上唯一一種只消費不生產的生物。他不產奶，不下蛋，力不能拉犁，跑不能逐兔，但他是所有動物的主人。他讓所有的動物為他工作，但他給動物們的食物卻只能勉強讓我們不致餓死，自己好從中掠奪剩下的產出。是我們在辛勤地耕地，是我們的糞便使大地肥沃，但兩手空空的也是我們。乳牛們，去年我看見你們擠出了成千加侖的奶，這本該餵養出強壯牛犢的奶水到哪裡去了？每一滴都流進了我們敵人的喉嚨裡！你們，母雞們，去年你們又生了多少個蛋？其中只有可憐的幾隻被孵成了小雞，剩下的都被送到市場上？瓊斯的人換得了錢幣。還有你，克羅薇，你生的四隻馬駒都到哪裡去了？有誰來供養和安慰你的晚年？

牠們都在剛滿一歲的時候被賣掉了，你再也沒有見過他們。而你又得到了什麼？不過是一口食物和一個窩。

「甚至，這樣的悲慘生活還不能讓我們安享天年。至於我，我是從來不為自己抱怨什麼的。我已經十二歲了，有了四百多個子孫。這只是每一頭豬都該享有的正常生活。但是，沒有哪一隻動物逃過刀斧。你們這些年輕人是不會像我這樣幸運的。你，拳師，當你老邁無力的時候，瓊斯先生會毫不猶豫地把你賣掉，你會被殘忍地割斷喉嚨，你的肉會成為狗食。狗老了也沒有好運，瓊斯先生會在他們的脖子上繫上磚頭，把它們溺死在最近的湖裡。

「這還不夠清楚嗎？同志們，所有的邪惡都源自人類的暴政。只有消滅了人類，我們的勞動果實才能真正被我們自己所有；只要消滅了人類，我們會在一夜之間變得富有而自由。同志們，這就是我要告訴你們的兩個字：革命！我不知道革命會在什麼時候開始，也許要等一個星期，也許要等上一百年，但我清清楚楚地知道，正義是終將來臨的。仔細看吧，也許就在你短暫的餘生裡。並且，把我的意思傳達給你們的後來人，讓我們的子子孫孫都為正義而奮鬥，直到有一天正義終於來臨。

「記住，做了決定就不能動搖。關於那些人和動物有著共同利益的話連聽都不要聽，那全是一派胡言。人都是自私的。我們動物要聯合起來與之戰鬥，所有的人類都是敵人，所有的動物都是同志。」

這時，聽眾中起了一陣騷動。四隻老鼠爬出洞來聆聽梅傑的演說，卻在狗的追逐下倉皇地逃回了洞裡。「同志們，」梅傑要求肅靜，「有一點必須要明確，那些野生的動物，比如老鼠、野兔，究竟是我們的朋友還是敵人？讓我們投票表決。」

表決很快地結束了，站在老鼠一邊的占了壓倒多數，只有三隻狗和一隻貓投了反對票。

梅傑繼續他的談話：「我要說的已經不多了，只是有一點還要強調：你們要永遠記住，兩條腿的是敵人，四條腿的是朋友。而且，我們不能模仿人類，即使我們已征服了他們，也不能沾染他們的惡習。我們不能住在房子裡，不能睡在床上，不能穿衣，不能喝酒，不能抽煙，更不能去摸錢、從事交易。人類的所有習性都是邪惡的。當然，最重要的是，任何動物都不能淩駕同類。無論是弱小的還是強壯的，無論是聰明的還是蠢笨的，全都是兄弟。動物決不能殘殺他的同類。所有的動物都是平等的。現在，我該告訴你們昨晚我到底夢見了什麼？這個夢難於描述。它展示了一個未來，一個人類已被全部消滅的未來。它讓我想起了一些我久已忘記的東西。那是多年以

前，當我還是一隻小豬的時候，媽媽和牠的同輩們經常唱起的一支老歌，那

個我曾熟悉的調子現在早已忘記。但在昨夜，它又重回到我的夢裡。這首歌

我要唱給你們聽：儘管我已年老，嗓音已沙啞，但當你們跟著我的旋律的

時候，你們會比我唱得更好。這首歌叫做「英格蘭的野獸」。大豬梅傑清了

清嗓子就唱了起來。儘管如他所說，它的嗓音確實有些沙啞，但依舊唱得很

好，況且這是一支很能打動人的旋律。歌詞是這樣的：

英格蘭的野獸，愛爾蘭的野獸，

所有地方的野獸們，

聆聽我這只歡快的歌，

唱的是我們金色的未來。

那一天遲早會到來：

人類的暴政將被推翻，

在英格蘭富饒的大地上，

只有野獸們在自由穿行。

皮鞭也不會再響。

馬刺會永遠的腐爛，

背上也不再有鞍韉，

我們的鼻子上不再戴著籠頭，

富饒得超過我們的想像，

所有的穀物，所有的糧食，

在那一天將全部屬於我們。

動物農莊

英格蘭的田野將會陽光普照，

流水清澈，微風和煦，

那一天我們將獲得自由。

牛，馬，鵝，驢各種動物

勞動是為了自由的緣故。

那時候我們都將工作，

儘管死亡仍不可避免，

英格蘭的野獸，愛爾蘭的野獸，

所有地方的野獸們，

聆聽我這只歡快的歌，

唱的是我們金色的未來。

歌聲使所有的動物激動不已，他們漸漸地都跟著梅傑開始了哼唱。最笨的動物也已明瞭了大意，聰明者如豬和狗早已經心領神會。終於，農莊裡爆發了輝煌的合唱：牛在哞哞地吼，狗在汪汪地吠，羊在咩咩地叫，馬在希律地嘶鳴。看他們這般極度亢奮的樣子，怕是要唱上整個通宵了。

不幸的是，這聲響驚動了瓊斯先生。他確信是溜進了狐狸，於是匆忙下床抓了一把槍，向著黑夜連射六彈，子彈射進了穀倉的牆裡。動物們的聚會便匆忙散場了，大家都飛也似的逃回了各自的樓所，農莊在一瞬間恢復了往日的寧靜。

人類是世上唯一一只消費不生產的生物，但為什麼人類可以成為所有動物的主宰？

020

第二章

三天後，大豬梅傑在睡夢中平靜地死去，遺體被埋在了花園的一角。

這是早春三月，接下來的三個月裡，有許多的活動在祕密地進行著。梅傑的話給了農莊裡那些愛思考的動物們嶄新的生存觀。雖然他們並不知道梅傑預言的革命會在何時開始，也完全沒有理由認為這場革命是今生今世的事情，但他們都很清楚，為這場革命鋪路已成了自己畢生的責任。宣傳與組織的工作自然地落在了豬的身上，因為他們被公認是動物當中最聰慧的。豬群當中，有兩隻公豬最為出類拔萃，一隻名叫雪球，另一隻名叫拿破崙，都是瓊斯先生準備養大了賣掉的。拿破崙是農莊裡唯一的一隻波克夏豬，體形碩大，面目略微有些猙獰，話不多，卻很有主見。雪球的性格比較開朗，講話快，富於創造性的活力，但總嫌不夠沉穩。農莊裡的其他公豬都是些食用豬，最有名的一隻叫做史奎爾，臉頰滾圓，愛眨眼，動作敏捷，嗓音尖銳。他是個高明的演說家，當爭論到某個問題的難點時，他總是踱來踱去，頗有說服力地不時揮動著尾巴。在其他動物的心目中，史奎爾確實有著顛倒黑白的口才。

這三個傢伙把梅傑的言論發展成了一套精密的思想體系，並為之冠名為「動物主義」。在瓊斯先生睡熟的夜裡，他們會把大家召集到穀倉，不厭其煩地把動物主義一遍又一遍地解說。起初，他們遇到不少冷淡以及一些惹人發笑的愚蠢問題。有的動物談到了「忠誠」——對「主人」瓊斯先生的忠誠：「是瓊斯先生在養活我們，如果瓊斯先生不在了，我們一定會餓死。」還有別的一些問題，諸如：「我們為什麼要在乎死後的事情？」或者是：「如果革命是注定要發生的，我們做不做什麼不都無關緊要嗎？」因此，三隻豬總是要費盡心力地指出：這些說法都是與動物主義的核心思想決不相容的。最蠢的問題都是來自母馬莫莉的，她問雪球的第一句話是：「革命以後還會有糖吃嗎？」

「沒有，」雪球斬釘截鐵地說，「在這片農莊裡，我們根本就沒有產糖的理由。況且，你並不需要糖，你會得到足夠的燕麥和乾草。」

「那我還能在頭髮上繫上絲帶嗎？」莫莉又問。

「我的同志呀，」雪球說，「你迷戀的那些絲帶正是奴役的標誌。難道你不明白，自由的價值更勝絲帶？」

莫莉雖然點了頭，但看上去還是沒有被完全說服。

更為費力的工作是，三隻豬要不斷去撲滅烏鴉摩西的謊言。摩西是瓊斯先生的寵物，是動物們當中的間諜，而且能言善辯。他聲稱瞭解那神祕的糖果山的底細，那裡是所有動物死後的歸宿。據摩西說，糖果山就坐落在天空的某處，在雲彩後面不遠的什麼地方。在那裡，天天都是週末，一年四季都生長著繁茂的苜蓿。動物們都不喜歡摩西，因為他只耍嘴皮子，卻從來不真正地參與工作。但是一些動物卻始終對糖果山抱有堅定的信仰，爲此，三隻豬不得不苦口婆心地解釋這樣的地方根本不存在。

拳師和克羅薇——兩匹駕車高頭大馬——是三隻豬最忠實的信徒，他們真正地把三隻豬視爲師長，對於三隻豬所說的一切照單全收，並用簡單的話把意思傳達給其他動物。他們從不缺席穀倉裡的祕密會議，並且擔任領唱，在散會之前讓「英格蘭的野獸」作爲結束曲響遍全場。

關鍵時刻就要來臨了，誰也沒有料到革命會爆發得如此之早而又如此的輕易。在過去的年頭裡，瓊斯先生雖然算不上是位溫和的主人，但至少還算是勤勞能幹，但最近的一段日子裡事情卻發生了變化。他先是在一次訴訟當中蒙受了財產損失，後又因此而沮喪，日日酗酒。經常是一整天，他倒在躺椅裡只是看報、喝酒，或用啤酒泡過的麵包渣餵餵摩西。農莊裡的員工們也變得懶散，所以田裡滿是荒草，漏雨的屋頂沒人修補，籬笆缺少照看，動物們有一頓沒一頓的。

六月來臨，該是收割乾草的時候了。星期六，一個仲夏之夜，瓊斯先生醉倒在威靈頓的紅獅酒館，直到第二天的中午才返回農莊。而員工們早晨擠完牛奶後就外出打野兔去了，沒人注意到動物們都還餓著肚子。瓊斯先生呢？一回來就躺進臥室沙發，胡亂抓了份《世界新聞報》遮在臉上一路睡到晚上，而動物們始終沒有進食。終於，大家實在無法忍受了。先是一頭牛破門而出，接著，所有的動物都紛紛衝出了圍欄。瓊斯先生這才醒了過來，忙和四名員工一起朝四面八方胡亂揮著鞭子。動物們再也忍無可忍，雖然事先並沒有反叛的念頭，此刻卻一齊朝著人類猛撲過去。當瓊斯一夥驚恐地發現自己被無處不在的蹄子踢打與犄角衝撞時，局面已經不是他們能控制的了。他們從未見過動物們這樣的舉動，無法明白這一向來逆來順受的動物們竟會如此兇猛。才一下子，他們便放棄抵抗各自逃命去了。於是，出現了一幅既驚人又滑稽的場面：瓊斯一夥往大路上沒命地飛奔，後面緊追著一群因突如其來的勝利趾高氣揚的動物。

瓊斯夫人從臥室的窗戶看到了這一切，便匆匆忙忙地收拾行李，從另一條路跑了。摩西尾隨在後，呱呱大叫著。

同一時間，凱旋的動物們關上了農莊的大門。在他們還沒有真正地意識到革命的勝利之前，革命已經成功地結束了：瓊斯一夥被逐出了境外，農莊已屬於動物們自己。

最初的幾分鐘裡，動物們對這場突如其來的勝利簡直覺得難以置信。他們開始大步走著搜索整座農莊，以確定不再有人類藏身其間，然後又回到房間裡，懷著揚眉吐氣的心情掃清所有瓊斯政權的痕跡。工具間的門被打開了：馬嚼子、狗項圈、還有瓊斯先生用來閹割豬羊的滿是血腥的刀具，一切一切，通通被扔進了井裡。韁繩、籠頭、眼罩、連同皮鞭，也全被扔進了院子裡熊熊燃燒的火堆。看到皮鞭在火焰中翻騰時，所有的動物都喜不自勝。雪球還把絲帶也扔進了火堆，這些絲帶曾是在趕集的日子裡用來裝飾馬的鬃毛的。

「絲帶，」他說，「也是一種服飾，而服飾正是人類的標誌之一。所有的動物都應是裸身的。」

拳師一聽到這話，忙把隨身的草帽也扔進了火堆。這草帽曾是他夏天裡抵禦蚊蟲入耳的最好的工具。

在很短的時間之內，動物們毀掉了所有能使他們回憶起瓊斯先生的東西。拿破侖又帶領大家來到儲藏室，給每個動物發放了雙份的飼料，每隻狗還能額外獲得兩塊餅乾。然後，他們又狂歡一樣地把「英格蘭的野獸」唱了無數遍，筋疲力盡之後便倒頭睡去——那酣眠的樣子簡直能讓人相信這是他們有生以來的第一次睡眠。

但在清晨，他們還是像往常一樣地醒來了，然後突然記起了昨天光榮的勝利，便一齊向草場奔去。到草場的路上有一座可以俯瞰幾乎整個農莊的小丘，動物們擠到高處，在清澈的晨光下向四周眺望：這是多麼奇妙的事啊！眼中所見的一切竟全屬於他們自己了！他們在狂喜中跳躍，直要跳到高高的空中。他們在露水裡打滾，他們把夏天裡香甜的草葉含了滿嘴，他們踢碎黑色的土塊去嗅那泥土裡馥鬱的香氣。他們又在沉靜的無言中審視這整片的大地：這果園、這池塘、這矮林，那神情就好像他們從來都沒有見過這些世間美景。甚至直到現在他們依然難以置信：這一切，這一切一切，都已真正地屬於他們自己。

然後，他們回到了農莊，在寂靜的農舍門外停下了腳步。這農舍也是他們的了，然而要進去的時候卻還是有些害怕。過了一會兒，雪球和拿破崙終於用肩膀撞開了大門，動物們便魚貫而入，輕輕地像是生怕驚擾了什麼。他們踮著腳尖走過了一間又一間屋子，不敢高聲說話，懷著敬畏的心情注視著屋子裡那一份份讓人難以置信的奢華：鋪著毛毯的大床、精美的鏡子、鬆軟的沙發、布魯塞爾地毯、維多利亞時代的版畫……忽然，在下樓梯的時候，大家回頭去找，見莫莉正留在最漂亮的那間臥室裡。她從瓊斯夫人的梳妝盒裡找到了一條藍色的絲帶，繫在肩上，對著鏡子搔首弄姿。這樣的舉動招致大家一片指責。除此,房間裡幾乎什麼都沒有被翻動過。大家當場就全體一致地作了一個決定:農舍應該保留下來作為博物館,作為人類的罪證昭示子孫後代,而動物則是不應該住在這裡的。

早餐後,雪球和拿破崙又把大家召集到一起。

「同志們,」雪球說,「現在剛剛六點半鐘,離天黑還有很長的時間。從現在起,我們要開始收割乾草。但在開始收割之前,有一件事情要請大家注意。」

豬在這時透露了在過去的三個月裡,他們已從一冊被瓊斯家的小孩扔進垃圾堆裡的識字課本裡學會了讀書寫字。拿破崙派人弄來一桶油漆,雪球(因為他的書法最好)抓起一把刷子,把大門上的「曼諾農莊」幾個字一把抹掉,隨後大力寫上了四個大字…動物農莊!農莊今後就叫這個名字了。這之後,他們又叫人找來一把梯子架在牆上,解釋說…經過三個月以來的學習,他們把動物主義歸納成了「動物七誡」,這七誡要被刻在牆上以便大家隨時

動物農莊

誦讀。在動物農莊裡生活的動物都要遵守這七誡。雪球費力地爬上梯子（對於一頭豬，在梯子上保持平衡可真不是件容易的事）開始落筆，史奎爾他們在下面爲他舉著油漆桶。「七誡」是用巨大的白字寫成的，在三十碼外都能看到。它的內容是這樣的：

動物七誡

1. 凡是有兩條腿的都是敵人
2. 凡是有四條腿的或是有翅膀的都是朋友
3. 不准穿衣
4. 不准睡在床上
5. 不准喝酒
6. 不准殺害同類
7. 所有動物一律平等

字跡清晰。除了「朋友」被寫成了「有朋」和一個「S」被轉錯了方向，全部的拼寫還是相當正確的。雪球又對著全體動物高聲朗讀了一遍。動物們紛紛點頭稱是，聰明一點的已經開始在默背了。

「現在，同志們，」雪球高聲喊道，扔掉手裡的刷子，「到草地裡去，我們收割的速度比瓊斯他們更快，這是一種榮耀！」

但在此時，那三頭乳牛卻不安分起來，因為已經整整二十四個小時沒有擠奶了，她們的乳房簡直要漲破。經過簡單的思考，三隻豬叫人拿來了大桶，親自為乳牛擠了奶，也因此才發現豬蹄子竟然很適合這項工作。很快地就有了五大桶鮮奶，所有的動物不由得都眼巴巴地望著這道美味。

某個聲音忍不住發問：「我們怎麼處置這些牛奶呢？」

「瓊斯先生有時會摻一些牛奶在我們的飼料裡。」一隻母雞說。

「不要在意這些牛奶，同志們，」拿破侖一邊說一邊用身體擋住了大桶，「收割才是更重要的。雪球同志會在前面指引大家，我幾分鐘後就到。

衝吧，同志們！乾草在召喚我們！」

於是，動物們前往草地開始收割。當他們黃昏歸來的時候，牛奶已經神祕地消失了。

想一想

將繁複的動物主義簡化成「七誡」供其他動物背誦，你覺得這樣的做法有什麼好處或壞處？

動物農莊

第三章

你想像不到這些動物們在收割乾草的戰役中流下了多少的汗水，但付出是有回報的：他們的收穫大大超出了預想。

有時候，工作是很辛苦的：各種為人類而設計的工具並不適合動物們使用。但三隻豬充分發揮了他們的聰明才智，克服了一切的困難。對於馬來說，他們熟悉這裡每一英吋的土地，比瓊斯他們的耕耘要做得更好。三隻豬並不真正參與工作，只負責指導和監督的工作。由於他們有著超卓的頭腦，他們理所當然地獲取了領袖的地位。拳師和克羅薇操作著收割機和馬拉摟耙（當然，他們已經不再需要嚼子和韁繩了）在草地裡一圈又一圈地繞著，一隻豬不停在身後吆喝：「前進，同志！」或是「後退，同志！」所有的動物

035

都不遺餘力地運送乾草，甚至鴨子和母雞也都在烈日之下一次次地銜著草葉往返奔波。最後，只用了兩天就完成了全部的收割工作，比起瓊斯時代的效率高得太多了。而且，這還是整個農莊有史以來收穫最豐盛的一次。也沒有絲毫的浪費，鴨子和母雞們銳利的眼睛確保即使是最小的草梗也沒有漏掉。

整個夏天，農莊裡的工作就像鐘錶一樣的按部就班。動物們都在感受著這從未想像過的快樂：每一小塊食物都真的屬於自己：自己耕耘，自己享用，不再是來自吝嗇主人的施捨。寄生的人類已經不在了，每隻動物都可以分到更多的食物。

閒暇的時光也多了起來，雖然動物們還不太適應這種閒暇。他們也遇到了無數的困難——比如，在年底收割穀物時，他們必須用很原始的方法一點一點地吹掉穀殼，因為農莊裡並沒有可供使用的打穀機——但幸好，三隻豬的智慧和拳師驚人的蠻力足以克服一切的困難。拳師的勤勞贏得了大家的崇敬。他在瓊斯時代就已經贏得了勤勞的美名，來到現在，他真是一個能頂三個；有時，似乎整個農莊的重負都壓在他強而有力的肩上。

從早到晚他都不停歇，而且總是出現在工作最繁重的地方。他讓一隻小公雞一大早就叫醒他，比別的動物都要早上半個小時，哪裡需要他幫忙，他就到哪裡去。他對每一個問題總是給以同樣的回答：「我會更努力的。」——這已經成了他的座右銘。

每一隻動物都盡其所能。在這裡，沒有誰偷竊，沒有誰抱怨他們沒有得到足夠的食物配給；在瓊斯時代屢見不鮮的爭吵、撕咬、嫉妒幾乎都已經絕跡。也沒有誰逃避工作——「幾乎」沒有。莫莉總是起得晚、走得早；貓的行為也有些離奇，在工作的場合經常找不到她，她會一連消失幾個小時，到了吃飯的時間或是一天的工作已經完成時才突然露面，而且表現得就像什麼都沒發生過。她總是能找出無數個精彩絕倫的藉口，讓人無法不相信她的缺席完全是出於好意。老驢本傑明在革命之後似乎沒有絲毫的改變，他依然頑固地保持著在瓊斯時代就已養成的慢吞吞的工作作風，既不多幹也不少幹。對於革命和革命的結果，本傑明從來沒有發表什麼意見。當被問及他是否因

038

為瓊斯被驅逐而感到高興，他總是給出讓人摸不著頭腦的答案：「驢的壽命太長了，你們看過死驢嗎？」其他動物也不得不就此打住。

星期天是休息時間，早飯比平常要晚一個小時，飯後有個例行的儀式。先是升旗，雪球在工具間裡找到了瓊斯夫人的一塊綠色桌布，在上面用白顏料畫上了一隻蹄子和一隻角。每星期天早晨，這面旗幟都會在農莊的花園中高高升起。旗幟是綠色的，雪球解釋這代表了英格蘭的綠色田野，蹄子和角標誌著未來的動物共和：到了那時，動物們將會是這片大地上真正的主人，人類政權已被澈底顛覆。升旗之後，所有的動物列隊走進穀倉舉行集會，制定下週的工作計畫和提案、討論。提出決議提案的總是那幾隻豬，其他的動物僅僅懂得投票表決。雪球和拿破侖是這裡最活躍的分子，但他們兩個的意見卻從來沒有一致過：一方提出的議案總是遭到另一方毫不留情的反對。會議的收尾照例是合唱「英格蘭的野獸」，散會後的下午就是娛樂的時間了。

豬把工具間當作了他們自己的高層會議室。晚上，他們在這裡學習從農莊的書本中得到的關於治鐵、木工和其他技術的各種知識。雪球還忙於組織其他動物成立一個叫做「動物委員會」的組織，並為此孜孜不倦。他為母雞們成立了「下蛋委員會」，為母牛成立了「淨尾團」，還成立了「掃盲與再教育委員會」（這個委員會的目的是馴服老鼠和野兔）等等。總體來說，這些專案全部以失敗告終。貓參加了「掃盲與再教育委員會」，而且在某一段

動物農莊

時間裡非常活躍。有天大家看到她坐在屋頂上和遠處的麻雀說著話。她說所有的動物現在都已是同志了，所以，她非常歡迎麻雀到她的腳爪上棲息。但儘管她說盡了難以抗拒的甜言蜜語，麻雀還是警戒地與她保持距離。

不過，讀寫班卻獲得了巨大的成功。到了秋天，幾乎每一隻農莊裡的動物都能夠在一定程度上識文斷字。

至於豬，他們的讀寫能力已經到了相當高的水準。狗的閱讀能力也已經稱得上高超，但除了「七誡」，他們對任何文字都提不起興趣。本傑明可以讀得像豬一樣好，但卻從不應用這種能力。他說據他所知，實在是沒有什麼東西值得一讀。克羅薇認識了全部的字母，卻始終拼不出一個完整的單詞。拳師總是學不過字母「D」，無論他為此下了多大的工夫。有幾次他居然也記住了「E，F，G，H」，但馬上發現「A，B，C，D」又給忘掉了。最後他終於滿足於認知這四個字母的程度了，每天還要默寫兩次來鞏固記憶。而莫莉呢，除了拼寫自己名字的六個字母以外，什麼都不願學。

農莊裡的其他動物都只是記下了字母「A」。此外，一些比較笨的動物——比如綿羊、母雞和鴨子根本連「七誡」都沒有記住。有鑒於此，雪球把「七誡」進一步歸納成一句：「四條腿的是好漢，兩條腿的是壞蛋。」他說，這一句話涵蓋了動物主義的最高準則。誰能夠真正領悟這句真理，誰就能遠離人類的邪惡。

「同志們，至於鳥的翅膀，」他說，「只是一種推動身體前進的器官，和腿的功用是一樣的。人類的最顯著標誌是手，憑著手，他們幹盡了一切壞事。」

鳥兒並不明白雪球的長篇大論，但接受了他的說法。所有較低等的動物都開始口誦心念這句新的口號。「四條腿的是好漢，兩條腿的是壞蛋。」這句話被刻在穀倉的牆上高過「七誡」的地方，字體也較大。綿羊對這句話有獨特的喜好，一天到晚總把這句話掛在嘴上，喋喋不休。

拿破侖對雪球的委員會毫無興趣。他說年輕人的教育是遠比對成年人的

042

教育還重要。在收割之後，傑西和藍鈴生下了九隻小狗。剛剛斷奶，拿破侖就把他們從媽媽的身邊帶走，說是自己要親自負責起對他們的教育。他把他們帶到工具間的閣樓上，只有架上梯子才能上去。教育的過程是如此的隱祕，以致動物們很快就忘記了這些小狗的存在。

牛奶的神祕失蹤事件終於水落石出了。每天都被混雜在豬食當中。

是蘋果成熟的季節了，被風吹落的果實落滿了花園的土地。動物們理所當然地認為這些應該由大家平分的東西，直到有一天，有道命令要求將這些蘋果收集起來送到工具間讓豬專門享用。對此，一些動物議論紛紛，但這沒用。所有的豬都一致贊同這項決議，雪球與拿破崙也不例外。最後，史奎爾被派出去向大家解釋。

「同志們！」他喊道，「我希望你們不要以為我們這樣做是出於自私和特權。事實上，我們大多並不喜歡牛奶和蘋果。這樣做的唯一目的只是為了保持健康。牛奶和蘋果（同志們，這是已被科學證實的）含有對豬的健康很有益處的物質。我們是腦力工作者，整個農莊的組織與管理工作都要由我們來做，我們日日夜夜地關注大家的福利。我們喝牛奶、吃蘋果都是為了你們好。

難道你們不知道如果我們失職意味著什麼？瓊斯會回來的！是的，瓊斯會回來的！是的，同志們！」史奎爾喊道，幾乎是用了懇請的語調，一邊踱來踱去，不停搖晃著尾巴，「你們絕對沒有人願意看到瓊斯回來吧！」

現在，大家唯一能肯定的一件事，就是他們絕不希望瓊斯回來。他們無話可說了。看來，確保豬的健康實在是至關重要的事。決議就這樣達成，牛奶和蘋果今後都是豬的禁臠，確切無疑。

為什麼牛奶和蘋果只能保留給豬吃？如果是你，你會不會出聲反對？

045

第四章

到了仲夏，關於動物農莊的各種消息已經傳遍了整個英格蘭大地。每天，雪球和拿破侖都將信鴿放出去，要牠們到鄰近的農莊去傳播革命的消息和教唱「英格蘭的野獸」。

在這段時間裡，瓊斯先生總是泡在紅獅酒吧，逢人便抱怨自己的苦難遭遇。他得到了足夠的同情，但實際幫助卻少得可憐。他哪知道，別的農莊主人們真正在想的只是如何能從中趁火打劫地撈上一把。但不幸中的萬幸是，臨近動物農莊的另外兩座農莊一直都不太景氣。其中之一是狐木農莊：面積大，有些荒廢，風格老舊，草場已不像樣子，籬笆年久失修。農莊主人名叫皮爾金頓，性格非常隨和，總是寧願把大部分時間花在釣魚和打獵這些休閒

活動上，而不願去整理一下他那早已慘不忍睹的莊院。另外一座農莊叫做平

徹菲爾德，面積較小，情況也稍好一點，產權是屬於弗雷德里克先生的。這

位先生總是面孔嚴峻、算計精明，彷彿一年到頭都有官司纏身，而且因為善

於討價還價而在這一帶享有不太好的名聲。這兩位農莊主人素來不睦，即使

有共同利益可尋也絕對無法達成共識。

　　但這一次，他們全被動物農莊的革命嚇住了，惟恐自己農莊裡的動物也

會群起效仿。一開始，他們對動物們自己經營農莊這件事嗤之以鼻。他們本

以為這場鬧劇不出兩週就會結束，還堅持說曼諾農莊（他們仍固執地沿用

「曼諾農莊」這個名字）裡的動物們會必然地陷入無止盡的爭鬥，最終的結

局除了餓死別無其他可能。再者，那裡的同類相殘和共產共妻根本就違反了

自然法則！

　　謠言滿天飛，關於動物農莊裡人類是怎樣被驅逐、動物們怎樣取得統治

地位的說法，如今已有了各式各樣的版本。那一年，革命的風潮席捲了整個

大地。一向馴順的公牛變得狂野十足，綿羊也每每衝破藩籬，「英格蘭的野獸」的旋律響徹了每一個有動物的角落。

人類雖然指斥這支歌曲的荒謬，但聽到時又每每壓抑不住心頭的怒火。他們不明白，動物們怎麼能唱出這樣可鄙的垃圾旋律？一發現有哪隻動物在唱歌，人類馬上就加以鞭撻。鴿子在樹枝上唱。教堂的鐘聲裡，村口的喧嘩裡，都隱隱約約摻和著這支旋律的回響。這歌聲可就是人類的喪鐘吧？人類也不由自主地相信了：今日喪鐘長鳴，明朝厄運當頭。

十月，穀子已收割完了，有些已經完成脫粒，儲藏的工作正在進行當中。一個早晨，鴿子帶來了一個讓整個農莊都為之不安的消息：瓊斯一夥和六名來自臨近農莊的幫手正朝著農莊走來。看他們全副武裝的樣子，是決心要奪回農莊了。

這是早在意料之中的事，這陣子雖然平和，但應戰的準備從來都沒有鬆懈過。雪球在一本描繪凱薩大帝的書中學會了古代名將們的種種攻殺戰守，理所當然地負責起整個防禦工作的組織籌備。在他嫻熟的調兵遣將之下，大家很快地列好了戰鬥隊形。

在瓊斯一夥剛剛抵達時，雪球立刻發動了他的第一輪攻擊：三十五隻鴿子衝上半空，把排泄物瘋狂地投下。瓊斯他們剛來得及應付空中打擊，就突然有鵝群從籬笆後面衝出，猛啄他們的小腿。這只是一場小規模的阻擊，隊伍很快就被瓊斯他們驅散。這時，雪球發動了第二輪的進攻。本傑明和整個羊群在雪球的帶領下從側翼發動兇猛的攻勢。老驢本傑明始終在隊伍的最前鋒，揚蹄四踏，勇冠三軍。但棍棒和皮靴實在太厲害了，動物們到底也是血肉之軀，隨著雪球的一聲令下，大家開始有秩序的撤退，從大門退進院子。

瓊斯他們為了這第一場勝利而歡呼。他們看到，並且也堅定地認為：敵人們正在抱頭鼠竄、落荒而逃，於是鼓譟一番，胡亂地向他們追去。沒想到，這正落入了雪球精心設計的圈套。瓊斯一夥剛剛追進院子時，埋伏已久的三匹馬、三頭牛和一大群豬立即包抄過來，把後路截斷。當瓊斯他們驚慌失措之際，雪球把握時機，發出了總攻擊令。雪球本著擒賊先擒王的打算直撲瓊斯本人。瓊斯開槍了，子彈帶著血劃過了雪球的脊背，一隻綿羊應聲倒地。雪球毫不遲疑，碩大的身體猛撞瓊斯的腿。瓊斯被這股蠻力推進了糞堆，槍也甩了出去。

但最激動人心的場面還是要屬拳師：拳師揚起後腿，用釘著鐵掌的蹄子重重踢向一個少年的腦袋。人們被嚇住了，丟掉武器只想逃命。恐慌迅速蔓延，現在是人類在抱頭鼠竄了。動物們或踢、或咬、或踩、或撞，用不同的方式來發洩復仇的快感。就連貓也加入了攻擊的隊伍，在一次突襲中得手，抓破了一個人的脖子。終於，這些人算是奪路逃了出來，沒命地奔上了他們曾經趾高氣揚的來路。

所有的人都逃光了，只除了一具屍體。拳師用蹄子捅了捅他，但屍體沒有任何反應。

「他死了，」拳師有些憂傷，「我不是故意的。我忘了我是釘了鐵掌的。我真的不是故意的。」

「同志，別再多愁善感了！」雪球喊道，不顧自己的背上還淌著血，「戰爭就是戰爭。只有死人才不會給我們帶來傷害。」

「我一點都不想殺生，就算對人也是一樣。」拳師還在重複著，眼裡滿是淚水。

「莫莉在哪裡？」有個聲音突然喊道。

莫莉失蹤了。大家一陣驚慌，猜想著種種可能：被人打傷了？還是被人抓走了？最後，大家在馬廄裡找到了莫莉……她把頭深深地埋在乾草堆裡；是的，從槍聲一響時她就這樣躲了起來。大家鬆了口氣，回到院子，卻發現那個「死人」其實只是昏了過去，剛剛已經甦醒並且逃掉了。

動物們重新恢復了勝利後狂喜的心態，每一位都扯著嗓子吹噓著自己的赫赫戰功。即興的慶祝活動隨即展開：旗幟被高高升起，「英格蘭的野獸」

被一遍遍地縱情歌唱，大家還為死於槍彈的那隻綿羊舉行了莊嚴的葬禮，並把一棵山楂樹種在他的墓地上。隨後，雪球簡短地講了些話，強調如有必要，所有動物都應不惜犧牲生命來保衛這座得來不易的動物農莊。

大家還一致決定了製作榮譽勳章來獎賞有功將士，恰好他們還在工具間裡找到了一些優質的黃銅。

「動物英雄，一級勳章」被授予雪球和拳師，「動物英雄，二級勳章」被公認給那隻死去的綿羊。

關於這場戰役的命名起了一些爭論。最後決定叫做「牛棚之役」，因為至關重要的那場伏擊就是在牛棚開始的。瓊斯先生的槍也在泥塘裡被找到了，動物們將槍像大炮一樣地掛在旗杆上，並且決定一年鳴槍兩次：一次是在十月十二日，作為「牛棚之役」的週年紀念；一次是在夏至日，那天正是革命的開始。

想一想

牛棚之役的起因為何？動物農莊的崛起對人類和動物們來說象徵了什麼樣的意義？

第五章

冬天到了，莫莉變得越來越惹人厭。她總會在每天早晨工作的時候遲到，還振振有辭地說是不小心睡過了頭。她一天到晚抱怨這裡疼那裡疼，食欲卻比豬還旺盛。她會找出各種藉口溜到飲水池邊，然後低著頭欣賞自己。

但這些還算小事，另外一些傳聞就讓人吃驚了。

一天，莫莉正在院子裡面閒逛，克羅薇突然攔住她的去路。

「莫莉，」她說，「有件事讓我很驚訝。今天早上，在動物農莊和狐木農莊交界那裡，我看見你和一個皮爾金頓先生的夥計在一起。雖然離得遠，但我敢肯定他是在對你說話，更過份的是，你還讓他摸你的鼻子。告訴我，莫莉，到底是怎麼回事？」

「什麼怎麼回事？他沒摸，我更沒讓他摸，根本是你胡編亂造！」莫莉大聲嚷嚷，蹄子跺著地。

「莫莉，你看著我，你敢向我發誓那人沒摸你的鼻子？」

「當然沒有，」莫莉的語氣堅決，但眼神遲疑。一段尷尬之後，她飛也似的奔向田野，轉眼就沒了蹤影。

望著莫莉離去，克羅薇的心裡忽然閃過一個念頭。她沒有跟任何動物說，只是跑到莫莉的廄棚裡，用蹄子在草間翻找——草下竟藏著一堆方糖和幾條五彩繽紛的絲帶。

三天後，莫莉不見了，接連幾個星期下落不明。後來是鴿子傳來消息，說是在威靈頓那裡看到她。當時，她正拉著一輛馬車。那是一輛很時髦的車，漆得光鮮亮麗，停在一所旅館的門口。一個紅臉的胖子穿著方格子馬褲和高筒靴，像是旅館的老闆，一邊撫摩莫莉的鼻子一邊餵糖給她。她的鬃毛修剪得煥然一新，額頭還綁著一條紅色絲帶，看來很是驕傲。

消息看來是可靠的。從此以後，再也沒有任何動物提起莫莉了。

一月份的天氣異常惡劣，田地硬得像一塊鐵板，讓任何的開墾工作都變得徒勞無功。穀倉裡召開了無數次的會議，聰明的豬都在忙於籌劃下一個季度的工作。他們的聰明才智使他們成為整個農莊裡的最高決策者，儘管他們的決策還需要經過全體動物的投票表決才能通過。

要是雪球和拿破崙之間沒有那麼多摩擦，會議本來能進行得相當流暢。但任何議題都能引發他們的爭執。

雪球如果建議應該擴大燕麥的種植面積，拿破崙就會說多種大麥才是真正的當務之急；拿破崙如果說某某地方最適合捲心菜的生長，雪球就非要說除了番薯以外那裡什麼也長不了。

他們兩個的爭辯有時相當激烈。雪球口才極佳，滔滔的雄辯極具說服力量；而拿破崙更擅長分別遊說，搞些「走廊外交」來拉取選票。他的這些手腕在羊群那裡獲得了巨大成功，後來，不管什麼樣的場合，羊群都會咩咩叫個不停：「四條腿是好漢，兩條腿是壞蛋」，並經常藉此（當然是在拿破崙的授意之下）擾亂會場秩序。

雪球曾在瓊斯先生的房間裡找到了一些過期的《農莊主人和畜牧業者》雜誌，並進行深入的研究，一些技術上的革新與發明的想法經常充斥他的腦袋。當他談起農田排水、飼料保鮮、鹼性爐渣之類的話題時總是頭頭是道，一副學究氣十足的樣子。他還真的設計出了一套複雜的系統，可以把動物們每天在不同地方排泄的糞便直接送到地洞裡，大大節省了繁重的運送工作。拿破崙在這一領域裡則是毫無建樹，但卻時常拐彎抹角地評論說雪球搞的這些東西不過是些雕蟲小技。在他們無止盡的各種爭論當中，最為激烈的應該是關於風車的議題了。

離農莊不遠的牧場上有一座不大的山丘，是整個農莊的制高點。在詳盡的勘察之後，雪球向大家宣布說沒有什麼地方能比那裡更適合建造風車了。風車能夠帶動發電機，可以為農莊提供電力，獸欄裡可以點亮電燈，冬天可以取暖，也可以帶動電鋸、鍘草機、切片機和電動擠奶機的運轉……動物們聽得瞠目結舌，這些都是前所未聞的東西（這座農莊比較老式，只有一台叫不出名字的老掉牙的機器）。雪球對機器繪聲繪色的描述讓動物們聽得如癡如醉：他說那些機器可以在他們正悠閒地吃草的時候、在他們聊天的時候，幫他們把該做的工作全都做好，而且任勞任怨、不知疲倦。

不出幾個星期，雪球的風車設計方案就擬訂完成。詳細的技術資料大多取自於《造屋千益事》、《泥水工需知》和《電學入門》等瓊斯先生的書。雪球將一間小棚子用來當作自己的工作間，在裡面閉門造車，一待就是幾個小時。

那間小棚子原是用來孵蛋的，裡面有光滑的木地板，適合用來畫圖。雪球經常把打開的書用石塊壓著，兩趾之間夾著一截粉筆，不時地踱來踱去，一邊發出興奮的哼哼聲，一邊一筆一筆地畫著線條。

漸漸地，設計圖已進階到充滿大量曲柄和齒輪的複雜部分，圖面覆蓋了大半個地板——這在其他動物們看來簡直太深奧了。但動物們也對此留下了極深的印象，他們每天至少要來一次，靜靜地在一旁觀看雪球繪圖。就連平時不太過問大家在做什麼的雞和鴨子也來了，還極為謹慎地避開地上那些粉筆線。

只有拿破崙自始至終都在迴避。他從一開始就反對這個專案，然而出乎意料的是，有一天，他也來察看風車的設計圖了：他一聲不吭地在棚子裡繞來繞去，仔細看著每一處細節，偶爾還冷哼兩聲，然後也斜著眼睛站在一旁。突然，他抬起腿來，對著設計圖撒了一泡尿，然後便一聲不吭地揚長而去了。

動物們在風車一事上截然分成了兩派。雪球並不否認建造風車要付出繁重的工作，需要採石築牆，需要塑造葉片，另外也需要發電機和電纜（一開始，他也沒說這些東西要怎麼弄來）。但他堅持，整個工程能在一年之內完

060

成；而且還信誓旦旦地許諾，風車建成後能節省大量勞力，動物們的勞動時間每週可以縮短至三天。但拿破崙卻有著截然不同的觀點，他認為，目前最緊要的是迅速增加糧食生產，如果在風車上浪費時間，到時大家就會餓死。

就這樣，在「擁護雪球的每週三天工作制」和「擁護拿破崙的糧食滿倉制」的不同口號之下，動物們分成了旗幟鮮明的兩派。老驢本傑明是唯一的中立者，對誰的話都不信。他說，不管有沒有風車，生活都會繼續下去。

除了風車問題外，還有另一個爭執長久以來困擾大家：農莊的防禦體系裡的動物們也開始蠢蠢欲動，人類也因此更有理由對動物農莊下手了。

根據拿破崙的意見，動物們的當務之急就是要迅速武裝自己，並且學習怎樣使用武器。但雪球卻說，他們應該放出更多鴿子，到其他農莊裡去煽動革命。拿破崙說如果不自衛就等同於坐以待斃，雪球說如果大地上革命四

——儘管瓊斯一夥在「牛棚之役」中大敗而回，但他們奪回農莊的企圖是不會因此打消的。進一步說，「牛棚之役」的消息已經傳遍了全國，鄰近農莊

起，他們也就沒有防禦的必要了。動物們聽誰的話都覺得有理，議案因此懸

而未決。

雪球的設計圖終於完成了，但是否眞的要開工建造則還要等到星期天大

會的表決。那一天，面對穀倉裡集合的全體動物，雪球再一次提出了他之所

以熱衷於這個專案的緣由。接著，拿破崙站起來反駁，他拐彎抹角地勸大家

要量力而爲。

雪球再也按捺不住，猛地站了起來，大聲喝住咩咩亂叫的羊群，爲了獲

得支持而再度慷慨陳詞。在這之前，動物們因爲各有所好，基本上是一半一

半地分成兩派，但頃刻間就全被雪球極富感染力的演說所折服。雪球熱切地

描述了當動物們擺脫了繁重的勞動時，整座動物農莊裡的嶄新氣象。他的構

想此時早已遠遠超出了鍘草機和切蘿蔔機。他說，電能帶動打穀機、犁、

耙、碾子、收割機和捆紮機，除此之外，還能讓每個獸欄裡都能使用電燈和

熱水，甚至是電爐。此時，全體動物們的表決傾向已經很明顯了。但就在這

個關頭，拿破崙忽然站了起來，古怪地瞥了雪球一眼，吹了一聲尖銳的口哨。

口哨的聲音剛落，外面就傳來一陣兇狠的狗叫聲，緊接著，九條大狗，戴著鑲有銅釘的項圈，跳進大穀倉裡，徑直撲向雪球。就在這千鈞一髮之際，雪球猛然跳了起來，一下子就跑出門外，九條狗在他後方窮追不捨。動物們都被這個景象嚇呆了，全都愣住不知所措。接著他們擠到門外注視這場追逐。

雪球使出渾身解數飛奔穿越牧場，而九條狗已經銜尾追來。突然間，他滑倒了，眼看著就要被逮住。可他又爬了起來，跑得更快了。狗又再次追了上去，其中一條狗幾乎就要咬住雪球的尾巴了，幸而雪球及時地把尾巴甩到一邊。接著他一個衝刺，和狗只差了一步之遙，從樹籬中的一個缺口竄了出去，再也不見蹤影。

動物們這才驚愕地回到穀倉，餘悸未消。不一會兒，那些狗又汪汪地叫著跑了回來。一開始，大家都不知道這些凶巴巴的傢伙是從哪裡冒出來

的，但問題很快就弄明白了：他們正是早先被拿破崙從他們的母親身邊以教育名義爲由帶走的那些小小狗，拿破崙一直偷偷地養著他們。儘管他們還沒有完全長大，但個頭都已經不算小了，看上去簡直凶得像狼。大家也都注意到，他們始終緊挨著拿破崙，對他親近地擺著尾巴。那姿勢，竟和以前別的狗對瓊斯先生的親熱法一模一樣。

這時，拿破崙在那些忠狗的跟隨下，登上梅傑當年的演說台，高聲宣布，星期天的全體會議從此取消，因爲那些會議實在是毫無必要，純屬浪費時間。此後，一切有關農莊的議題將由一個由豬組成的特別委員會集體定奪，而這個委員會將由他自己親自統管。

委員會會把每次會議的決議及時傳達給全體動物。但動物們仍要在星期天早晨集合，舉行升旗儀式，唱誦「英格蘭的動物們」，並接受下一週的工作安排。但討論是再也不會有了。

雪球被驅逐給了動物們不小的刺激，拿破崙這番話更無異於火上澆油。

有幾隻動物想要抗議，一時之間卻不知道該說些什麼。就連拳師也困惑不已。他豎起耳朵，抖抖鬃毛，努力想理出頭緒。四隻在前排的小肉豬尖聲叫著，當場跳起來準備發言。但突然間，圍坐在拿破侖身邊的那群狗發出讓人毛骨悚然的咆哮聲。四隻小肉豬只得重新坐下，緘口不語。接著，羊群的叫聲又響起來：「四條腿是好漢，兩條腿是壞蛋！」在這樣的氣氛下，大家根本已經無從討論了。

後來，史奎爾受命在農莊裡晃了一圈，就這個新的安排向動物們解釋。

「同志們，」他說，「我希望農莊裡的每個動物都對拿破侖同志為承擔這些額外的勞動所作出的犧牲心存感激。同志們，千萬不要以為當領導是一種享受！恰恰相反，它意味著艱難而繁重的職責。沒有誰能比拿破侖同志更堅信所有動物一律平等了。他確實很想讓大家自己作主。可是，萬一你們失策了，那麼同志們，會怎樣呢？要是你們真的跟從了雪球那荒誕無稽的風車夢，現在的農莊又會是怎樣的一番景象呢？雪球這東西，就我所知，不比一個壞蛋好上多少。」

「可他在『牛棚之役』中表現得很勇敢。」有隻動物忍不住說了一句。

「光是勇敢是不夠的，」史奎爾說，「忠誠和服從要更為重要。就『牛棚之役』而言，我相信我們終有一天會發現雪球的功勞言過其實。紀律，同志們，鐵的紀律！這才是我們今天的口號。只要走錯一步，我們的仇敵便會來侵犯我們。同志們，你們肯定不想讓瓊斯再回來吧？」

這番論證是無可辯駁的。毫無疑問，動物們害怕瓊斯回來；如果星期天早晨召集的會議有導致他回來的可能，那麼會議就應該停止。拳師細細琢磨了好一陣子，終於說了句：「如果這是拿破侖同志說的，那就一定沒錯。」以此來表達他的感受。從此以後，他在他的座右銘「我會更努力的」後面又補充了一句，那就是：「拿破侖同志永遠正確。」

到了春暖花開、春耕開始的時候，雪球之前那間小棚子還一直被封著，大家猜想著那些設計圖肯定早已從地板上被抹掉了。

每個星期天的早晨十點鐘，動物們照例聚集在穀倉，聆聽下一週的工作安排。大豬梅傑的顱骨已經從墓穴裡挖了出來，被安放在旗桿下的一個木墩上。升旗之後，動物們得要按規定恭恭敬敬地列隊經過那個顱骨，然後才能進入穀倉。

近來，大家不再像以前那樣坐在一起了。拿破崙、史奎爾和一頭叫做繆斯的豬一同坐在前臺。繆斯他天賦非凡，善於吟詩譜曲；九條狗圍著他們坐成半圓，其他豬坐在後臺，其餘的動物們則是面對著他們坐在穀倉中央。拿破崙用一種粗暴的軍人風格，宣讀下一週的工作安排，最後，全體動物們只唱了一遍「英格蘭的動物們」，就宣布解散了。

雪球被驅逐後的第三個星期天，拿破崙竟然宣布要建造風車。動物們聽到這個消息都很吃驚。而拿破崙也沒有為他的改變主意表示任何理由，只是簡單地告誡動物們，額外的風車修建任務將意味著非常艱苦的勞動：也許有必要因此縮減大家的食物。幸運的是，設計圖已經全部畫好了，只剩下最後一些細節。一個由豬組成的特別委員會爲了這個專案，在過去的三週內一直忙碌著。風車的修建，加上其他要做的諸多改善，預期要花費兩年時間。

當天晚上，史奎爾一直私下對其他動物解釋，說拿破崙從來沒有真正反對過建造風車。相反的，整個風車專案還是他最早建議的。雪球的那份設計圖，實際上是他早些時候從拿破崙的筆記中剽竊的。事實上，風車完全是拿破崙的創造。

動物們於是更加困惑，有的動物問道，那爲什麼拿破崙一直把風車說得那麼壞？關於這一點，史奎爾表現出他高超的圓滑功力。他說，這正是拿破崙同志的老練之處：他假裝反對風車，那只是一個計謀，目的在於驅除雪球這個隱患，這個十惡不赦的壞東西。既然現在雪球已經逃跑了，計畫也就能在沒有雪球妨礙的情況下順利進行了。

史奎爾說，這就是策略。他重複了好幾遍，「策略，同志們，策略！」他一邊歡快地笑著，一邊甩動著尾巴，活蹦亂跳。

動物農莊

動物們一時間還搞不懂這些話的含意，可是史奎爾的話如此有說服力，加上剛好有三條氣勢洶洶的狗陪在他身邊，大家也就沒有再追問下去，糊里糊塗地接受了他的說法。

想一想

拿破崙和雪球兩者之間有何不同？你覺得為什麼拿破崙要驅逐雪球？

第六章

整整一年，動物們像奴隸一樣地終日工作。但好在他們樂在其中，無論流血還是流汗都毫無怨言。他們知道，雖然辛苦，但付出的一點一滴都是為了自己，而不再是為了養活那遊手好閒、寄生成性的人類。

從初春到夏末，他們每週都要工作六十個小時。八月，拿破侖又規定了星期天下午也不能休息。雖然理論上，這段時間要不要工作是大家的自由，不過，無論是誰，凡是缺勤的都會被減去一半的糧食。但即使加班，大家還是發覺有些工作根本是做不完的。今年的收穫略遜於去年，而且，因為耕作沒有及早完成，本來該在初夏就播種番薯的兩塊地至今毫無收獲。冬天該怎麼度過呢？悲觀的預想灰濛濛地籠在大家頭上。

風車的事引起了一連串意外的難題。照理說，農莊裡有一個質地很好的石灰石礦，動物們又在一間小屋裡發現大量沙子和水泥，所有的建材很順利地齊備了。但問題是，沒有任何動物有砌石和建築的經驗，一個個全都手足無措。十字鎬和撬棍看來是必要的工具，可是，沒有動物能單獨用後腿站立，無法使用這些只適合人類的工具。

在徒勞了幾個星期後，才有動物想出利用重力的點子：採石場上到處都是巨大的圓石，大家用繩子綁住這些圓石，再由牛、馬、羊和所有能抓住繩子的動物——甚至豬有時也會在關鍵時刻支援——一起拖著石頭，慢慢沿著斜坡拖到礦頂。到了那裡，再把石頭從邊上堆下去摔成碎塊。這樣一來，運輸工作就顯得簡單一些了。馬用貨車拉，羊零碎地拖運，就連莫莉和本傑明也套上了一輛破舊的兩輪座車，盡了他們微薄的心力。就這樣到了夏末，石料積累充足了。接著，在豬的監督下，風車工程終於正式啓動。

不幸的是，整個採石過程進展緩慢。光是把一塊圓石拖到礦頂，常常就要花上整整一天。另外有些時候，雖然順利地將石頭從崖上推了下去，但石頭卻毫無損傷。

幸好拳師幫了很大的忙，要是沒有他那身萬夫不擋的蠻力，恐怕什麼事都做不成。當圓石開始往下滑，拉石頭的動物因此而大聲哀哭地被拖下山坡時，拳師總是能及時趕到，拉住繩索，制止了迫在眉睫的悲劇。

拳師的全力以赴與任勞任怨爲他贏得了全體動物們衷心的欽佩和讚歎。

克羅薇經常會叮囑他要多加小心，不要勞累過度傷了身體，但他從來不放在心上。只是一如往常地用「我會更努力的」和「拿破侖同志永遠正確」這兩句口頭禪回答所有的問題。他甚至和那隻報曉的小公雞商量好，把叫醒他的時間由原先的半小時改爲提早四十五分鐘。同時，儘管日常的工作已把時間幾乎都占滿了，但他仍會抽空，獨自到採石場去，自己一人，裝上一整車碎石，悶著頭朝風車的工地拉去。

這年夏天，儘管工作艱辛，但大家的境況還不算太壞，雖然他們能夠得到的食物並不比瓊斯時代多上多少，但比起來至少也不算少。關鍵在於，除了自己食用之外，大家再也不必去供養那些寄生的人類了。有了這至關重要的一點，其他的事情就顯得微不足道了。

另外，動物們的工作效率也大大提升。比如鋤草這類工作，動物們執行的程度可說是完美無缺，是人類永遠也做不到的。再者，動物們並沒有偷盜的行爲，用來隔開牧場和耕地的籬笆也因此而撤掉，大量的維護工作自然也完全可以省去。

但儘管如此，夏季剛過，就有各式各樣意料不到的困難紛湧而來……農莊裡需要煤油、釘子、線繩、狗食餅乾以及馬蹄上釘的鐵掌，但農莊裡並沒有生產這些東西。後來，又有了對種子和化肥的需求，還要有各類工具和風車零件。這些東西該從哪裡獲得呢？大家都沒有頭緒。

一個星期天的早晨，動物們照例集合起來準備接受新的指令。拿破崙忽然宣布，他已經決定執行一項新的政策，允許動物農莊和鄰近的農莊做些交易——當然這不包含任何商業目的，僅僅是為了獲得某些稀缺物資。

他說，為了風車工程，我們要不惜一切代價。因此，他決定賣掉一些乾草和小麥，而且，如果還需要更多的錢，那就得賣雞蛋了，畢竟雞蛋在威靈頓一直是很搶手的。拿破崙沒忘記告訴母雞，為風車工程而做的任何犧牲將是她們最高的榮耀。

動物們再次感到一種說不出來的彆扭。「決不和人來往，決不從事交易，決不用錢。」早年的宣言不是早已經確立了嗎？從前信誓旦旦的情形至今都還歷歷在目，綱領性的東西怎麼能這麼輕易加以篡改呢？

那四隻曾在拿破崙宣布廢除會議時提出過些許抗議的年輕公豬膽怯地準備發言，但一聽到狗的咆哮聲後便很快閉上了嘴。接著，羊又照例咩咩地叫起來：「四條腿是好漢，兩條腿是壞蛋！」一時的難堪場面也算順利地對付過去了。

最後，拿破崙抬起前蹄，示意大家安靜，宣布他已作好妥善安排，任何動物都不必介入和人打交道這項可鄙的事務當中，因為作為領袖，他將把全部重擔都壓在自己肩上。一個住在威靈頓的律師，名叫溫普爾，已經同意擔任動物農莊和外面社會的仲介人，他將在每個星期一的早晨來訪以處理全部的對外交易事項。最後，拿破崙照例以一聲：「動物農莊萬歲！」的高呼結束談話。動物們便齊聲高唱「英格蘭的野獸」，會議就此散場。

會後的安撫工作是史奎爾的拿手好戲，他向大家打包票，反對從事交易和反對用錢的宣言從來沒有獲得通過，搞不好連相關的提議都是子虛烏有的事。如果追溯謠言的根源，那很可能是來自雪球的陰謀詭計。對那些仍然半信半疑的動物，史奎爾厲聲問道：「你們一定是把夢裡的事和現實生活搞混了！同志們，你們見過這個宣言的記錄嗎？它寫在哪裡了？」當然，類似的宣言並沒有以文字記載。因此，動物們便真的相信是他們自己搞錯了。

那個叫溫普爾的律師，留著落腮鬍，矮個子，一臉奸詐。他的業務規模不大，但他本人相當精明，早就看出了動物農莊會需要經紀人，而且傭

動物農莊

金會相當可觀。按照協議，每個星期一，溫普爾都會過來農莊一趟。動物們對人類還是相當畏懼的，看著他來來去去，各個都避之惟恐不及。

不過，在他們這些四條腿的動物看來，拿破崙對著兩條腿的溫普爾發號施令的情景，提昇了他們的自信，某種程度也讓他們覺得這個新政策是相當不錯的。

如今，他們和人類的關係早已今非昔比。但是，人們對動物農莊的敵意非但沒有因為農莊的興旺而有所和緩，反倒更加劇烈。而且每個人都堅信：動物農莊破產只是遲早的事。他們還在小酒店的聚會裡，希望透過圖表證明風車計畫注定是要失敗的；或者，即便它能建成，也只會是個無法運轉的廢物。雖然如此，他們對動物們管理農莊的能力也不得不刮目相看。他們在稱呼動物農莊時，不再固執地沿用「曼諾農莊」這個名字，而是認可了動物的說法，開始使用「動物農莊」這個原本被公認為離經叛道的名字。所有人都放棄了對瓊斯先生的支援，而瓊斯先生自己也早已放棄，不再抱有任何奪回農莊的希望，靜悄悄地移居到國外去了。如今，多虧溫普爾，動物農莊才有了和外面世界相接觸的機會。但小道消息總是不斷，說是拿破侖正準備和狐木農莊的皮爾金頓先生，或者是平徹菲爾德的弗雷德里克先生簽訂一商業協定，不過，這個協定只會和兩家中的一家簽訂。

約莫就是在這個時候，豬突然搬進莊主的院子，在那裡住下了。這一回，動物們又隱約地想起，在早先的宣言裡有一條是反對這樣做的。可是史奎爾又及時出現，告訴大家事實並非如此。他說，豬是農莊的首腦，理所當然應該擁有一個安靜的工作場所，這樣才能保證各項決策工作的順利進行。再說，為了領袖（近來他在談到拿破侖的時候，已經開始使用「領袖」這一尊稱）的尊嚴，一所潔淨遠勝豬圈的房子是有必要的。儘管這樣，但在聽到豬不但使用廚房煮東西吃外，還占用客廳當作娛樂室之後，仍有一些動物為此深感不安。只有拳師滿不在乎，淡淡地說了一句：「拿破侖同志永遠正確。」但克羅薇卻認為的確存在一條反對使用床鋪的誡律。

她跑到穀倉那裡，試圖從「七誡」當中找出答案。結果發現自己已經連字母都認不出來了。她只好找來穆勒。

「穆勒，」她說，「你替我念一下第四條誡律，它是不是說動物絕不能睡在床上什麼的？」

穆勒費了好大的氣力才拼讀出來。

「上面寫著，『任何動物不得睡在床鋪上使用棉被』。」最後她總算念了出來。

克羅薇覺得有些困惑，她從不記得第四條誡律提到過棉被，但既然它就寫在牆上，那一定本來就是如此了。恰好，史奎爾在幾條狗的陪同下路過這，他提出了特殊的見解。

「同志們，你們已經聽到我們豬睡在床上的事了？這有什麼不好的嗎？你們想想，真的有過什麼誡律反對睡床嗎？床只不過是指稱一個睡覺的地方，從這一點來說，獸欄裡的稻草堆就是一張床。這條誡律只是在反對棉被，因為棉被是屬於人類的發明。我們已經把床上的棉被全撤掉，另外換上了幾條毛毯。可是同志們，我得告訴你們，我們的工作需要消耗大量的腦力，和我們如此多的付出相比，使用這些東西並不過分。同志們，你們總不能不讓我們好好休息吧？你們一定也不願讓我們因為勞累過度而失職吧？更重要的是，你們當中有誰願意看到瓊斯那傢伙回來嗎？」

大家總算消除了疑慮，此後也不再議論這件事了。幾天之後，又有消息宣布，今後豬的起床時間比其他動物晚上一個小時，對此，也不再有誰表示不滿。

到了秋天，大家都累得不行了，不過心情還不錯。說起來他們已經在各種艱難困苦中熬足了整整一年，在賣掉了一些乾草和穀物之後，用來過冬的食物就不太充裕了，好在風車補償了這一切。

工程已近一半了，秋收以後，是一連串秋高氣爽的日子，大家的幹勁因此而提高了不少。他們整天都在拖運石塊，奔忙不休。看著牆壁在一尺尺地

082

加高，覺得自己的辛勤勞動充滿了無窮的意義。拳師甚至在夜裡也不閒著，總會藉著月光再多工作個一兩個小時。大家的樂趣就是在忙裡偷閒時繞著進行了一半的工程走來走去，讚歎著牆壁的強度和近乎完美的線條，讚歎著自己用數不清的汗水換來的成果，對一件如此偉大的工程能夠在自己的手裡完成而開心不已。唯獨老本傑明對風車毫無熱情，他如同往常一樣，除了不斷地重複著「驢的壽命都很長」這句飽含玄機的名言之外，就再也無所表示了。

十一月到了，刮起了猛烈的西北風。一直多雨，沒辦法和水泥了，風車工程只得中斷。一天晚上，忽然間狂風大作，整個農莊都被撼動得發抖，穀倉的頂棚瓦片翻飛。雞群突然被驚醒，嘎嘎亂叫，彷彿在夢中聽見遠處有槍聲響起。好不容易熬到早晨，動物們走出獸欄，發現旗桿已被風吹倒，果園邊上的一棵榆樹也被連根拔起。突然，大家一齊驚呼，一個令人絕望的畫面：風車毀了。

大家發瘋似地衝向前去。一向沉著幹練的的拿破崙跑在最前頭。是的，他們全部的奮鬥成果倒塌，只留下一地狼籍，他們好不容易弄碎又好不容易才運來的石塊散亂在四處。大家呆呆地望著這些碎石塊，心都碎了。拿破崙默默地踱步，偶爾趴在地上聞一聞。他的尾巴僵直，不時左右抽動幾下，這正是他深思的表現。突然，他停住了，好像是拿定了主意。

「同志們，」他的聲調非常平和，「你們知道這是誰做的嗎？你們知道昨天晚上究竟是誰毀了我們的風車嗎？是雪球！」他突然吼道：「這是雪球幹的！這個叛徒！這個居心回測的傢伙！他摸黑潛入這裡，毀了我們近一年的辛勤付出。是的，他企圖阻撓我們偉大的計畫，他像瘋狗一樣地報復我們！同志們，我宣布對雪球處以死刑。無論是誰，只要能夠活抓雪球，並依據我的判決對他行刑，就將被授予『二等動物英雄』勳章和半籃蘋果。」

竟然是雪球犯下如此滔天大罪！動物們既驚愕又憤慨，開始商量如何對付這個窮兇極惡的敵人。幾乎在這同時，離小山丘不遠的草地上，發現了模糊的豬蹄印。雖然那些蹄印只有幾步，但看得出是通向樹籬缺口的方向。拿破崙對著蹄印仔細地聞了一番，然後一口咬定那就是雪球，並推測雪球有可能是從狐木農莊來的。

「別再猶豫了，同志們！」拿破崙又抬起了頭：「還有工作在等著我們，我們要重建風車，就從今天早晨開始！在這個冬天之內我們一定要完工！我們要投入全副精力，不管颳風下雨。我們要讓這個卑鄙的叛徒知道，我們的宏圖偉業不會這樣輕易就被破壞的！記住，同志們，我們的計畫不僅不會有任何改變，反而會更一心一意地進行下去。前進吧，同志們！風車萬歲！動物農莊萬歲！」

豬不停地隨意更改七誡，然而為什麼其他動物雖然起初有些質疑，最後卻又都被說服了？

第七章

這是一個寒冷的冬天。彷彿永遠都不會停歇的狂風暴雨總算是過去了，但很快的，天氣又是雨雪交加，雪片大如席。曠日的嚴寒直到二月才見和緩。動物們都在全力以赴地趕建風車，因為他們都很清楚，外界的眼光從來就沒有離開過他們，如果重建風車的行動又告失敗，那些人類肯定會為此幸災樂禍。

那些不懷好意的人類揚言他們根本就不相信風車是被雪球破壞的。他們寧願相信風車會倒塌純粹是因為牆壁的厚度不夠。雖然動物們從來不這麼覺得，但還是決定牆的厚度不能少於三英尺，而非上次的一英尺半。一方面，這意味著動物們更加小心謹慎，另一方面也意味著採石的工作量加重。但採石場上有長久不化的積雪，嚴重阻礙了工作進行。後來，天氣漸漸乾燥，才勉強開工，但大家再也不像先前那樣滿懷希望、信心十足。總有難以驅散的冷意、難以壓制的飢餓感。只有拳師和克羅薇依然保持當初的幹勁。史奎爾不時做出華麗的陳述，把勞動的樂趣與工作所帶來的神聖感闡述得淋漓盡致。但真正鼓舞大家的卻是拳師無與倫比的任勞任怨，和他時刻不離嘴的那句格言：「我會更努力的。」

一月份，食物開始短缺。大家突然發現糧食儲備已經嚴重不足。上面通知說要額外發些土豆給大家，但隨後卻發現由於地窖遮蓋得不夠嚴密，絕大部分的土豆都已嚴重凍傷，只剩一小部份還能吃。這段日子裡，穀糠和蘿蔔成了大家唯一的食物，雖然上面說禍根是一場小型的自然災害，但實際上大家面臨的差不多就是饑荒了。

對外遮掩實情已成了當務之急。因為風車的倒塌而壯了膽的人類更因此捏造出種種新奇的謊言。比如有謠傳說這裡所有的動物都在饑荒和瘟疫中垂死掙扎，並爆發了一次又一次的內鬨，同類相食和吞食幼獸的慘境更是每天都在發生。拿破侖深知其中利害，決意利用溫普爾先生的中立身份來闢謠。

本來，溫普爾每次來訪時都很少與動物們接觸。但這次，拿破侖卻挑選了羊和其他的一些動物，要他們在溫普爾能聽得到的地方故意閒聊，內容都圍繞著食物增加的主題。不僅如此，拿破侖又下令把儲藏室裡那些空箱子填滿沙土，再把僅存的一些糧食薄薄地蓋在上面，一切就緒之後，便找個適當的藉口，引領溫普爾到儲藏室去，不經意地讓他瞥了一眼。溫普爾就這樣被騙了過去，如大家所意料地為闢謠出力。

但掩蓋問題並不等於解決問題。一月底，剩下的食物已經實在無法再維持下去，如果再沒有糧食，農莊就真的完蛋了。這些天來，拿破侖不再輕易露面，整天待在莊主的院子裡，氣勢洶洶的狗把守那裡的每一道門。一旦外出，總是頗具威儀，六條狗前呼後擁，對任何走近的動物報以兇猛的吼叫。即使是星期天早晨大家也很少見到他，總是史奎爾來發布他的最新指示。

一個星期天的早晨，史奎爾鄭重宣布：從今以後，所有的母雞都必須交出雞蛋。透過溫普爾的協調，拿破侖已經簽署了一份每週出售四百顆雞蛋的合約。這筆生意所賺的錢可以解決迫在眉睫的食物短缺問題，農莊也就可以維持到夏天。到了夏天，情況就會好轉了。

這項指示引起了雞群的強烈抗議。雖然之前就已經提過，說這種犧牲恐怕是必不可少的，但雞群從不相信這種事會真的發生。此時，他們備好的蛋是準備在春天用來孵化小雞的，因而抗議說道，拿走雞蛋就等於謀財害命。於是，為了維護自身的權利，在三隻年輕的黑米諾卡雞的帶領下，他們索性豁出去了。

他們飛到椽子上產蛋，讓雞蛋落到地面因而粉碎。這是農莊自瓊斯被逐以來，第一次的反叛行動。

對此，拿破侖立即採取了嚴厲的措施。他指示停發雞的食物，同時下令，任何動物對雞的同情行為都將等同於反叛行動，當事人將被處以極刑。

動物農莊

由狗負責執法。

堅持了五天之後，雞終於投降了。這期間內共有九隻雞死去，遺體都埋在果園，對外則宣稱他們是死於雞瘟。溫普爾對此事毫不知情。雞蛋嚴格地按時交付，每週都有一輛食品車來農莊裡取貨。

雪球再也沒有蹤影。但關於他的傳聞始終不斷。有的說他就躲在附近的農莊裡，不是在狐木農莊就是在平徹菲爾德農莊。此時，拿破崙和其他農莊的關係也比以前稍有改善。

碰巧，農莊的院子裡，有一堆已經放了十年的木料，於是溫普爾建議把它賣掉。皮爾金頓先生和弗雷德里克先生願意出價，可拿破崙還在猶豫應該賣給誰比較好。

大家注意到，每當他似乎要和弗雷德里克先生達成協定的時候，就有謠傳說雪球正躲在狐木農莊；而當他轉而聯絡皮爾金頓時，就又有謠傳說雪球是躲在平徹菲爾德。

初春時節，突然有件事震驚整個農莊，不知從哪裡傳來的消息指出，說，雪球常在夜間祕密潛入農莊！動物們全都嚇壞了，躲在獸欄裡夜不能寐。據說，每晚他都在夜幕的掩護下偷偷溜進來，蓄意報復，無惡不作。他偷走穀子，弄翻牛奶桶，打碎雞蛋，踐踏苗圃，咬掉果樹皮。不論什麼時候，什麼事情搞糟了，都會把責任推到雪球身上，要是一扇窗子壞了或者下水道堵住了，就會有誰斷定這是雪球在晚上弄的。儲藏室的鑰匙不見了，大家都堅信是被雪球扔到井裡去了。但奇怪的是，在終於發現鑰匙原來是被放在一袋麵粉底下之後，他們還是對雪球的罪惡堅信不移。乳牛異口同聲地稱雪球在她們睡覺時溜進牛棚，偷喝了她們的奶。那些在冬天曾給大家帶來無盡煩惱的老鼠，也被指責為雪球的同夥。

有鑒於此，拿破侖下令對雪球的行蹤進行全面調查。他在狗的護衛下親自執行這項工作，其他動物全都謙恭地尾隨在後。每走幾步，拿破侖就會停下來，聞一聞地面上是否有雪球的氣味。他聞遍了每一個角落，從穀倉、牛棚到雞窩和蘋果園，幾乎到處都有雪球的蹤跡。每到一處，他就把嘴伸到地上，深深吸進幾口氣，隨即驚異地大叫道：「雪球！他到過這裡！我聞得出來！」一聽到「雪球」這兩個字，所有的狗都一齊齜牙咧嘴，發出一陣令大家膽顫心驚的咆哮聲。

大家全被嚇壞了。對他們來說，雪球就像某種隱身的惡魔，無聲無息地出沒在他們的周圍，伺機施展他的邪惡。到了晚上，史奎爾把大家召集起來，惶惶恐恐地做出宣告：「同志們！我們發現了一件可怕的事情，雪球已經向平徹菲爾德農莊的弗雷德里克賣身投靠。而弗雷德里克那傢伙正在計劃著襲擊我們，妄圖霸占我們的農莊！雪球將作為他的嚮導出賣大家。更糟的是，我們一向以為，雪球的反叛僅是出於他自己的野心。可我們錯了，同志們，你們知道什麼才是他真正的動機嗎？雪球打從一開始就和瓊斯是一夥的！他自始至終都是瓊斯的奸細。我們剛剛發現了一些他遺留下來的文件，這才發現了這個實在難以令人相信的大祕密！同志們，依我看，很多問題可以在這裡找到答案。在牛棚之役中，雖然幸虧他的陰謀沒有得逞，但他想毀滅我們的企圖難道不是昭然若揭嗎？」

大家都愣住了。和破壞風車的罪名比起來，這件事可要嚴重得太多了。但大家實在難以接受這一事實。他們都還記得，牛棚之役中，雪球英勇的衝鋒陷陣是有目共睹的，而且，即使瓊斯的子彈已經射進他的脊背時他也毫不退縮。現在，就連拳師也搞不懂了。他趴在地上，前腿縮在身子底下，眼睛緊閉著，絞盡腦汁想把思路理順。

「我不信，」他說道，「雪球在牛棚之役中奮勇衝殺，這是我親眼看到的。戰鬥一結束，我們不是就立刻授予他『一等動物英雄』勳章了嗎？」

「那是我們的失誤。同志們，現在我們才知道，其實他是想引誘我們走向全軍覆滅。在我們發現的那些祕密文件當中，這一點寫得清清楚楚。」

「但他的確受傷了，」拳師說，「我們都看見他邊流血邊衝鋒陷陣。」

「那也是他陰謀中的一部分！」史奎爾叫道，「瓊斯的子彈只不過擦了一下他的皮。要是你識字的話，我會把他自己寫的文件拿給你看。他們的陰謀，就是要在關鍵時刻發出一個信號，讓雪球逃跑並把農莊留給人類。他差不多就要成功了，我甚至敢說，要是沒有我們英勇的領袖拿破崙同志，他的奸計早就得逞了。難道你們不記得了，就在瓊斯一夥衝進院子的時候，雪球突然轉身就逃，很多動物跟著他就跑？還有，就在那一會兒，大家全亂套了，幾乎就要完蛋了，是拿破崙同志突然衝上前去，大喊：『消滅人類！』

同時一口咬住了瓊斯的腿，難道你們不記得了嗎？你們肯定記得！」史奎爾一邊左蹦右跳，一邊大聲叫喊。

既然史奎爾把當時的場景描述得如此逼真，大家便相信是確有其事了。

不管怎麼說，他們記得在激戰的關鍵時刻，雪球的確曾經掉頭逃過。但是拳師還是有些疑惑。

他慢吞吞地說：「我還是不能相信雪球從一開始就是叛徒。他後來的所作所為是另一回事，但我認為在牛棚之役中，他是一個好同志。」

「我們的領袖，拿破崙同志，」史奎爾以緩慢而堅定的語氣宣告，「已經明確地——明確地，同志們——聲明雪球從一開始就是瓊斯的奸細，是的，遠在籌劃起義之前他就是奸細。」

「噢，那這就不一樣了！如果這是拿破崙同志說的，那就肯定不會錯。」拳師說。

「這就是事實的真相，同志們！」史奎爾大叫。但動物們注意到他那閃亮的小眼睛向拳師怪模怪樣地瞥了一下。他轉身要走，又忽然停下來強調：

「我要提醒農莊裡的每個動物，你們要睜大眼睛。我們有理由相信，現下，雪球的密探正潛伏在我們中間！」

四天以後的一個下午，拿破崙召集所有的動物在院子裡開會。集合完畢之後，拿破崙威嚴地從屋裡出來了，佩戴著他的兩枚勳章（他最近已授予自己一枚「一等動物英雄」和一枚「二等動物英雄」勳章），還帶著他那九條大狗。那些狗圍著他蹦來蹦去，發出讓所有動物都毛骨悚然的吼叫。大家默

默蜷縮著，心裡有種不祥
的預感。

　　拿破崙嚴厲地站在那
裡，向四周巡視一番，接
著便發出一聲尖細的驚
叫。於是，那些狗立刻衝
上前去，咬住了四頭年輕
公豬的耳朵，將他們向外
拖。那四頭公豬在疼痛和
恐懼中嚎叫著被拖到拿破
崙腳下，耳朵流出血來。
狗嘗到了血腥味，發狂了
好一會兒。更讓大家吃驚

的是，有三條狗竟然向拳師撲了過去。拳師看到他們撲來，不慌不忙地伸出巨掌，在半空中踢翻一條狗，又把他踩在腳下。那條狗發出了尖利的叫聲，慌忙求饒，另外兩條狗見狀便夾著尾巴飛奔回來。拳師不解地看著拿破侖，不知道是該把那狗踩死還是放掉。拿破侖變了臉色，對拳師厲聲呵斥。拳師便抬起腳掌，那條狗就帶著傷在哀號中溜走了。

喧囂立即平靜下來。那四頭公豬渾身發抖地等待發落。有的動物還記得，他們正是曾公開抗議拿破侖廢除星期天大會的那四頭公豬。接著，拿破侖喝令他們坦白罪行。他們沒頭沒尾地交代說，自雪球被驅逐後他們一直和他祕密保持聯絡，毀壞風車的罪行也有他們的份，並且還和雪球達成一項協定，打算把動物農莊拱手讓給弗雷德里克先生。他們還補充說雪球曾私下對他們透露過，過去幾年來他一直都是瓊斯的奸細。話才剛說完，他們的喉嚨就被狗的厲齒咬穿了。

行刑完畢，拿破侖聲色俱厲地質問還有誰要坦白什麼。在這種恐怖氣氛的壓迫下，那三隻曾經在雞蛋事件中領頭鬧事的雞戰戰兢兢地走上前去，說雪球曾托夢給他們，煽動他們違抗拿破崙的命令。坦白完畢，他們也沒能逃過被殺掉的命運。接著上來的是一隻鵝，說他曾在去年的收穫季節私藏了六穗穀子，並在當天晚上吃掉了。一隻羊也坦白說他曾在飲水池裡撒尿，但這是雪球慫恿他的。另外兩隻羊則說，他們曾經謀殺了一隻老公羊，那是一隻十分忠實的拿破崙的信徒，他們在他正患咳嗽時，追著他圍著火堆跑來跑去。這些動物當場被處以死刑。拿破崙的腳前已屍體成堆，空氣中彌漫著濃重的血腥味，聞所未聞的事情就這樣開始了。

等一切都過去，豬狗以外的動物，便都擠成一堆溜走了。他們既驚又懼，但卻說不清到底什麼更使他們害怕——是那些和雪球結為同盟的叛徒呢，還是剛剛目睹的殘忍懲罰更可怕？過去，雖然類似的流血場景也時常可見，但遠不如這次來得陰森恐怖，因為這是發生在動物之間的事。從瓊斯逃離農莊直到現在，還從沒有發生過動物之間相互殘殺的慘劇，就連老鼠也未曾受過傷害。

這時，大家已經走到小山丘上，尚未完工的風車孤零零地矗立在那裡。躺在那裡吧，擠在一起可以取暖。克羅薇、穆勒、本傑明、牛、羊，鵝群和雞群，除了貓之外全都在這裡了，貓在集合的時候就已經失蹤了。一時間沒人說話，只有拳師站著，一邊煩躁不安地走動，一邊用尾巴不斷地在身上拍打，最後，他終於說話了：「我不明白，我真不敢相信這種事發生在我們的農莊裡，一定是因為我們做錯了什麼。如果說有什麼補救辦法，我想關鍵就是要更加努力地工作。從今天起，早上我要再提前一個小時起床。」

他步履沉重地離開了，走向採石場。一到那裡，便連續採了兩車石頭，直拉到風車的建設基地，忙到晚上才收工回去。

大家都擠在克羅薇的周圍默默不語。在他們躺著的地方，可以俯視整個村莊：狹長的牧場伸向那條大路，耕地裡長著碧綠的麥苗，還有草灘、樹林、池塘，以及農莊裡的紅色屋頂和那煙囪裡冒出的裊裊青煙。這是一個春天的傍晚，夕陽的光輝灑在青草地和茂盛的叢林之上，蕩漾著片片金輝。他們忽然意識到，這是他們自己的農莊，每一寸土地都歸他們自己所有，他們為此驚訝，在此之前，他們從未發現這裡竟是如此的美麗，如此的令他們心馳神往。

克羅薇已經止不住奪眶而出的熱淚。如果她有辦法能夠說出此時的想法，她肯定會說：我們已經背離了當年為推翻人類而許下的諾言，這些殘酷的殺戮並不是我們在大豬梅傑鼓動起義的那天晚上所嚮往的。

對於未來，如果說她還曾有過什麼想望，那一定會是這樣的一個社會：在那裡，沒有飢餓，沒有鞭子，一切平等，大家各盡所能，弱者能夠得到保護：就像在大豬梅傑講演的那天晚上，她曾經彎曲著前腿保護著那一群遲到的小鴨子一樣。

但她不明白，為什麼現在卻處在一個不能講真話的世界裡，四周隨時有氣勢洶洶的狗到處咆哮，還必須眼看著自己的同志在坦白了可怕的罪行後被撕成碎片。但她的心裡沒有任何反叛或者違命的念頭。她知道，即便現狀慘不忍睹，也還是比瓊斯時代好太多了；再說，當務之急還是要防備人類再次捲土重來。不管發生什麼事，她都要忠心耿耿，辛勤勞動，服從拿破崙的領導，完成他交付的一切任務。

但她也確實相信，她和其他的動物曾滿懷期望並為之不懈奮鬥的，並不是今天的這般場景；他們建造風車，勇敢地冒著瓊斯一夥的槍林彈雨衝鋒陷陣，也不是為了眼前這般結果。這就是她此刻的深切感受，只是千頭萬緒竟然無法以言語表達。

於是她張開喉嚨，低低地唱起「英格蘭的野獸」。這曲調忽然有了異乎尋常的感染力，漸漸地，越來越多的聲音加入了這支旋律，一遍又一遍，和諧卻緩慢，低沉卻淒然。這是第一次，第一次大家以這樣的心態、這樣的嗓音唱起這支不能再熟悉的歌曲，別有一番滋味湧上了心頭。

突然，歌聲被史奎爾打斷了。他在兩條狗的陪同下，宣布了拿破崙同志的一項特別命令：「英格蘭的野獸」已被廢止。從今以後禁唱這首歌。

大家怔住了。

「爲什麼？」穆勒嚷道。

「不再需要了，同志們，」史奎爾冷冷地說，『英格蘭的野獸』是革命歌曲。但革命已經成功，今天下午對叛徒的處決就是整個革命的最後行動。另外，敵人已經全部被打垮了。我們在『英格蘭的野獸』中所表達的是在當時對未來美好社會的渴望，但這個社會現在已經建立起來。這首歌已明顯不再有任何意義了。」

大家感到一種莫名的恐懼，正有些動物想抗議的時候，羊群便大聲地咩咩叫起來：「四條腿是好漢，兩條腿是壞蛋。」一直叫嚷了好幾分鐘，於是淹沒了這場爭議。

於是，「英格蘭的野獸」再也聽不到了，取而代之的，是豬中的才子繆斯寫的另外一首歌曲，它是這樣開頭的：

動物農莊，動物農莊，

吾輩誓不讓汝受損罹傷！

從此，每個星期天早晨的升旗之後就改唱這首歌了。但對大家來說，無論歌詞還是曲調，這首作品遠不能和「英格蘭的野獸」相提並論。

想一想

你認同拿破崙為了剷除異己所採取的各種行動嗎？你覺得這會為動物們帶來什麼樣的影響？

第八章

幾天以後，行刑的恐慌已經平息下來，一些動物這才想起了第六條誡律中彷彿有過這樣一條規定：「任何動物都不得傷害同類」。在討論這個話題時，大家總是儘量地避開那些豬狗，他們隱約覺得這次殺戮與第六誡律是有衝突的。克羅薇請求本傑明為她念一下第六誡律，但本傑明只是像往常一樣置身事外。最後是穆勒念給她聽：「任何動物不得無緣無故地傷害同類。」對「無緣無故」這幾個字，動物們幾乎沒有印象。但他們明白了拿破侖的暴力行為並不是沒有理論依據的，當年的誡律並沒有被違反。

這一年，動物們比前些年更加辛苦。重建風車，不但要把牆築上兩倍厚，還有著緊迫的時間期限；再加上日常的例行性工作，工作量相當驚人。

大家發現，現在的工作時間已明顯地比瓊斯時代長了，但食物卻並不比那時候多。

每到星期天早上，史奎爾的蹄子上就捏著一張長紙條，向大家宣布各類食物產量增加的資料，根據內容分門別類，有的增加了百分之二百，有的增加了百分之三百或百分之五百。動物們覺得沒有任何理由不聽信他的話，尤其是他們再也想不起起義前的情況了。不過，他們寧願少聽點數據而多分些食物。

現在，所有命令都透過史奎爾或另一頭豬宣布，拿破侖則兩星期也難得露一次面。一旦他公開現身，不僅狗侍衛會前呼後擁，還有一隻黑色小公雞鳴鑼開道：拿破侖講話前，小公雞會先響亮地啼叫一下。據說，即使在莊主的院子裡，拿破侖也是和別的豬分開住的，用餐由兩條狗伺候，餐具用的是上好的瓷器。另外，每逢拿破侖的生日也要鳴槍致敬，就像另外的兩個紀念日一樣。稱呼上也有了改變，直呼其名是大不敬的，必需改稱：「偉大的領袖拿破侖同志」，此外，豬還喜歡錦上添花地為他冠上各式頭銜，如「動物之父」、「人類剋星」、「羊之守護者」、「鴨子之友」等等。每次史奎爾演講時，總會淚流滿面地暢談拿破侖無上的智慧和慈悲心腸，說他對普天之下的動物，尤其是那些還生活在其他農莊裡飽受歧視與奴役的動物，滿懷深摯的愛。農莊裡，大家已習於把每一件幸運的事和每一項榮譽都歸功於偉大的拿破侖。可以常常聽到一隻雞對另一隻雞這樣講：「在偉大領袖拿破侖的指引下，我在六天之內下了五顆蛋。」或者兩頭正在喝水的牛高聲讚美：

「多虧偉大領袖拿破侖同志的領導，這水喝起來真甜！」農莊裡，動物們的精神狀態充分體現在一首名為「拿破侖同志」的詩中，詩是繆斯寫的：

偉大的拿破侖同志！

讓我總是有仰望的狂熱，

讓我總是有激情如火，

您的雙眼堅毅沉著，

哦，主，是您賜給了我們糧食！

幸福的源頭！

孤兒的好友！

每日的兩餐飽飯，

每夜那潔淨的草墊，

恩主呀，都歸功於您無私的賞賜！

偉大的拿破侖同志！

都是因為有了您的撫慰，

連夢都做得很美，

每隻動物都能安睡，

我要是有頭幼獸，

幼小得惹人憐愛，

哪怕他還太小，還不太懂事，

他也應該學會

忠誠地聆聽您的教誨，

第一聲一定要這樣叫，我的寶貝：

「偉大的拿破侖同志！」

拿破崙對這首詩非常滿意，讓手下把它刻在穀倉的牆上，就在與「七誡」相對的另一頭。詩的上方是史奎爾用白漆畫的拿破崙的一幅畫像。

這期間，由溫普爾牽線，拿破崙正針對那堆木材與弗雷德里克及皮爾金頓進行一系列繁冗的談判。在這兩個人中，弗雷德里克比較急著要買，但又不肯出一個公道的價錢。與此同時，有一個過時的消息重新開始流傳，說弗雷德里克和他的夥計們正在密謀襲擊動物農莊，並想把那個他嫉恨已久的風車毀掉，而雪球就藏身在平徹菲爾德農莊。仲夏時節，大家又驚訝地聽說，另外有三隻雞也坦承罪行，說他們曾受雪球的煽動，參與過一起刺殺拿破崙的陰謀。那三隻雞立即被處決了。而有鑒於此，為了拿破崙的安全，戒備措施更加完善：夜間，每個床腳都有一條狗作為守衛，枕戈待旦；一頭名叫平克埃的豬在拿破崙吃飯之前先替他試試食物，以防有人下毒。

差不多同時，有消息說拿破崙決定把那堆木材賣給皮爾金頓先生；他還擬訂了一項關於動物農莊和狐木農莊之間以物易物的長期協定。儘管還是通過溫普爾牽線，但拿破侖和皮爾金頓先生現在的關係可以說是相當不錯的。對於皮爾金頓這個人，動物們並不信任。但他們更不信任弗雷德里克，他是個讓動物們又怕又恨的傢伙。

夏天過去了，風車即將竣工，那個關於弗雷德里克將要襲擊農莊的風聲也越來越大。據說鬥爭已經迫在眉睫，而且，弗雷德里克他們人數更多，裝備更好，還聽說他已經買通了地方官和警察，這樣，一旦他能把動物農莊的地契弄到手，就可以成為合法的所有人了。更有甚者，平徹菲爾德農莊傳出了許多可怕的消息，說弗雷德里克對他農莊裡的動物極為殘酷：他用鞭子抽死了一匹老馬，讓他的牛挨餓，還把一條狗扔到爐子裡燒死了，到了晚上，他就把刮鬍刀的碎片綁在雞爪子上看鬥雞取樂。

聽到這些消息，動物們群情激憤，他們不時叫嚷著要一起去進攻平徹菲爾德農莊，趕走那裡的人類，解放那裡的動物。他們之所以把火氣暫時壓了下來，是因為史奎爾一再告誡大家，要避免草率行動，要相信拿破侖的戰略布署。儘管如此，反對弗雷德里克的情緒還是越來越高漲。一個星期天早上，拿破侖來到穀倉，他解釋說他從來沒打算把那堆木料賣給弗雷德里克。他說，和那個惡棍打交道實在有辱他的身份。作為起義宣傳員的鴿子，以後不准在狐木農莊落腳。他還下令，把他們過去的口號「打倒人類」換成「打倒弗雷德里克」。

夏末，雪球的另一個陰謀又被揭露了：麥田裡之所以長滿雜草，是因為他曾在某個夜晚潛入農莊，往糧種裡拌了草籽。一隻與此事件有牽連的雄雞向史奎爾坦白了罪行後，就吞食劇毒草莓畏罪自殺了。大家還被告知，事實並不像他們一直認為的那樣：雪球從來都沒有獲頒過「一等動物英雄」勳章。受獎的事不過是他在戰鬥中怯懦的表現而受盡了譴責。這種解釋的確不有這回事，倒是因為他在戰鬥中怯懦的表現而受盡了譴責。這種解釋的確不是人人都能夠輕易接受的，但史奎爾的如簧之舌，很快就使動物們把這些歸咎於自己遲鈍的記憶力。

到了秋天，大家竭盡全力，在不耽誤收割的前提下終於使風車竣工了。

接下來的事就是安裝機器。溫普爾正在爲購買機器的事到處奔忙，但不管怎樣，風車的主體總算是完成了——不管他們的經驗多麼不足，工具多麼原始，運氣多麼不佳，雪球的詭計多麼陰險，整個工程到此總算是在計畫之內如期完成了！驕傲遠遠壓過了早已過度的疲憊，他們繞著自己的這一傑作轉個不停。在他們眼裡，風車要比第一次做得漂亮多了，另外，牆座也比第一次的厚了一倍以上。除了炸藥以外，它堅固的外牆已經能夠抵禦任何侵襲！

回想當初爲此流過的血與汗，大家依然湧現疲憊，但一想到當風車的翼板帶動了發電機，此後他們的生活將會發生巨大改變，他們就忘記了疲勞，開始歡呼，雀躍不已。拿破侖在狗和公雞的前呼後擁下，親自視察，並親自對大家的豐功偉績表示祝賀，還莊重地以「拿破侖」三個字爲風車命名。

兩天後，大家被召集到穀倉，召開一次特別會議。拿破侖宣布，他已經把那堆木材賣給了弗雷德里克，明天就是交貨的日子。頓時，大家都驚訝得

114

目瞪口呆。原來，拿破崙只是和皮爾金頓虛與委蛇，實際上他已和弗雷德里克達成了祕密協定。

與狐木農莊的關係完全破裂了，他們去信向皮爾金頓發出了極盡能事的謾罵與侮辱，通知鴿子們要視平徹菲爾德農莊為禁地，還把「打倒弗雷德里克」的口號改成了「打倒皮爾金頓」。同時，拿破崙親自出面進行闢謠，說所謂動物農莊面臨襲擊的說法是徹頭徹尾的謊言，弗雷德里克虐待動物的傳聞也純屬無稽之談。所有的謠言都很有可能是來自雪球及其同夥。總之，照現在的情況看來，雪球並非藏在平徹菲爾德農莊，而是一直住在狐木農莊裡面。身為皮爾金頓最得力的心腹，他每天都過著極為靡爛的生活。

拿破崙精明的算計使群豬欣喜若狂：與皮爾金頓的表面友好迫使了弗雷德里克把價錢提高了十二英鎊。史奎爾說，拿破崙思想上的卓越之處就在於其實他根本就不相信任何人，即使對弗雷德里克也是如此。弗雷德里克曾打算用一種叫做支票的東西支付木料錢，那個東西不過是一張白紙，只是寫著保證支付之類的許諾而已，但拿破侖根本不是他能糊弄得了的，他要求用真正的五英鎊鈔票付款，而且要拿到錢才交貨。這筆錢弗雷德里克已經如數付清，金額剛好夠爲風車添置機械。

木料很快就被載走了，貨車才剛剛離開，拿破侖便迫不及待地在穀倉裡又召開了一次特別會議，內容是讓動物們觀看弗雷德里克給付的鈔票。拿破侖笑顏逐開，心花怒放，他戴著他的兩枚勳章，端坐在草墊上，錢就在他身邊整齊地堆放著。動物們排成一行慢慢走過，無不大飽眼福。拳師還伸出鼻子聞了聞那堆鈔票，聞到一股新鮮的油墨味道。

三天以後，在一陣嘈雜聲中，只見溫普爾飛車趕到，面如死灰。他把自行車就地一扔，徑直衝了進去。很快，拿破侖的房間裡響起了一陣哽噎著嗓子的怒吼。出事了！這消息迅速傳遍整個農莊：鈔票是假的！弗雷德里克沒有花一毛錢就載走了木料！

拿破侖立即召集所有動物，咬牙切齒地當眾判處弗雷德里克死刑。他

說，要是抓住他，非把他活活煮死不可。同時他也告誡大家，繼這個背信棄義的行動之後，會有更糟的事情將發生。弗雷德里克和他的同夥隨時都可能發動他們蓄謀已久的襲擊。因此，得馬上在所有通向農莊的路口設置崗哨。

另外，派四隻鴿子給狐木農莊去信修好，希望皮爾金頓先生能夠不念舊惡。

但襲擊就在第二天的早晨突然開始了。當時正是早飯時間，哨兵飛報，說弗雷德里克已經氣勢洶洶地逼近了。動物們懷著滿腔的怒火，立刻給敵人以迎頭痛擊，但這一回可不比「牛棚之役」了。敵方有十五個人，六把槍，可怕的槍聲和惡毒的子彈已不是動物們的血肉之軀可以抵擋。雖然拿破崙和拳師不斷集結攻勢，但始終不能衝進敵人的五十碼之內。隨著傷員的增多，大家對戰鬥開始絕望，於是四散奔逃，各自尋找藏身之地。不一會兒，整個牧場，還有風車，都已落入了敵手。拿破崙也已不知所措了，他一言不發地踱著步，尾巴變得僵硬，不停地抽搐。他不時朝著狐木農莊的方向投射渴求的眼光。如果皮爾金頓的人願意幫他們的話，這場戰鬥不是沒有機會。不過雪上加霜的是，前一天派出的四隻鴿子飛回來了，但其中一隻帶著皮爾金頓寫下的一張紙條，上面寫著：「你們活該。」

這時，弗雷德里克一夥人已停在風車周圍。動物們一邊窺視他們，一邊不安地嘀咕起來。有兩個人拿出鐵鍬和大鐵錘：他們竟然要拆掉風車！

「這不可能！」拿破侖喊道，「我們已把牆築得那麼厚實，他們休想在一個星期之內拆掉它。不要怕，同志們！」

但本傑明仍在急切地注視著那些人的活動。拿著鐵鍬和大鐵錘的兩個人正在風車的地基附近打孔。終於，本傑明帶著幾乎是戲謔的神情，慢騰騰地呶了呶他那長長的嘴巴。

「我知道他們要幹嘛了，」他說，「過一會兒，他們就要往打好的孔裡裝填炸藥。」

果然，幾分鐘之後，眼看那些人朝四下散開，接著，響起了一聲震耳欲聾的爆炸。頓時，鴿子們飛到空中，其他動物（除了拿破侖外）全都轉過臉

動物農莊

119

去，猛地趴倒在地。當他們起來後，只看到風車上空飄蕩著一團巨大的黑色煙雲。煙消雲散之後，風車已化作了一地碎石！

動物們被激怒了。他們發出一陣強烈的復仇吶喊，不等指示，便一齊向敵人衝去。這次，他們顧不得那如冰雹一般掃射而來的子彈。這是一場殘酷、激烈的戰鬥。那群人不斷發射子彈，等動物接近他們時，他們就拿起棍棒大打出手。一頭牛、三隻羊、兩隻雞就這樣死在他們的手裡。每隻動物都留下了傷痕，就連一直在後面指揮作戰的拿破侖也被子彈削去了尾巴尖。但人類也為此付出了代價：三個人的頭顱被拳師的鐵蹄打破；一個人的肚子挨了重重的一下牛犄角；還有一個人，褲子幾乎都被撕掉了。身為拿破侖貼身警衛的那九條狗，奉命在樹籬的遮掩下偷偷繞過去，突然出現在敵人的側翼，兇猛地吼叫起來。一見苗頭不對，弗雷德里克便和他的同夥倉皇地撤出去。

動物們勝利了，但早已疲憊不堪，鮮血淋漓。他們一瘸一拐地走回農

莊。看到昨日還是親愛的同志今天卻橫屍在草地上，不禁悲從中來，淚流滿面。他們在那個曾矗立著風車的地方靜默了好長時間。風車沒了，甚至地基也被炸毀了一部分。如此一來，要想再建風車，情況也非同上一次可比了。上一次還可以利用剩下的石頭，可這次卻連石頭也不見了⋯爆炸把石頭拋到幾百碼以外，好像這裡原本就是一片空地。

走近農莊的時候，史奎爾朝他們蹦蹦跳跳地走了過來，沒有誰記得曾在戰鬥的時候看到過他，但此時他卻高興得搖頭擺尾。「勝利了！」他喊道。

接著，典禮的槍聲從農莊裡傳了出來。

「為什麼要開槍？」拳師不解地問。

「為什麼？當然是為了慶祝我們的勝利！」史奎爾嚷道。

「什麼勝利？」拳師問。他的膝蓋還在流血，又丟了一隻蹄鐵，蹄子也綻裂了，另外還有十二顆子彈擊中了他的後腿。

「什麼勝利？同志們，難道我們沒有在我們的領土上——在神聖的動物農莊領土上趕跑敵人嗎？」

「但他們毀了風車，我們已經為了風車辛苦了整整兩年！」

「那有什麼？我們會再蓋一座。高興的話我們就蓋六座。同志們，你們不瞭解，我們已經完成了一件多麼偉大的事。敵人曾占領我們腳下這塊土地。但現在呢，多虧拿破崙同志的領導，我們重新奪回了每一寸土地！」

「可是我們奪回本來就屬於我們的。」拳師又說道。

「這就是我們的勝利。」史奎爾不以為然。

他們一瘸一拐地走進大院。拳師腿皮下的子彈使他疼痛難忍。他知道，擺在他面前的，將是一項從地基開始再建風車的沉重勞動，他知道應該振作起來。但是，他第一次想到，自己已經十一歲了，身體的狀況已今非昔比。

但當動物們看到那面綠旗在飄揚，聽到再次鳴槍──共響了七下，聽到拿破崙的談話，聽到他對他們的行動的祝賀，他們似乎覺得，說起來，他們的確是取得了巨大的勝利。

大家爲在戰鬥中死難的動物們安排了隆重的葬禮。拳師和克羅薇拉著靈車，拿破崙親自走在隊伍最前方。用了整整兩天的時間舉行各種慶祝活動：唱歌、演講，還少不了鳴槍，每一隻動物都得了一個作爲特殊紀念物的蘋果，每隻家禽還得到了二盎司穀子，每條狗有三塊餅乾。有通知說，這場戰鬥將被命名爲「風車之役」，拿破崙還爲此設立了一個新的「綠旗勳章」，並授予他自己。在一片歡天喜地之中，那個不幸的鈔票事件也就被忘掉了。

慶祝活動過後幾天，豬偶然在地下室裡發現了一箱威士忌酒。當天晚上，莊主院子裡傳出一陣響亮的歌聲，令大家驚奇的是，中間還夾雜著「英格蘭的野獸」的旋律。大約在九點半左右，只見拿破崙戴著一頂瓊斯先生的舊圓頂禮帽，從後門出來，在院子裡飛快地跑了一圈，又閃進門不見了。但第二天早晨，院子內卻是一片沉寂，看不到一頭豬走動，快到九點鐘時，史奎爾出來了，目光呆滯，尾巴無力地掉在身後，渾身上下病懨懨的。他把大家叫道一起，傳達了一個沉痛的消息……拿破崙同志病危！

124

動物農莊

一陣哀嚎油然而起。莊主院子的門外鋪著稻草，於是，大家踮著蹄尖從那裡走過。他們眼中含著熱淚，相互之間不安地詢問：要是領袖拿破侖離開了，我們可該怎麼辦？農莊裡此刻到處都在風傳，說雪球最終還是成功地設法把毒藥摻到拿破侖的食物中了。十一點，史奎爾出來發布另一項公告，說是拿破侖同志在彌留之際宣布了一項神聖的法令：飲酒者要處死刑。

可是到了傍晚，拿破侖卻顯得好多了，次日早上，史奎爾就告訴他們說拿破侖正在康復。當天晚上，拿破侖又重新開始工作了。又過了一天，動物們才知道，他早先讓溫普爾在威靈頓買了一些有關蒸餾及釀酒的書。一週後，拿破侖下令，要將蘋果園那邊的小牧場翻一遍土。那片牧場原先是打算為退休動物留作養老用的，現在卻說牧草已經耗盡，需要重新耕種；但不久以後便真相大白了──拿破侖準備在那裡播種大麥。

大概就在這時，發生了一件奇怪的事情，幾乎每個動物都百思不得其解。這事發生在一天夜裡十二點鐘左右，當時，院子裡傳來一聲巨大的跌撞

125

聲，大家立刻衝出獸欄去看。

那晚月光皎潔，在穀倉一頭寫著「七誡」的牆角下，橫著一架斷為兩截的梯子。史奎爾平躺在梯子邊上，昏迷不醒。他手邊有一盞燈，一把油漆刷子，一筒打翻的白漆桶。狗圍著史奎爾，等他甦醒過來，馬上就護送他回莊主院子。大家都想不通這是怎麼回事，只有本傑明吸了吸他那長嘴巴，露出一副若有所思的神情，似乎看出了一點端倪，但卻什麼也沒說。

幾天後，穆勒在閱讀七誡時注意到，又有另外一條誡律大家記錯了。他們本來以為，第五條誡律是「任何動物不得飲酒」，但有兩個字他們卻都忘記了。事實上，那條誡律應該是：「任何動物不得飲酒過度」。

想一想

風車計畫對動物們來說究竟意味著什麼？為什麼歷經了這麼多次失敗，拿破崙卻還是堅持不斷重建？

126

動物農莊

第九章

拳師身上的傷口過了很久才好。慶祝活動結束後第二天，大家就又開始為風車奔忙了。拳師不肯好好休息，強忍著傷痛，不讓大夥察覺。晚上，他悄悄地告訴克羅薇，他的蹄子疼得厲害，克羅薇就嚼了些草藥給他敷上。她和本傑明都一再地勸過拳師：工作要適可而止，用不著太賣命。但拳師一句也聽不進去。他說，他實在很希望在能退休之前親眼看到風車竣工。

說到退休，還是有必要回顧一下當初的律法。律法規定不同動物的退休年齡分別為：馬和豬十二歲，牛十四歲，狗九歲，羊七歲，雞和鵝五歲，而且，退休以後還會按時領取一份優厚的養老津貼。雖然至今為止還沒有一個動物真正領到過這份津貼，但近來有關這個話題的討論卻越來越多了。蘋果園那邊的小牧場已被用來種植大麥，就又有小道消息傳說養老院的占地改為大牧場的一角——但願這話不是出自哪隻動物的一廂情願。據說，每匹馬的養老津貼是每天五磅穀子，到冬天改為每天十五磅乾草，節日裡還發給一根胡蘿蔔或是一個蘋果。拳師的十二歲生日就在來年的夏末。

這段日子裡大家的生活並不輕鬆。和去年冬天相比，寒冷有增無減，食物卻更少了。除了豬和狗以外，所有動物的食物再次減少。史奎爾解釋，糧食分配太平均是違背動物主義原則的。無論如何，他都能極其輕鬆地向其他動物證明，無論表面上看起來是怎樣，事實上他們並不欠缺糧食。當然，有時會出於暫時考慮而稍微調整一下供應量（他總是強調「調整」而從來不提「減少」）。但與瓊斯時代相比，現在已有了驚人的進步。史奎爾的論據十分有力，他會用他尖細的嗓音一口氣念完一大串數據。這些數據顯示，和瓊斯時代相比，現在他們有了更多的燕麥、乾草、蘿蔔，工作的時間更短，飲用水的水質更好，現在他們有了更多的燕麥、乾草、蘿蔔，工作的時間更短，飲用水的水質更好，大家的平均壽命也延長了，幼獸的存活率提高了，獸欄裡有了更多的草墊，甚至連跳蚤都少多了。在這樣強大的宣傳攻勢下，大家終於對一切信以為真。說實話，在他們的記憶中，瓊斯和他所代表的過去的一切幾乎已經被時間沖刷得一乾二淨。他們知道，近來的生活的確艱難，常常是饑寒交迫，全部的時間都得工作、吃飯、睡覺，別無其他。但毫無疑問，如果這樣很糟的話，那過去就一定比這更糟。再說，從前他們都是奴隸，而現在卻擁有自由。正像史奎爾常說的：這一點使一切都有了天壤之別。

嗷嗷待哺的動物更多了。這天，四頭母豬差不多同時都生了小豬，共有三十一頭之多，全都帶著黑白條斑。誰是他們的父親呢？這並不難猜，因為拿破侖是農莊裡唯一的一頭種豬。有消息說，過些時候，等買好了磚頭和木材，就要在院子的花園裡為這些小豬蓋一間學校。目前則是由拿破侖在廚房裡親自為孩子們擔任教師。這些小豬平常都在花園裡活動，而且不許他們和其他動物的幼獸一起玩耍。大約與此同時，上面又頒布了一項規定，說是當其他動物在路上遇到豬時，必須馬上讓到路邊；另外，所有的豬，不論地位高低，均享有星期天在尾巴上戴絲帶的特權。

這一年總算是無災無難地過去了，只是經濟上稍嫌拮据。建學校用的磚頭、沙子、石灰和完善風車要用的機器都是不小的開銷。莊主院子裡需要的燈油和蠟燭，拿破侖的食用糖（他禁止其他豬吃糖，因為吃糖會讓他們變胖）也得花錢去買。再加上數目不少的日用品，諸如釘子、繩子、煤、鐵絲、鐵塊和狗食餅乾等等，開銷同樣不小。看來最要緊的就是存錢了。剩下的那些乾草和一部分土豆已經賣掉，雞蛋的購銷合約便又增加到每週六百顆。因此，在這一年中孵出的小雞數量極少，二月份又被削減了一次；為了省油，獸欄裡也禁止點燈。只有豬的生活水準沒有絲毫下降。事實上，即使有著種種的不利情況，他們的體重卻總是有增無減。二月底的一個下午，有一股動物們從來沒有聞過的、令他們垂涎欲滴的香味，從廚房那一邊的小釀造房裡飄過院子。有動物說，這是蒸大麥的味道。他們貪婪地聞著香氣，心裡都在暗自

130

動物農莊

猜測：這是不是在為他們的晚餐準備熱呼呼的大麥糊？但是，晚飯時並沒有見到熱呼呼的大麥糊。而且接下來的那個星期天，大家又接獲一個新的公告，說是往後大麥將成為豬的專用品。大家這才想起，蘋果園那邊的田裡就早就種上大麥了。不久，又傳出了這樣一個消息，說是現在每頭豬每天都可以領用一品脫啤酒，拿破崙的定額則是半磅。

但是，不管受了什麼氣，不管日子多難熬，只要一想到現在活得比從前體面，大家也就覺得還說得過去。現在是歌聲多，演講多，活動多。拿破崙已經指示，每週要舉行一次叫做「自發遊行」的活動，目的在於慶祝動物農莊的奮鬥成果和繁榮興旺。每到既定時刻，大家便紛紛放下工作，列隊繞著農莊的邊界遊行：豬帶頭，然後是馬、牛、羊，接著是家禽。狗在隊伍兩側，為拿破崙開道的公雞走在隊伍的最前方。拳師和克羅薇還會拿著一面綠旗，旗上畫著蹄子和犄角以及「拿破崙同志萬歲！」的標語。遊行之後，大家爭先恐後地背誦對拿破崙的贊詩；接著是演講，由史奎爾報告糧食產量增

131

長的最新資料，一逢高潮還要鳴槍慶賀。羊對「自發遊行」活動最為熱心，如果哪個動物抱怨（有些動物有時會趁豬和狗不在場時發些牢騷）說這是浪費時間，羊肯定就會響亮地重覆說著：「四條腿是好漢，兩條腿是壞蛋」，頓時就叫得他們啞口無言。但大體上說來，大家對慶祝活動還是相當興致勃勃的。說到底，他們發現正是這些活動讓他們感到自己是真正當家做主，他們所做的一切都是在追求自身的幸福。想到這些，大家也就心滿意足了。在歌聲中，在遊戲中，在史奎爾列舉的數據中，在鳴槍聲中，在公雞的啼叫聲中，在綠旗的飄揚中，至少他們還能在這些時候忘掉自己的饑腸轆轆。

四月份，動物農莊宣告成立「動物共和國」。這就意味著要選舉一位總統。可候選人只有一個：拿破崙，他在大家的一致推舉下就任總統。同一天，又公布了有關雪球和瓊斯串通勾結的新證據，其中涉及到很多具體事例。從這些事例中不難看出，雪球不僅詭計多端地破壞過「牛棚之役」，而且還公開為瓊斯作幫兇。他在參加混戰之前，還高喊過「人類萬歲！」有些動物仍記得雪球背上帶了槍傷，但那實際上是被拿破崙咬傷的。

仲夏，失蹤數年的烏鴉摩西突然出現。他幾乎沒有變，照舊不工作，喋喋不休地講著「糖果山」的事。誰要是願意聽，他就一本正經，還用他的大鳥喙指著天空——「在那裡，同志們，」他一本正經，還用他的大鳥喙指著天空——「在那裡，同志們，」他一本正經，還用他的大鳥喙指著天空——「在那裡，同志們，」他滔滔不絕地說著：「在那裡，就在那團烏雲那邊，那裡有座『糖果山』。那個幸福的國度將是我們可憐動物擺脫了塵世後的最後歸宿！」不但如此，他甚至還聲稱曾在一次高空飛行中到過那，看到一望無際的苜蓿草地，無數的亞麻子餅和方糖就長在低矮的樹籬上。很多動物為此而神往。他們想，現實生活滿是飢餓和勞累，那麼，死後的歸宿應該是無限美好的吧？只有豬對他相當輕蔑，他們說那些關於「糖果山」的事全是一派胡言，但他們並沒有採取什麼措施，甚至還默許他的不勞而獲，每天分給他一其爾的啤酒。

拳師的蹄子痊癒之後，工作更拼命了。其實這一年，所有的動物工作起來都像奴隸一般。除了日常工作和第三次重建風車外，還要為小豬蓋學校：

工程是在三月份動工的。有時，在食不果腹的情況下，長時間的工作令人難以忍受，但拳師從沒退縮過。從他工作賣力的程度是看不出他的老態的，他只是外貌上有了小小的變化：皮毛沒有以前那麼光亮，粗壯的腰部似乎也有點萎縮。別的動物說：「等春草茂盛時，拳師就會慢慢恢復過來了」；但是，春天來了，拳師並沒有長胖。有時，當他在通往礦頂的坡上，用盡全身氣力頂著那些巨型圓石時，支撐他的彷彿只剩不懈的意志。這種時候，他總是一聲不吭，但從旁看過去，似乎還隱約見到他口中念念有辭：「我會更努力的」。克羅薇和本傑明再三警告他要當心身體，但拳師絲毫不予理會。他的十二歲生日快到了，但他沒有放在心上，一心一意只想在退休之前收集足夠的石頭。夏天的一個傍晚，突然有動物說拳師出事了。在這之前，他獨自外出，往風車那裡拉了一車石頭。果然，消息是真的。幾分鐘後，兩隻鴿子急速飛來，說：「拳師倒下去了！他現在躺在風車那裡，站不起來了！」

農莊裡大約有一半動物衝了出去，趕到建風車的小山丘上。拳師就躺在那裡。他在車轅中間伸著脖子，連頭也抬不起來，眼睛眨著，身體兩側的毛被汗水黏得一團一團的，嘴角流出一股稀稀的鮮血。看到這般情景，克羅薇跪倒在他的身邊。

「拳師！」她喊道，「你怎麼了？」

「我的肺，」拳師聲音微弱，「沒關係，我想沒有我你們也能建成風車，備用的石頭已經收集夠了。我充其量也只剩一個月可活了。不瞞你說，我一直盼望著退休。眼看著本傑明也老了，說不定他們會讓他也同時退休，和我作個伴。」

「會有人來幫我們的，」克羅薇叫道，「快點，誰快去告訴史奎爾這裡出事了！」

大家全都跑回農莊向史奎爾報告，只有克羅薇和本傑明留下來。本傑明趴在拳師身邊，一語不發地用他的長尾巴為拳師驅趕蒼蠅。十五分鐘後，史奎爾趕到，滿臉關切。他說拿破崙同志已得知此事，對農莊裡最忠誠的成員發生這樣的不幸感到十分悲傷，正安排將拳師送往威靈頓的醫院治療。

聽到這些，大家不免有些不安，因為除了莫莉和雪球之外，其他動物從未離開過農莊，他們不想把一位生病的同志交給人類。然而，史奎爾毫不費力地說服了他們，他說在威靈頓的獸醫院比在農莊裡能更好地治療拳師的病。大約過了半個小時，拳師有些好轉了，他好不容易才站起來，一步一步地走回到他的馬廄，克羅薇和本傑明已經為他鋪好了一張舒適的稻草床。

此後兩天，拳師就待在他的馬廄裡。豬送來了一大瓶紅色的藥，那是他們在藥櫃裡和他聊天，由克羅薇在飯後餵給拳師服用，每天兩次。晚上，她躺在他的棚子裡和他聊天，本傑明為他趕蒼蠅。拳師說他對發生的一切並不後悔。如果能澈底康復，他希望自己還能再活上三年。他盼望能在大牧場的一角平平靜靜地住上一陣子。那樣的話，他就能抽空學習新事物以增長才智。他說，他打算利用自己的餘生學習字母表上剩下的二十二個字母。

然而，本傑明和克羅薇只有在工作結束之後才能和拳師待在一起。一天中午，來了一輛車載走了拳師。當時，大家在一頭豬的監視下正忙著在蘿蔔地裡除草，忽然，他們驚訝地看見本傑明從農莊獸欄飛奔而來，還一邊扯著嗓子大叫。這是他們第一次見到本傑明如此激動，也是第一次看到他沒命地奔跑。「快，快！」他大聲喊著，「快來！他們要載走拳師了！」沒等豬下命令，大家全都放下了手上的工作，趕緊跑回去了。果然，院子裡停著一輛大篷車，由兩匹馬拉著，車邊上寫著字，駕駛的位置上坐著一個男人，臉色陰沉，頭戴一頂低簷圓禮帽。而拳師的馬廄眞的空了。

大家圍住車，傷感地說：「再見了，拳師！再見！」

「笨蛋！傻瓜！」本傑明喊著，一邊跳，一邊用他的蹄掌敲打著地面，「傻瓜！你們沒看見車子上寫著什麼嗎？」

這下子，大家猶豫了，全都安靜下來。穆勒試圖去拼讀那些字。可本傑明把她推到了一邊，他在死一般的寂靜中念道：「『威靈頓，艾夫列·西蒙茲，屠馬商兼煮膠商，皮革商兼供應狗食的骨粉商。』你們不知道這是什麼意思嗎？他們要把拳師載到宰馬場去！」

聽到這些，所有的動物突然迸發一陣恐懼的哭嚎。就在這時，坐在車上的那個人揚鞭催馬，馬車迅速離開院子。大家跟在後面，拼命地叫喊著。克羅薇擠到最前面去。這時，馬車開始加速，克羅薇也越跑越快，「拳師！」她哭喊道，「拳師！拳師！」此時，拳師好像聽到了外面的喧囂聲，他的臉出現在車後的小窗子裡。

「拳師！」克羅薇淒厲地哭喊，「拳師！快出來！他們要送你去死！」所有動物一齊跟著哭喊起來，「出來，拳師，快出來！」但馬車加速，離他們越來越遠了。誰也不知道拳師到底有沒有聽見克羅薇的那些話。但不一會，他的臉從窗上消失了，接著車內響起一陣巨大的馬蹄踢蹬聲。他正試圖踹開車子出來。若是從前，拳師只要幾下就能把車廂踢個粉碎。可是，唉！他已不如從前，沒有力氣了；不一會兒，馬蹄的踢蹬聲漸漸變弱，漸漸消失。。絕望的動物們開始懇求拉車的兩匹馬停下來，「朋友，朋友！」他們

大聲呼喊，「別把你們的同類拉去送死！」但是那兩匹愚蠢的動物，竟然傻得不知道這是怎麼回事，只是豎起耳朵加速奔跑。拳師的臉再也沒有出現在窗子上。有的動物想跑到前面去關上柵門，但是太遲了，一瞬間，馬車就已衝出大門，飛快地消失在大路上。就這樣，再也見不到拳師了。

三天之後，據說拳師已死在威靈頓的醫院裡。但是，作為一匹馬，他已經得到了無微不至的照顧。這個消息是由史奎爾當眾宣布的，他說，在拳師生前的最後幾小時裡，他一直守候在場。

「那是我見過的最感人的場面！」他說，抬起蹄子抹去了一滴淚水，「最後一刻，我守在他床邊，他衰弱得幾乎說不出話來，他湊在我耳邊，說唯一的遺憾是沒有看到風車建成。最後他還低聲說著：『同志們，前進！以革命的名義前進，動物農莊萬歲！拿破侖同志萬歲！拿破侖永遠正確。』同志們，這些就是他的臨終遺言。」講到這裡，史奎爾忽然變了臉色。他沉默了一會兒，用他那雙小眼睛疑神疑鬼地掃視了一下全場，才繼續講下去。

他說，據他所知，拳師被載走後，農莊裡流傳著一個愚蠢的、不懷好意的謠言。有的動物注意到，拉走拳師的馬車上有「屠馬商」的標記，就草率地認為拳師被送到宰馬場了。「我真是不敢相信有這麼傻的動物！」他擺著尾巴左蹦右跳，責問大家：「從這一點看來，你們真的敢說自己很瞭解敬愛的領袖拿破崙同志嗎？其實只是因為那輛車以前曾歸一個屠馬商所有，但獸醫院買下了它，不過他們還沒將舊名字塗掉。是因為這樣，才會引起大家的誤會。」聽到這裡，大家才如釋重負地鬆了一口氣。接著，史奎爾繼續繪聲繪影地描述著拳師臨終的囑託，和他所受到的優厚優待，還有拿破崙為他不惜一切代價購置貴重藥品等等細節。於是，大家打消了最後一絲疑慮，想到他們的同志是在幸福中死去的，悲傷也就不再了。

接下來的星期天會議中，拿破崙親自出席，為拳師宣讀了一篇簡短的悼辭。他說，已經不可能把大家已故的同志遺體載回來安葬在農莊裡了。但他已指示，用莊主院子花園裡的月桂做一個大花圈，送到拳師的墓前。而且他

141

打算幾天後爲拳師舉行一場追悼會。最後，拿破侖以「我會更努力的」和「拿破侖同志永遠正確」這兩句拳師心愛的格言總結談話。他說，所有動物都應該把這兩句格言當作自己的借鑒，並認真地將之貫徹到實際行動中去。

宴會當天，一輛雜貨商的馬車從威靈頓駛來，在莊主院子裡交付了一隻大木箱。當晚，莊主院子裡傳來了一陣鼓噪的歌聲，在此之後，又響起了另外一種聲音，聽上去像是在激烈地吵鬧，吵鬧聲直到十一點左右的時候，才在一陣打碎了玻璃的巨響中平靜下來。一直到第二天中午，莊主院子裡不見任何動靜。同時，又流傳這樣的消息，說豬先前不知從哪弄到了一筆錢，爲他們自己買了一整箱的威士忌。

想一想

拳師爲動物農莊鞠躬盡瘁，爲什麼最後卻落得這樣的下場？

第十章

春去秋來，年復一年。在時光的無情流逝中，壽命較短的動物已經一個個地相繼死去。現下，除了克羅薇、本傑明、烏鴉摩西和幾頭老豬之外，已經沒有一個能記起革命前的那段歲月了。

穆勒死了，傑西死了，就連瓊斯也死了，死在他的某個酒鬼朋友家裡。雪球更是早被大家忘掉了，「拳師」也成了一個陌生而模糊的名字。克羅薇也老了，身體已胖得有些過份，關節不再柔韌有力，眼角也總是沾滿黏液。兩年前她就應該退休了，但實際上，從來沒有一隻動物真正地享受過退休的待遇，將大牧場一角作為養老院的話題也早就不再有人提起。

如今，拿破侖已是一頭超級雄壯的公豬，體重將近三百四十磅。史奎爾更是胖得連睜眼往外看都覺得費力。只有老驢本傑明似乎超脫得置身於歲月之外，除了鼻子和嘴的周圍有點轉灰之外，其餘幾乎就和過去一個樣子。只是，自從拳師死後，他比以前更孤僻了。

現在，農莊裡的動物要比以前多得多了，儘管沒有比從前所預料得多。很多動物是在農莊裡出生長大的，還有一些則是來自別的地方。對於前者來說，革命在他們的腦子裡只不過是一個朦朦朧朧的傳說，而對於後者，那些二往日的光榮與夢想他們更是一無所知。現在的農莊裡，除了克羅薇，另外還有三匹馬。他們都是好同志，都很勤勞，也很溫順，只可惜腦筋都不太好。照現在的樣子看來，他們之中要是有誰能學到字母表上的「B」那就真要謝天謝地了。對於有關革命和有關「動物主義」的事情，他們是聽到什麼就相信什麼，完全不經大腦思考，如果某件事情是由克羅薇告訴他們的那就更是如此了，他們視克羅薇為母親，對她言聽計從。不過，他們究竟是不是真能體會話中的涵義就沒有人知道了。

現在的農莊更加欣欣向榮，也更加井然有序。農莊裡增加了兩塊地，是從皮爾金頓先生那裡買來的。風車最終還是建成了，其中的艱辛當然不用多說。另外，農莊裡還有了自己的一台打穀機，新的建築也說得上是鱗次櫛比。就連溫普爾也為自己添置了一輛馬車。稍微有些遺憾的，就是風車最終還是沒能用來發電，而是用來磨穀了，這讓磨穀成為了農莊的支柱產業，著實獲利良多。如今，大家又忙著修建另一座風車。據說，等這一座風車建成了，就要裝上發電機來實現當年的夢想。雖然，當年雪球為大家描述的那種舒適、那種有電燈和熱水的獸欄、那種每週三天工作制，如今已不再有人提起了。拿破侖早就斥責，這些想法與動物主義精神是背道而馳的。他說，真正的幸福就在於勤奮工作和儉樸生活中。

不知道為什麼，從表面看上去，農莊似乎已經變得富裕了，但動物們卻仍是毫無餘裕，只有豬和狗確實是走進了新的生活中。也許，部分原因是由於豬和狗的家族比較龐大吧？和大家不同的是，豬和狗都是用他們自己的方

145

式在從事勞動的。就像史奎爾總愛掛在嘴上說的那樣，農莊的監督和組織會以一種獨特的方式耗費驚人的工作量，但這卻是其他動物無法理解的。例如，史奎爾說，豬每天要耗費大量的精力，用來處理那些叫做「文件」、「報告」、「會議記錄」和「備忘錄」等等神祕的事宜。這類文件為數眾多，必須仔細填寫，而一旦填寫完畢，又得把它們在爐子裡燒掉。史奎爾說，為了農莊的幸福，沒有什麼工作比這更重要了。但說歸說，迄今為止，無論是豬還是狗，都並沒有親自產出過任何糧食，即便他們為數眾多，食欲也總是出奇旺盛。

至於其他動物，生活還是一如既往。他們仍然在挨餓，睡的是草墊，喝的是髒水，做的是辛勤的農耕工作，冬天受寒受凍，夏天蚊蠅纏身。有時，會有些上了年紀的動物絞盡腦汁，從那些淡漠的印象中搜索回憶，他們追問、判斷，到底革命以後的那段日子，剛趕走瓊斯那時，情況是比現在更好還是更糟？但誰也不記得了，沒有一件事情可以拿來和現在比對，除了史奎爾時常公布的一系列沒完沒了的數據以外，他們沒有任何憑據用來比較，而史奎爾的數據總是千篇一律地表明，所有的事物正變得越來越好。大家發現這個問題解釋不清，不管怎麼說，他們現在已很少有時間去思索這類事情。唯有老本傑明，他聲稱對自己漫長一生中的每個細節都記憶猶新，還說他已經體認到，一切事物，過去沒有、將來也不會有更好或更糟的分別。因此，飢餓、艱難、失望的現實，都是生活中必然要面臨的困境。這就是生活，誰也無法改變。

　不過，大家仍然沒有放棄希望。確切地說，他們身為動物農莊的一員，從來沒有喪失自己的榮譽和優越感——一下子也沒有過。他們的農莊依然是整個英格蘭境內唯一一所動物自給自足、並由動物自行管理的農莊。他們之中，就連最年輕的、或是那些來自十幾英里以外農莊的新成員，每每想到這一點時，自豪感都會油然而生。當他們聽到槍鳴，看到旗桿上綠旗飄揚，豪情壯志就湧上心頭，話題一轉，也就常提起那史詩般的過去，以及驅除瓊斯、刻寫「七誡」、擊退人類來犯者的偉大戰鬥等等。其實，舊日的夢想一個也沒有被丟棄。當年梅傑預言過的「動物共和國」，以及英格蘭的綠色田野上不再有人類足跡的夢想，至今依然是他們的信仰。他們依然相信：總有一天，那個時代會到來。也許不是立刻，也許今生已無望看到，但它終究會到來。而且至今，說不定就連「英格蘭的野獸」這支曲子還在被偷偷地傳唱著，反正農莊裡的每個動物都熟悉它，儘管誰都不敢放聲高歌。也許，他們處境險惡；也許，他們的希望並沒有全部實現，但他們很清楚，他們和別的動物不一樣。如果他們沒有吃飽，不是因為將食物分給暴虐的人類；如果他們工作太過辛苦，那至少也是在為自己而努力。他們之中，沒有誰用兩條腿走路，沒有誰稱呼誰為「主人」，所有動物一律平等。

148

動物農莊

初夏的一天，史奎爾把羊叫了出去。他帶領他們前往農莊另一頭一塊長滿樺樹苗的地方。在史奎爾的監督下，羊在那裡吃了整整一天的樹葉，到了晚上，他告訴羊，既然天氣相當暖和，他們就繼續待在那裡。然後，他獨自返回莊主院子。羊就在那裡待了整整一個星期——對大家來說，也就是失蹤了一個星期。史奎爾每天都花很多時間和他們待在一起。他說他正在教唱羊群一首新歌，需要清靜的地方。

一天傍晚，羊回來了。當時，大家才剛剛結束工作，正走在返回農舍的路上。突然，庭院裡傳來了一聲馬的嘶鳴，大家嚇了一跳，全都停下了腳步：是克羅薇的聲音。此時她再次發出慘叫聲。於是，大家全都衝進了庭院。他們全都看見了讓克羅薇吃驚大叫的情景——有隻豬正用後腿走路。

是的，是史奎爾。他還有點笨拙，好像還不大習慣用這種姿勢支撐他巨大的身體，不過已能平衡。不一會兒後，莊主院子裡又走出一群豬，都用後腿行走。他們走得好壞不一，有一、兩頭豬還有點不大穩，看上去應該要找

149

一根棍子支撐比較好。不過，每頭豬大致上還算走得成功。最後，在一陣非常響亮的狗叫聲和公雞尖細的啼叫聲中，拿破侖也走出來了。他大搖大擺地站著，眼睛朝四周傲慢地瞥了一下，那群狗則活蹦亂跳地簇擁在他的周圍。

他的蹄子裡握著一根鞭子。

一陣死一般的寂靜。驚訝、恐懼的動物們擠在一起，看著那群豬慢慢地繞著院子用雙腳行走。這世界彷彿已經完全顛倒了。接著，當他們從這場震驚中稍微冷靜下來時，有那麼一瞬間，他們已經顧不得任何事——顧不得他們對狗的害怕，顧不得他們多年來養成的，無論發生什麼事都不抱怨、不批評的習慣——準備要大聲抗議。但就在這時，羊群突然齊聲叫嚷：「四條腿是好漢，兩條腿更是好漢！四條腿是好漢，兩條腿更是好漢！四條腿是好漢，兩條腿更是好漢！四條腿是好漢，兩條腿更是好漢！」

喊叫聲持續了足足有五分鐘。等羊安靜下來以後，大家發現已經錯過抗議的機會了，因為豬已列隊走回了院子。

本傑明感覺到有一個鼻子在他肩上磨蹭。回頭一看，是克羅薇。只見她那一雙勞累的眼睛比以往更加灰暗。她沒說一句話，只是輕輕地拽了他的鬃毛，領著他前往大穀倉，那裡是寫著「七誡」的地方。他們站在那裡注視著有白字的柏油牆。

「我的眼睛不行了，」她終於說話了，「即使是年輕時，我也看不懂那上面寫的東西。可是今天，我覺得這面牆和以前已經不一樣了。『七誡』還是過去那樣嗎？本傑明？」

只有這一次，本傑明為她破例，將牆上寫的東西念給她聽，那上面已經沒有別的了，只有一條誡律，它是這樣寫的：

　所有動物一律平等

　但有些動物比其他動物

　更平等

從此以後，大家對一切都見怪不怪了：第二天，所有的豬在農莊監督工作時，蹄子上都握著一根鞭子，這不稀奇；豬爲他們自己買了一台無線電收音機，而且正準備安裝一台電話，這不稀奇；他們訂閱了《約翰牛報》、《珍聞報》及《每日鏡報》，這不稀奇；拿破侖在莊主院子花園裡散步時，嘴裡叼著一根煙斗，這也不稀奇。是的，不必再大驚小怪了。如今，拿破侖已經穿上了一件黑外套和一條特製的馬褲，還綁上了皮革綁腿，同時，他心愛的母豬也穿上了一件紋綢洋裝，那是瓊斯夫人過去常在星期天穿的。

一個禮拜後，一輛馬車駛進農莊。一個由鄰近農莊主人組成的代表團接受邀請來此考察觀光。他們參觀了整個農莊，對一切都讚不絕口，尤其是那座風車。當時，動物們正在蘿蔔地裡除草，他們正費力工作，不敢抬起頭，搞不清楚自己怕的究竟是人還是豬。

那天晚上，莊主院子裡傳來一陣陣哄笑聲和歌聲。大家突然被吸引住，他們相當好奇，既然這是動物和人類第一次在對等關係下齊聚一堂，究竟會發生什麼事呢？大家便不約而同地悄悄往莊主院子的花園過去。

到了門口，他們又停住了，或許是因為害怕，誰也不敢再往前走，最後是克羅薇帶頭進去。他們踮著蹄子，走到房子前，個頭較高的動物就從餐廳的窗戶往裡面看。屋子裡面，在那張長桌子周圍，分別坐著六個農莊莊人和六頭地位崇高的豬，拿破侖則坐在桌子前方的主位上。讓大家吃驚的是，豬在椅子上表現出的舒適自在遠勝於他們在泥地裡的模樣。賓主們一直都在專注地玩著牌，但是中場休息了一下子，他們端起酒杯來準備乾杯。有個很大的酒壺在他們之間傳來傳去，他們在杯子裡添滿了啤酒。沒人注意到窗戶外有很多詫異的面孔正往裡面窺探。

狐木農莊的皮爾金頓先生舉著杯子站了起來。他說在乾杯之前，有幾句話得先講一下。

他說，他相信，他自己還有在場的各位都十分慶興，人類和動物農莊之

154

155

間長久以來的猜疑和誤解終於得以化解了。過去，無論是他自己，還是在座的各位，都無法想像會有今天的情形。當時，可敬的動物農莊的所有者，曾受到人類鄰居的關注，不過，他會說這些關注是出於某種程度的顧慮而非敵意。錯誤與不幸都曾發生過，不正確的說法也曾廣為流行過。一個由豬所有並經營的農莊多少曾讓人類覺得有些不正言不順，且讓鄰近農莊有種不安的感受。相當多的農莊主人並未詳加調查就信口開河地推斷，說動物農莊裡的歪風邪氣正在到處蔓延。他們擔心這種狀況會影響到他們自己的動物，甚至影響到他們的雇員。但現在，所有疑慮都已煙消雲散了。今天，他和他的朋友們拜訪了動物農莊，用他們自己的眼睛觀察了農莊的每一個角落。他們發現了什麼呢？這裡不僅有著最先進的工作方法，而且紀律嚴明，秩序井然，應該成為各地農莊的典範。他相信，也敢肯定，動物農莊裡的下層動物，做的工作比任何動物都多，吃的飯比任何動物都少。他和他的代表團成員今天看到了這裡的很多特色，也準備立即在自己的農莊中貫徹實施。

在即將結束發言之際，他再次重申了動物農莊及其鄰居間已經建立的、和應該建立的友好情感。豬和人之間不存在任何意義上的利害衝突。他們奮鬥的目標和遭遇的困難是一樣的。勞工問題不是到哪裡都相同嗎？講到這裡，皮爾金頓先生好一會兒樂不可支，他竭力憋笑，下巴憋得都發紫了，最後才說：「如果你們有你們的下層動物在作對，」他說，「我們也有我們的下層階級要應付！」這一句話引起一陣哄堂大笑。皮爾金頓先生再次為他在動物農莊看到的飼料供給少、勞動時間長，生活簡約樸素等諸多良好現象向豬表示敬意。

最後他請各位站起來，斟滿酒杯：「先生們，先生們，我敬你們一杯，為動物農莊的繁榮昌盛乾杯！」

一片熱烈的喝彩聲和跺腳聲隨即響起，惹得拿破侖心花怒放。他離開座位，繞著桌子走向皮爾金頓先生，和他碰了杯便一口喝乾了，待喝采聲一靜下來，始終以後腿站立著的拿破侖舉蹄示意：他也有幾句話要講。

這番談話就像拿破崙所有的演講一樣，簡明扼要而又一針見血。他說，他也為誤解時代的結束而感到高興。曾經有很長一段期間，流傳著各式各樣不懷好意的謠言，他有理由認為，這些謠言是一些居心叵測的仇敵散佈的，說他和他的同僚的觀念中，有一種主張顛覆的、甚至根本是屬於破壞性的東西。他們一直被認為是在企圖煽動鄰近農莊的動物造反。但是，事實絕非如此。他們唯一的願望，無論是過去、現在還是將來，都是與他們的鄰居們和平共處，維持正常的貿易關係。他補充說，他有幸掌管的這個農莊是一家協作營運企業。他自己手中的那張地契是歸豬共同所有的。

他說，他相信任何猜疑都會消失，近來他在農莊裡的一些例行改革能夠更加堅定大家的信心。長期以來，農莊裡的動物們流傳著一個愚蠢的習慣，那就是互相以「同志」相稱。這要廢止。還有一個不知從何而來的怪習慣，就是在每個星期天早上，要列隊走過花園裡一個釘在木樁上的雄豬頭蓋骨。這也要廢止。頭蓋骨已經埋了。客人們也許已經看到那面旗杆上飄揚著的那

158

動物農莊

面綠旗，他們或許已經注意到，過去旗面上畫著的白色蹄子和犄角現在已經消失了。從今以後那面旗將是完全的綠色。

他說，關於皮爾金頓先生精采而友好的演講，只有一點他要作些簡單的補充修正。皮爾金頓先生一直提到「動物農莊」，當然，事前他不可能知情，因為拿破侖是第一次宣布這件事：「動物農莊」這個名字從今作廢，今後，農莊的名字將改為「曼諾農莊」。他相信，這個名字才是它應有的。

「先生們，」皮爾金頓再次總結道，「請容我向剛才一樣致意，但內容稍有不同。請斟滿你們的酒杯，先生們，我要向你們祝賀：為曼諾農莊的繁榮昌盛乾杯！」

一陣同樣熱烈而真誠的喝采聲轟然響起，酒一飲而盡。但當外面的動物們目不轉睛地看著這一情景時，他們似乎看到了有一些怪事正在發生。豬的面孔上似乎有了些變化。克羅薇那一雙昏花的眼睛掃過了一個接一個面孔：他們有的有五個下巴，有的有四個，有的有三個，但是有什麼東西似乎正在

159

融化消失。接著，熱烈的掌聲結束了，他們又拿起撲克牌，繼續剛才中斷的遊戲。外面的動物們這才悄悄地離開。

但他們才走不到二十碼的距離又突然停住了。莊主院子裡傳出一陣吵鬧聲。他們跑回去，再次透過窗子往裡看。果然，裡面正在大吵大鬧：有人大喊大叫，也有人捶打桌子；一邊是疑神疑鬼的銳利目光，另一邊則咆哮矢口否認。混亂的原因似乎是因為拿破崙和皮爾金頓先生同時打出一張黑桃A。

十二個聲音一齊憤怒地吼著，他們竟是如此相似！而今，不必再問豬的面孔上到底發生什麼變化了。外面的眼睛從豬看到人，又從人看到豬，再從豬看回到人：他們已分不出究竟誰是豬，誰是人了。

想一想

在整篇小說中，豬究竟運用了哪些手段，控制農莊動物們的思想和行動？你覺得如果是你，有辦法不任由豬擺布嗎？

動物農莊
Animal Farm

George Orwell

中英雙語版

晨星出版

01 ╱

Mr. Jones, of the Manor Farm, had locked the hen-houses for the night, but was too drunk to remember to shut the popholes. With the ring of light from his lantern dancing from side to side, he lurched across the yard, kicked off his boots at the back door, drew himself a last glass of beer from the barrel in the scullery, and made his way up to bed, where Mrs. Jones was already snoring.

As soon as the light in the bedroom went out there was a stirring and a fluttering all through the farm buildings. Word had gone round during the day that old Major, the prize Middle White boar, had had a strange dream on the previous night and wished to communicate it to the other animals. It had been agreed that they should all meet in the big barn as soon as Mr. Jones was safely out of the way. Old Major (so he was always called, though the name under which he had been exhibited was

snore [snor] **v** 打鼾
communicate [kəˈmjunəˌket] **v** 傳達；傳遞

Willingdon Beauty) was so highly regarded on the farm that everyone was quite ready to lose an hour's sleep in order to hear what he had to say.

At one end of the big barn, on a sort of raised platform, Major was already ensconced on his bed of straw, under a lantern which hung from a beam. He was twelve years old and had lately grown rather stout, but he was still a majestic-looking pig, with a wise and benevolent appearance in spite of the fact that his tushes had never been cut. Before long the other animals began to arrive and make themselves comfortable after their different fashions. First came the three dogs, Bluebell, Jessie, and Pincher, and then the pigs, who settled down in the straw immediately in front of the platform. The hens perched themselves on the window-sills, the pigeons fluttered up to the rafters, the sheep and cows lay down behind the pigs and began to chew the cud. The two cart-horses, Boxer and Clover, came in together, walking very slowly and setting down their vast hairy hoofs with great care lest

regard [rɪ'gɑrd] *v* 把……看作，把……認為
ensconce [ɛn'skɑns] *v* 使安頓；使安坐
majestic [mə'dʒɛstɪk] *adj* 崇高的
benevolent [bə'nɛvələnt] *adj* 仁慈的，有愛心的

there should be some small animal concealed in the straw. Clover was a stout motherly mare approaching middle life, who had never quite got her figure back after her fourth foal. Boxer was an enormous beast, nearly eighteen hands high, and as strong as any two ordinary horses put together. A white stripe down his nose gave him a somewhat stupid appearance, and in fact he was not of first-rate intelligence, but he was universally respected for his steadiness of character and tremendous powers of work. After the horses came Muriel, the white goat, and Benjamin, the donkey. Benjamin was the oldest animal on the farm, and the worst tempered. He seldom talked, and when he did, it was usually to make some cynical remark — for instance, he would say that God had given him a tail to keep the flies off, but that he would sooner have had no tail and no flies. Alone among the animals on the farm he never laughed. If asked why, he would say that he saw nothing to laugh at. Nevertheless, without openly admitting it, he was devoted to Boxer; the two of them usually spent their

conceal [kənˈsil] **v** 隱蔽，隱藏
tremendous [trɪˈmɛndəs] **adj** 巨大的，極度的，驚人的
cynical [ˈsɪnɪkl] **adj** 憤世嫉俗的；挖苦的
devote to [dɪˈvot] [tu] 將……奉獻給；致力於，專心於

Sundays together in the small paddock beyond the orchard, grazing side by side and never speaking.

The two horses had just lain down when a brood of ducklings, which had lost their mother, filed into the barn, cheeping feebly and wandering from side to side to find some place where they would not be trodden on. Clover made a sort of wall round them with her great foreleg, and the ducklings nestled down inside it and promptly fell asleep. At the last moment Mollie, the foolish, pretty white mare who drew Mr. Jones's trap, came mincing daintily in, chewing at a lump of sugar. She took a place near the front and began flirting her white mane, hoping to draw attention to the red ribbons it was plaited with. Last of all came the cat, who looked round, as usual, for the warmest place, and finally squeezed herself in between Boxer and Clover; there she purred contentedly throughout Major's speech without listening to a word of what he was saying.

All the animals were now present except Moses, the tame raven, who slept on a perch behind the back door. When Major saw that they had all made themselves comfortable and were waiting attentively, he cleared his

promptly [promptlɪ] *adv* 立即地
attentively [əˈtɛntɪvlɪ] *adv* 聚精會神地

throat and began:

"Comrades, you have heard already about the strange dream that I had last night. But I will come to the dream later. I have something else to say first. I do not think, comrades, that I shall be with you for many months longer, and before I die, I feel it my duty to pass on to you such wisdom as I have acquired. I have had a long life, I have had much time for thought as I lay alone in my stall, and I think I may say that I understand the nature of life on this earth as well as any animal now living. It is about this that I wish to speak to you.

"Now, comrades, what is the nature of this life of ours? Let us face it: our lives are miserable, laborious, and short. We are born, we are given just so much food as will keep the breath in our bodies, and those of us who are capable of it are forced to work to the last atom of our strength; and the very instant that our usefulness has come to an end we are slaughtered with hideous cruelty. No animal in England knows the meaning of happiness or leisure after he is a year old. No animal in England is free.

comrade [ˈkɑmræd] *n* 夥伴，同事；（共產黨的）同志
miserable [ˈmɪzərəbl] *adj* 痛苦的；不幸的
slaughter [ˈslɔtɚ] *v* 宰殺，屠宰

The life of an animal is misery and slavery: that is the plain truth.

"But is this simply part of the order of nature? Is it because this land of ours is so poor that it cannot afford a decent life to those who dwell upon it? No, comrades, a thousand times no! The soil of England is fertile, its climate is good, it is capable of affording food in abundance to an enormously greater number of animals than now inhabit it. This single farm of ours would support a dozen horses, twenty cows, hundreds of sheep — and all of them living in a comfort and a dignity that are now almost beyond our imagining. Why then do we continue in this miserable condition? Because nearly the whole of the produce of our labour is stolen from us by human beings. There, comrades, is the answer to all our problems. It is summed up in a single word — Man. Man is the only real enemy we have. Remove Man from the scene, and the root cause of hunger and overwork is abolished for ever.

"Man is the only creature that consumes without

fertile ['fɜtl] *adj* （土地）肥沃的，富饒的
labour ['lebə-] *n* 勞動
abolish [ə'bɑlɪʃ] *v* 廢除，廢止

producing. He does not give milk, he does not lay eggs, he is too weak to pull the plough, he cannot run fast enough to catch rabbits. Yet he is lord of all the animals. He sets them to work, he gives back to them the bare minimum that will prevent them from starving, and the rest he keeps for himself. Our labour tills the soil, our dung fertilises it, and yet there is not one of us that owns more than his bare skin. You cows that I see before me, how many thousands of gallons of milk have you given during this last year? And what has happened to that milk which should have been breeding up sturdy calves? Every drop of it has gone down the throats of our enemies. And you hens, how many eggs have you laid in this last year, and how many of those eggs ever hatched into chickens? The rest have all gone to market to bring in money for Jones and his men. And you, Clover, where are those four foals you bore, who should have been the support and pleasure of your old age? Each was sold at a year old — you will never see one of them again. In return for your four confinements and all your labour in the fields, what have you ever had except your bare rations and a stall?

hatch [hætʃ] **v** （蛋）孵化
confinement [kən'faɪnmənt] **n** 分娩（期）

"And even the miserable lives we lead are not allowed to reach their natural span. For myself I do not grumble, for I am one of the lucky ones. I am twelve years old and have had over four hundred children. Such is the natural life of a pig. But no animal escapes the cruel knife in the end. You young porkers who are sitting in front of me, every one of you will scream your lives out at the block within a year. To that horror we all must come — cows, pigs, hens, sheep, everyone. Even the horses and the dogs have no better fate. You, Boxer, the very day that those great muscles of yours lose their power, Jones will sell you to the knacker, who will cut your throat and boil you down for the foxhounds. As for the dogs, when they grow old and toothless, Jones ties a brick round their necks and drowns them in the nearest pond.

"Is it not crystal clear, then, comrades, that all the evils of this life of ours spring from the tyranny of human beings? Only get rid of Man, and the produce of our labour would be our own. Almost overnight we could become rich and free. What then must we do? Why, work night and day, body and soul, for the overthrow of the

grumble ['grʌmb!] **v** 抱怨，發牢騷
fate [fet] **n** 命運；結局

human race! That is my message to you, comrades: Rebellion! I do not know when that Rebellion will come, it might be in a week or in a hundred years, but I know, as surely as I see this straw beneath my feet, that sooner or later justice will be done. Fix your eyes on that, comrades, throughout the short remainder of your lives! And above all, pass on this message of mine to those who come after you, so that future generations shall carry on the struggle until it is victorious.

"And remember, comrades, your resolution must never falter. No argument must lead you astray. Never listen when they tell you that Man and the animals have a common interest, that the prosperity of the one is the prosperity of the others. It is all lies. Man serves the interests of no creature except himself. And among us animals let there be perfect unity, perfect comradeship in the struggle. All men are enemies. All animals are comrades."

At this moment there was a tremendous uproar. While Major was speaking four large rats had crept out of their holes and were sitting on their hindquarters, listening

rebellion [rɪˈbɛljən] *n* 反叛，造反：叛亂
prosperity [prɑsˈpɛrətɪ] *n* 成功
unity [ˈjunətɪ] *n* 團結

to him. The dogs had suddenly caught sight of them, and it was only by a swift dash for their holes that the rats saved their lives. Major raised his trotter for silence.

"Comrades," he said, "here is a point that must be settled. The wild creatures, such as rats and rabbits — are they our friends or our enemies? Let us put it to the vote. I propose this question to the meeting: Are rats comrades?"

The vote was taken at once, and it was agreed by an overwhelming majority that rats were comrades. There were only four dissentients, the three dogs and the cat, who was afterwards discovered to have voted on both sides. Major continued:

"I have little more to say. I merely repeat, remember always your duty of enmity towards Man and all his ways. Whatever goes upon two legs is an enemy. Whatever goes upon four legs, or has wings, is a friend. And remember also that in fighting against Man, we must not come to resemble him. Even when you have conquered him, do not adopt his vices. No animal must ever live in a house, or sleep in a bed, or wear clothes, or drink alcohol, or

overwhelming [ˌovɚˈhwɛlmɪŋ] *adj* 壓倒的；勢不可擋的
majority [məˈdʒɒrətɪ] *n* 多數，過半數
resemble [rɪˈzɛmbl] *v* 像，類似

smoke tobacco, or touch money, or engage in trade. All the habits of Man are evil. And, above all, no animal must ever tyrannise over his own kind. Weak or strong, clever or simple, we are all brothers. No animal must ever kill any other animal. All animals are equal.

"And now, comrades, I will tell you about my dream of last night. I cannot describe that dream to you. It was a dream of the earth as it will be when Man has vanished. But it reminded me of something that I had long forgotten. Many years ago, when I was a little pig, my mother and the other sows used to sing an old song of which they knew only the tune and the first three words. I had known that tune in my infancy, but it had long since passed out of my mind. Last night, however, it came back to me in my dream. And what is more, the words of the song also came back — words, I am certain, which were sung by the animals of long ago and have been lost to memory for generations. I will sing you that song now, comrades. I am old and my voice is hoarse, but when I have taught you the tune, you can sing it better for yourselves. It is called *Beasts of England*."

vanish ['vænɪʃ] **v** 消失；絕跡
hoarse [hors] **adj** （嗓音）嘶啞的；粗啞的

Old Major cleared his throat and began to sing. As he had said, his voice was hoarse, but he sang well enough, and it was a stirring tune, something between *Clementine* and *La Cucaracha*. The words ran:

Beasts of England, beasts of Ireland,
Beasts of every land and clime,
Hearken to my joyful tidings
Of the golden future time.

Soon or late the day is coming,
Tyrant Man shall be o'erthrown,
And the fruitful fields of England
Shall be trod by beasts alone.

Rings shall vanish from our noses,
And the harness from our back,
Bit and spur shall rust forever,
Cruel whips no more shall crack.

trod [trɑd] **v** 踩，踏；在……上面走（**tread** 的動詞過去式、過去分詞）
rust [rʌst] **v** 生鏽

Riches more than mind can picture,
Wheat and barley, oats and hay,
Clover, beans, and mangel-wurzels
Shall be ours upon that day.

Bright will shine the fields of England,
Purer shall its waters be,
Sweeter yet shall blow its breezes
On the day that sets us free.

For that day we all must labour,
Though we die before it break;
Cows and horses, geese and turkeys,
All must toil for freedom's sake.

Beasts of England, beasts of Ireland,
Beasts of every land and clime,
Hearken well and spread my tidings
Of the golden future time.

The singing of this song threw the animals into the wildest excitement. Almost before Major had reached the

toil [tɔɪl] **v** 苦幹：艱難地行進

end, they had begun singing it for themselves. Even the stupidest of them had already picked up the tune and a few of the words, and as for the clever ones, such as the pigs and dogs, they had the entire song by heart within a few minutes. And then, after a few preliminary tries, the whole farm burst out into *Beasts of England* in tremendous unison. The cows lowed it, the dogs whined it, the sheep bleated it, the horses whinnied it, the ducks quacked it. They were so delighted with the song that they sang it right through five times in succession, and might have continued singing it all night if they had not been interrupted.

Unfortunately, the uproar awoke Mr. Jones, who sprang out of bed, making sure that there was a fox in the yard. He seized the gun which always stood in a corner of his bedroom, and let fly a charge of number 6 shot into the darkness. The pellets buried themselves in the wall of the barn and the meeting broke up hurriedly. Everyone fled to his own sleeping-place. The birds jumped on to their perches, the animals settled down in the straw, and the whole farm was asleep in a moment.

preliminary [prɪˈlɪməˌnɛrɪ] *adj* 預備的；初步的
seize [siz] *v* 抓住

02 ╱

Three nights later old Major died peacefully in his sleep. His body was buried at the foot of the orchard.

This was early in March. During the next three months there was much secret activity. Major's speech had given to the more intelligent animals on the farm a completely new outlook on life. They did not know when the Rebellion predicted by Major would take place, they had no reason for thinking that it would be within their own lifetime, but they saw clearly that it was their duty to prepare for it. The work of teaching and organising the others fell naturally upon the pigs, who were generally recognised as being the cleverest of the animals. Pre-eminent among the pigs were two young boars named Snowball and Napoleon, whom Mr. Jones was breeding up for sale. Napoleon was a large, rather fierce-looking Berkshire boar, the only Berkshire on the farm, not much of a talker, but with a reputation for getting his own way.

pre-eminent [pri'ɛmɪnənt] *adj* 卓越的;顯著的

Snowball was a more vivacious pig than Napoleon, quicker in speech and more inventive, but was not considered to have the same depth of character. All the other male pigs on the farm were porkers. The best known among them was a small fat pig named Squealer, with very round cheeks, twinkling eyes, nimble movements, and a shrill voice. He was a brilliant talker, and when he was arguing some difficult point he had a way of skipping from side to side and whisking his tail which was somehow very persuasive. The others said of Squealer that he could turn black into white.

These three had elaborated old Major's teachings into a complete system of thought, to which they gave the name of Animalism. Several nights a week, after Mr. Jones was asleep, they held secret meetings in the barn and expounded the principles of Animalism to the others. At the beginning they met with much stupidity and apathy. Some of the animals talked of the duty of loyalty to Mr.

vivacious [vaɪˈveʃəs] *adj* 活潑的；有生氣的
inventive [ɪnˈvɛntɪv] *adj* 善於創新的，有新意的
persuasive [pəˈswesɪv] *adj* 有說服力的
elaborate [ɪˈlæbəˌret] *v* 詳盡說明；闡述
expound [ɪkˈspaʊnd] *v* 解釋；詳細述說

Jones, whom they referred to as "Master," or made elementary remarks such as "Mr. Jones feeds us. If he were gone, we should starve to death." Others asked such questions as "Why should we care what happens after we are dead?" or "If this Rebellion is to happen anyway, what difference does it make whether we work for it or not?", and the pigs had great difficulty in making them see that this was contrary to the spirit of Animalism. The stupidest questions of all were asked by Mollie, the white mare. The very first question she asked Snowball was: "Will there still be sugar after the Rebellion?"

"No," said Snowball firmly. "We have no means of making sugar on this farm. Besides, you do not need sugar. You will have all the oats and hay you want."

"And shall I still be allowed to wear ribbons in my mane?" asked Mollie.

"Comrade," said Snowball, "those ribbons that you are so devoted to are the badge of slavery. Can you not understand that liberty is worth more than ribbons? "

contrary [kənˈtrɛrɪ] _adj_ 相反的，對立的
firmly [ˈfɝmlɪ] _adv_ 堅定地；堅決地
badge [bædʒ] _n_ 標誌；象徵
liberty [ˈlɪbɚtɪ] _n_ 自由

Mollie agreed, but she did not sound very convinced.

The pigs had an even harder struggle to counteract the lies put about by Moses, the tame raven. Moses, who was Mr. Jones's especial pet, was a spy and a tale-bearer, but he was also a clever talker. He claimed to know of the existence of a mysterious country called Sugarcandy Mountain, to which all animals went when they died. It was situated somewhere up in the sky, a little distance beyond the clouds, Moses said. In Sugarcandy Mountain it was Sunday seven days a week, clover was in season all the year round, and lump sugar and linseed cake grew on the hedges. The animals hated Moses because he told tales and did no work, but some of them believed in Sugarcandy Mountain, and the pigs had to argue very hard to persuade them that there was no such place.

Their most faithful disciples were the two cart-horses, Boxer and Clover. These two had great difficulty in thinking anything out for themselves, but having once

convinced [kənˈvɪnst] *adj* 確信的
counteract [ˌkaʊntəˈækt] *v* 對⋯⋯起反作用；抵消
tame [tem] *adj* （動物）經馴養的，馴服的
tale-bearer [ˈtelˌbɛrɚ] *n* 打小報告的人；散播謠言者

accepted the pigs as their teachers, they absorbed everything that they were told, and passed it on to the other animals by simple arguments. They were unfailing in their attendance at the secret meetings in the barn, and led the singing of *Beasts of England*, with which the meetings always ended.

Now, as it turned out, the Rebellion was achieved much earlier and more easily than anyone had expected. In past years Mr. Jones, although a hard master, had been a capable farmer, but of late he had fallen on evil days. He had become much disheartened after losing money in a lawsuit, and had taken to drinking more than was good for him. For whole days at a time he would lounge in his Windsor chair in the kitchen, reading the newspapers, drinking, and occasionally feeding Moses on crusts of bread soaked in beer. His men were idle and dishonest, the fields were full of weeds, the buildings wanted roofing, the hedges were neglected, and the animals were underfed.

June came and the hay was almost ready for cutting.

absorbed [əbˈsɔrbd] **v** 汲取，理解（知識等）
disheartened [dɪsˈhɑrtnd] **adj** 沮喪的，灰心的
lawsuit [ˈlɔ‚sut] **n** 訴訟
idle [ˈaɪd!] **adj** 不工作的；無所事事的

On Midsummer's Eve, which was a Saturday, Mr. Jones went into Willingdon and got so drunk at the Red Lion that he did not come back till midday on Sunday. The men had milked the cows in the early morning and then had gone out rabbiting, without bothering to feed the animals. When Mr. Jones got back he immediately went to sleep on the drawing-room sofa with the *News of the World* over his face, so that when evening came, the animals were still unfed. At last they could stand it no longer. One of the cows broke in the door of the store-shed with her horn and all the animals began to help themselves from the bins. It was just then that Mr. Jones woke up. The next moment he and his four men were in the store-shed with whips in their hands, lashing out in all directions. This was more than the hungry animals could bear. With one accord, though nothing of the kind had been planned beforehand, they flung themselves upon their tormentors. Jones and his men suddenly found themselves being butted and kicked from all sides. The situation was quite out of their control. They had never seen animals behave like this before, and this sudden uprising of creatures

accord [əˈkɔrd] *n* 一致，符合

whom they were used to thrashing and maltreating just as they chose, frightened them almost out of their wits. After only a moment or two they gave up trying to defend themselves and took to their heels. A minute later all five of them were in full flight down the cart-track that led to the main road, with the animals pursuing them in triumph.

Mrs. Jones looked out of the bedroom window, saw what was happening, hurriedly flung a few possessions into a carpet bag, and slipped out of the farm by another way. Moses sprang off his perch and flapped after her, croaking loudly. Meanwhile the animals had chased Jones and his men out on to the road and slammed the five-barred gate behind them. And so, almost before they knew what was happening, the Rebellion had been successfully carried through: Jones was expelled, and the Manor Farm was theirs.

For the first few minutes the animals could hardly

thrash [θræʃ] **v** （用鞭，棍）打，痛擊
maltreat [mælˈtrit] **v** 虐待；粗暴對待
triumph [ˈtraɪəmf] **n** 勝利（或成功）的喜悅，歡欣
possession [pəˈzɛʃən] **n** 所有物；財產
slam [slæm] **v** 猛地關上
expel [ɪkˈspɛl] **v** 驅逐，趕走

believe in their good fortune. Their first act was to gallop in a body right round the boundaries of the farm, as though to make quite sure that no human being was hiding anywhere upon it; then they raced back to the farm buildings to wipe out the last traces of Jones's hated reign. The harness-room at the end of the stables was broken open; the bits, the nose-rings, the dog-chains, the cruel knives with which Mr. Jones had been used to castrate the pigs and lambs, were all flung down the well. The reins, the halters, the blinkers, the degrading nosebags, were thrown on to the rubbish fire which was burning in the yard. So were the whips. All the animals capered with joy when they saw the whips going up in flames. Snowball also threw on to the fire the ribbons with which the horses' manes and tails had usually been decorated on market days.

"Ribbons," he said, "should be considered as clothes, which are the mark of a human being. All animals should go naked."

When Boxer heard this he fetched the small straw hat

gallop [ˈɡæləp] **v** （馬等）疾馳，飛跑
wipe out [waɪp] [aʊt] 消滅；澈底摧毀
castrate [ˈkæstret] **v** 閹割

which he wore in summer to keep the flies out of his ears, and flung it on to the fire with the rest.

In a very little while the animals had destroyed everything that reminded them of Mr. Jones. Napoleon then led them back to the store-shed and served out a double ration of corn to everybody, with two biscuits for each dog. Then they sang *Beasts of England* from end to end seven times running, and after that they settled down for the night and slept as they had never slept before.

But they woke at dawn as usual, and suddenly remembering the glorious thing that had happened, they all raced out into the pasture together. A little way down the pasture there was a knoll that commanded a view of most of the farm. The animals rushed to the top of it and gazed round them in the clear morning light. Yes, it was theirs — everything that they could see was theirs! In the ecstasy of that thought they gambolled round and round, they hurled themselves into the air in great leaps of excitement. They rolled in the dew, they cropped mouthfuls of the sweet summer grass, they kicked up

biscuit [ˈbɪskɪt] *n* 餅乾
glorious [ˈglorɪəs] *adj* 光榮的，榮耀的
gambol [ˈgæmbl] *v* 跳躍，嬉戲

clods of the black earth and snuffed its rich scent. Then they made a tour of inspection of the whole farm and surveyed with speechless admiration the ploughland, the hayfield, the orchard, the pool, the spinney. It was as though they had never seen these things before, and even now they could hardly believe that it was all their own.

Then they filed back to the farm buildings and halted in silence outside the door of the farmhouse. That was theirs too, but they were frightened to go inside. After a moment, however, Snowball and Napoleon butted the door open with their shoulders and the animals entered in single file, walking with the utmost care for fear of disturbing anything. They tiptoed from room to room, afraid to speak above a whisper and gazing with a kind of awe at the unbelievable luxury, at the beds with their feather mattresses, the looking-glasses, the horsehair sofa, the Brussels carpet, the lithograph of Queen Victoria over the drawing-room mantelpiece. They were lust coming down the stairs when Mollie was discovered to be missing.

scent [sɛnt] **n** 氣味，香味
tiptoe [ˈtɪpˌto] **v** 踮起腳走；躡手躡腳地走
luxury [ˈlʌkʃərɪ] **n** 奢侈，奢華
mantelpiece [ˈmæntḷˌpis] **n** 壁爐

Going back, the others found that she had remained behind in the best bedroom. She had taken a piece of blue ribbon from Mrs. Jones's dressing-table, and was holding it against her shoulder and admiring herself in the glass in a very foolish manner. The others reproached her sharply, and they went outside. Some hams hanging in the kitchen were taken out for burial, and the barrel of beer in the scullery was stove in with a kick from Boxer's hoof, — otherwise nothing in the house was touched. A unanimous resolution was passed on the spot that the farmhouse should be preserved as a museum. All were agreed that no animal must ever live there.

The animals had their breakfast, and then Snowball and Napoleon called them together again.

"Comrades," said Snowball, "it is half-past six and we have a long day before us. Today we begin the hay harvest. But there is another matter that must be attended to first."

The pigs now revealed that during the past three months they had taught themselves to read and write from an old spelling book which had belonged to Mr. Jones's children and which had been thrown on the rubbish heap.

reproach [rɪˈprotʃ] *v* 責備；斥責
unanimous [juˈnænəməs] *adj* 一致同意的；無異議的

Napoleon sent for pots of black and white paint and led the way down to the five-barred gate that gave on to the main road. Then Snowball (for it was Snowball who was best at writing) took a brush between the two knuckles of his trotter, painted out MANOR FARM from the top bar of the gate and in its place painted ANIMAL FARM. This was to be the name of the farm from now onwards. After this they went back to the farm buildings, where Snowball and Napoleon sent for a ladder which they caused to be set against the end wall of the big barn. They explained that by their studies of the past three months the pigs had succeeded in reducing the principles of Animalism to Seven Commandments. These Seven Commandments would now be inscribed on the wall; they would form an unalterable law by which all the animals on Animal Farm must live for ever after. With some difficulty (for it is not easy for a pig to balance himself on a ladder) Snowball climbed up and set to work, with Squealer a few rungs below him holding the paint-pot. The Commandments

trotter [ˈtrɑtɚ] *n* 豬蹄
onwards [ˈɑnwɚdz] *adv* （時間）從……起
commandment [kəˈmændmənt] *n* 戒律
unalterable [ʌnˈɒltərəbl] *adj* 不可改變的；堅定不移的

were written on the tarred wall in great white letters that could be read thirty yards away. They ran thus:

THE SEVEN COMMANDMENTS

1. *Whatever goes upon two legs is an enemy.*
2. *Whatever goes upon four legs, or has wings, is a friend.*
3. *No animal shall wear clothes.*
4. *No animal shall sleep in a bed.*
5. *No animal shall drink alcohol.*
6. *No animal shall kill any other animal.*
7. *All animals are equal.*

It was very neatly written, and except that "friend" was written "freind" and one of the "S's" was the wrong way round, the spelling was correct all the way through. Snowball read it aloud for the benefit of the others. All the animals nodded in complete agreement, and the cleverer ones at once began to learn the Commandments by heart.

"Now, comrades," cried Snowball, throwing down the paint-brush, "to the hayfield! Let us make it a point of honour to get in the harvest more quickly than Jones and his men could do."

But at this moment the three cows, who had seemed uneasy for some time past, set up a loud lowing. They had not been milked for twenty-four hours, and their udders

were almost bursting. After a little thought, the pigs sent for buckets and milked the cows fairly successfully, their trotters being well adapted to this task. Soon there were five buckets of frothing creamy milk at which many of the animals looked with considerable interest.

"What is going to happen to all that milk?" said someone.

"Jones used sometimes to mix some of it in our mash," said one of the hens.

"Never mind the milk, comrades!" cried Napoleon, placing himself in front of the buckets. "That will be attended to. The harvest is more important. Comrade Snowball will lead the way. I shall follow in a few minutes. Forward, comrades! The hay is waiting."

So the animals trooped down to the hayfield to begin the harvest, and when they came back in the evening it was noticed that the milk had disappeared.

bursting [ˈbɝstɪŋ] *adj* 脹滿的
considerable [kənˈsɪdərəbl] *adj* 相當大的
mash [mæʃ] *n* 飼料
troop [trup] *v* 群集；成群結隊地走

03 /

How they toiled and sweated to get the hay in! But their efforts were rewarded, for the harvest was an even bigger success than they had hoped.

Sometimes the work was hard; the implements had been designed for human beings and not for animals, and it was a great drawback that no animal was able to use any tool that involved standing on his hind legs. But the pigs were so clever that they could think of a way round every difficulty. As for the horses, they knew every inch of the field, and in fact understood the business of mowing and raking far better than Jones and his men had ever done. The pigs did not actually work, but directed and supervised the others. With their superior knowledge it was natural that they should assume the leadership. Boxer and Clover would harness themselves to the cutter or the horse-rake (no bits or reins were needed in these days, of

implement ['ɪmplə,mɛnt] **n** 工具；裝備
drawback ['drɔ,bæk] **n** 缺點，短處，不利條件

course) and tramp steadily round and round the field with a pig walking behind and calling out "Gee up, comrade!" or "Whoa back, comrade!" as the case might be. And every animal down to the humblest worked at turning the hay and gathering it. Even the ducks and hens toiled to and fro all day in the sun, carrying tiny wisps of hay in their beaks. In the end they finished the harvest in two days' less time than it had usually taken Jones and his men. Moreover, it was the biggest harvest that the farm had ever seen. There was no wastage whatever; the hens and ducks with their sharp eyes had gathered up the very last stalk. And not an animal on the farm had stolen so much as a mouthful.

All through that summer the work of the farm went like clockwork. The animals were happy as they had never conceived it possible to be. Every mouthful of food was an acute positive pleasure, now that it was truly their own food, produced by themselves and for themselves, not doled out to them by a grudging master. With the worthless parasitical human beings gone, there was more for everyone to eat. There was more leisure too,

wastage [ˈwestɪdʒ] *n* 浪費
parasitical [pærəˈsɪtɪkəl] *adj* 寄生的

inexperienced though the animals were. They met with many difficulties — for instance, later in the year, when they harvested the corn, they had to tread it out in the ancient style and blow away the chaff with their breath, since the farm possessed no threshing machine — but the pigs with their cleverness and Boxer with his tremendous muscles always pulled them through. Boxer was the admiration of everybody. He had been a hard worker even in Jones's time, but now he seemed more like three horses than one; there were days when the entire work of the farm seemed to rest on his mighty shoulders. From morning to night he was pushing and pulling, always at the spot where the work was hardest. He had made an arrangement with one of the cockerels to call him in the mornings half an hour earlier than anyone else, and would put in some volunteer labour at whatever seemed to be most needed, before the regular day's work began. His answer to every problem, every setback, was "I will work harder!" — which he had adopted as his personal motto.

But everyone worked according to his capacity The

ancient ['enʃənt] *adj* 古代的；古老的
cockerel ['kakərəl] *n* 小公雞
motto ['mato] *n* 座右銘；格言

hens and ducks, for instance, saved five bushels of corn at the harvest by gathering up the stray grains. Nobody stole, nobody grumbled over his rations, the quarrelling and biting and jealousy which had been normal features of life in the old days had almost disappeared. Nobody shirked — or almost nobody. Mollie, it was true, was not good at getting up in the mornings, and had a way of leaving work early on the ground that there was a stone in her hoof. And the behaviour of the cat was somewhat peculiar. It was soon noticed that when there was work to be done the cat could never be found. She would vanish for hours on end, and then reappear at meal-times, or in the evening after work was over, as though nothing had happened. But she always made such excellent excuses, and purred so affectionately, that it was impossible not to believe in her good intentions. Old Benjamin, the donkey, seemed quite unchanged since the Rebellion. He did his work in the same slow obstinate way as he had done it in Jones's time, never shirking and never volunteering for extra work either. About the Rebellion and its results he would express no opinion. When asked whether he was not happier now that Jones was gone, he would say only

obstinate [ˈɑbstənɪt] *adj* 頑固的，固執的

"Donkeys live a long time. None of you has ever seen a dead donkey," and the others had to be content with this cryptic answer.

On Sundays there was no work. Breakfast was an hour later than usual, and after breakfast there was a ceremony which was observed every week without fail. First came the hoisting of the flag. Snowball had found in the harness-room an old green tablecloth of Mrs. Jones's and had painted on it a hoof and a horn in white. This was run up the flagstaff in the farmhouse garden every Sunday morning. The flag was green, Snowball explained, to represent the green fields of England, while the hoof and horn signified the future Republic of the Animals which would arise when the human race had been finally overthrown. After the hoisting of the flag all the animals trooped into the big barn for a general assembly which was known as the Meeting. Here the work of the coming week was planned out and resolutions were put forward and debated. It was always the pigs who put forward the resolutions. The other animals understood how to vote, but could never think of any resolutions of their own. Snowball and Napoleon were by far the most active in the

overthrown [ovə·'θron] **v** 打倒；推翻（**overthrow** 的動詞過去分詞）

debates. But it was noticed that these two were never in agreement: whatever suggestion either of them made, the other could be counted on to oppose it. Even when it was resolved — a thing no one could object to in itself — to set aside the small paddock behind the orchard as a home of rest for animals who were past work, there was a stormy debate over the correct retiring age for each class of animal. The Meeting always ended with the singing of *Beasts of England*, and the afternoon was given up to recreation.

The pigs had set aside the harness-room as a headquarters for themselves. Here, in the evenings, they studied blacksmithing, carpentering, and other necessary arts from books which they had brought out of the farmhouse. Snowball also busied himself with organising the other animals into what he called Animal Committees. He was indefatigable at this. He formed the Egg Production Committee for the hens, the Clean Tails

oppose [əˈpoz] *v* 反對；反抗
aside [əˈsaɪd] *adj* 在旁邊；到（或向）旁邊
headquarters [ˈhɛdˈkwɔrtəz] *n* 總部，總署
indefatigable [ˌɪndɪˈfætɪɡəbl] *adj* 不倦的；不屈不撓的
committee [kəˈmɪtɪ] *n* 委員會

League for the cows, the Wild Comrades' Re-education Committee (the object of this was to tame the rats and rabbits), the Whiter Wool Movement for the sheep, and various others, besides instituting classes in reading and writing. On the whole, these projects were a failure. The attempt to tame the wild creatures, for instance, broke down almost immediately. They continued to behave very much as before, and when treated with generosity, simply took advantage of it. The cat joined the Re-education Committee and was very active in it for some days. She was seen one day sitting on a roof and talking to some sparrows who were just out of her reach. She was telling them that all animals were now comrades and that any sparrow who chose could come and perch on her paw; but the sparrows kept their distance.

The reading and writing classes, however, were a great success. By the autumn almost every animal on the farm was literate in some degree.

As for the pigs, they could already read and write perfectly. The dogs learned to read fairly well, but were not interested in reading anything except the Seven Commandments. Muriel, the goat, could read somewhat

generosity [ˌdʒɛnəˈrɑsətɪ] **n** 寬宏大量；慷慨

better than the dogs, and sometimes used to read to the others in the evenings from scraps of newspaper which she found on the rubbish heap. Benjamin could read as well as any pig, but never exercised his faculty. So far as he knew, he said, there was nothing worth reading. Clover learnt the whole alphabet, but could not put words together. Boxer could not get beyond the letter D. He would trace out A, B, C, D, in the dust with his great hoof, and then would stand staring at the letters with his ears back, sometimes shaking his forelock, trying with all his might to remember what came next and never succeeding. On several occasions, indeed, he did learn E, F, G, H, but by the time he knew them, it was always discovered that he had forgotten A, B, C, and D. Finally he decided to be content with the first four letters, and used to write them out once or twice every day to refresh his memory. Mollie refused to learn any but the six letters which spelt her own name. She would form these very neatly out of pieces of twig, and would then decorate them with a flower or two and walk round them admiring them.

None of the other animals on the farm could get

faculty [ˈfækḷtɪ] *n* 能力；技能
admire [ədˈmaɪr] *v* 欣賞；欽佩

further than the letter A. It was also found that the stupider animals, such as the sheep, hens, and ducks, were unable to learn the Seven Commandments by heart. After much thought Snowball declared that the Seven Commandments could in effect be reduced to a single maxim, namely: "Four legs good, two legs bad." This, he said, contained the essential principle of Animalism. Whoever had thoroughly grasped it would be safe from human influences. The birds at first objected, since it seemed to them that they also had two legs, but Snowball proved to them that this was not so.

"A bird's wing, comrades," he said, "is an organ of propulsion and not of manipulation. It should therefore be regarded as a leg. The distinguishing mark of man is the *hand*, the instrument with which he does all his mischief."

The birds did not understand Snowball's long words, but they accepted his explanation, and all the humbler animals set to work to learn the new maxim by heart.

essential [ɪˈsɛnʃəl] *adj* 本質的；必要的
thoroughly [ˈθɝˑolɪ] *adv* 澈底地；完全地
propulsion [prəˈpʌlʃən] *n* 推進（力）
manipulation [məˌnɪpjʊˈleʃən] *n* 操作，運用

FOUR LEGS GOOD, TWO LEGS BAD was inscribed on the end wall of the barn, above the Seven Commandments and in bigger letters When they had once got it by heart, the sheep developed a great liking for this maxim, and often as they lay in the field they would all start bleating "Four legs good, two legs bad! Four legs good, two legs bad!" and keep it up for hours on end, never growing tired of it.

Napoleon took no interest in Snowball's committees. He said that the education of the young was more important than anything that could be done for those who were already grown up. It happened that Jessie and Bluebell had both whelped soon after the hay harvest, giving birth between them to nine sturdy puppies. As soon as they were weaned, Napoleon took them away from their mothers, saying that he would make himself responsible for their education. He took them up into a loft which could only be reached by a ladder from the harness-room, and there kept them in such seclusion that

bleat [blit] **v** （羊，小牛等）咩咩叫
whelp [hwɛlp] **v** （尤指母狗）生下（小動物）
wean [win] **v** 使斷奶
seclusion [sɪˈkluʒən] **n** 隔絕；孤立

the rest of the farm soon forgot their existence.

The mystery of where the milk went to was soon cleared up. It was mixed every day into the pigs' mash. The early apples were now ripening, and the grass of the orchard was littered with windfalls. The animals had assumed as a matter of course that these would be shared out equally; one day, however, the order went forth that all the windfalls were to be collected and brought to the harness-room for the use of the pigs. At this some of the other animals murmured, but it was no use. All the pigs were in full agreement on this point, even Snowball and Napoleon. Squealer was sent to make the necessary explanations to the others.

"Comrades!" he cried. "You do not imagine, I hope, that we pigs are doing this in a spirit of selfishness and privilege? Many of us actually dislike milk and apples. I dislike them myself. Our sole object in taking these things is to preserve our health. Milk and apples (this has been proved by Science, comrades) contain substances absolutely necessary to the well-being of a pig. We pigs are brainworkers. The whole management and

ripen ['raɪpən] **v** 使成熟
privilege ['prɪvlɪdʒ] **n** 特權

organisation of this farm depend on us. Day and night we are watching over your welfare. It is for your sake that we drink that milk and eat those apples. Do you know what would happen if we pigs failed in our duty? Jones would come back! Yes, Jones would come back! Surely, comrades," cried Squealer almost pleadingly, skipping from side to side and whisking his tail, "surely there is no one among you who wants to see Jones come back?"

Now if there was one thing that the animals were completely certain of, it was that they did not want Jones back. When it was put to them in this light, they had no more to say. The importance of keeping the pigs in good health was all too obvious. So it was agreed without further argument that the milk and the windfall apples (and also the main crop of apples when they ripened) should be reserved for the pigs alone.

welfare [ˈwɛlˌfɛr] *n* 福利；健康安樂

04 /

By the late summer the news of what had happened on Animal Farm had spread across half the county. Every day Snowball and Napoleon sent out flights of pigeons whose instructions were to mingle with the animals on neighbouring farms, tell them the story of the Rebellion, and teach them the tune of *Beasts of England*.

Most of this time Mr. Jones had spent sitting in the taproom of the Red Lion at Willingdon, complaining to anyone who would listen of the monstrous injustice he had suffered in being turned out of his property by a pack of good-for-nothing animals. The other farmers sympathised in principle, but they did not at first give him much help. At heart, each of them was secretly wondering whether he could not somehow turn Jones's misfortune to his own advantage. It was lucky that the owners of the two farms

mingle [ˈmɪŋgl] **v** 往來
monstrous [ˈmɑnstrəs] **adj** 極端荒謬的
sympathise [ˈsɪmpəˌθaɪz] **v** 同情；憐憫

which adjoined Animal Farm were on permanently bad terms. One of them, which was named Foxwood, was a large, neglected, old-fashioned farm, much overgrown by woodland, with all its pastures worn out and its hedges in a disgraceful condition. Its owner, Mr. Pilkington, was an easy-going gentleman farmer who spent most of his time in fishing or hunting according to the season. The other farm, which was called Pinchfield, was smaller and better kept. Its owner was a Mr. Frederick, a tough, shrewd man, perpetually involved in lawsuits and with a name for driving hard bargains. These two disliked each other so much that it was difficult for them to come to any agreement, even in defence of their own interests.

Nevertheless, they were both thoroughly frightened by the rebellion on Animal Farm, and very anxious to prevent their own animals from learning too much about it. At first they pretended to laugh to scorn the idea of animals managing a farm for themselves. The whole thing would be over in a fortnight, they said. They put it about that the animals on the Manor Farm (they insisted on calling it the Manor Farm; they would not tolerate the

bargain [ˈbɑrgɪn] *n* 協議；買賣
scorn [skɔrn] *v* 輕蔑；嘲笑；奚落

name "Animal Farm") were perpetually fighting among themselves and were also rapidly starving to death. When time passed and the animals had evidently not starved to death, Frederick and Pilkington changed their tune and began to talk of the terrible wickedness that now flourished on Animal Farm. It was given out that the animals there practised cannibalism, tortured one another with red-hot horseshoes, and had their females in common. This was what came of rebelling against the laws of Nature, Frederick and Pilkington said.

However, these stories were never fully believed. Rumours of a wonderful farm, where the human beings had been turned out and the animals managed their own affairs, continued to circulate in vague and distorted forms, and throughout that year a wave of rebelliousness ran through the countryside. Bulls which had always been tractable suddenly turned savage, sheep broke down hedges and devoured the clover, cows kicked the pail over, hunters refused their fences and shot their riders on to the other side. Above all, the tune and even the words of

wickedness [ˈwɪkɪdnɪs] *n* 邪惡之事
flourish [ˈflɝɪʃ] *v* 繁茂；興旺
vague [veg] *adj* 不明確的；曖昧的，含糊的

Beasts of England were known everywhere. It had spread with astonishing speed. The human beings could not contain their rage when they heard this song, though they pretended to think it merely ridiculous. They could not understand, they said, how even animals could bring themselves to sing such contemptible rubbish. Any animal caught singing it was given a flogging on the spot. And yet the song was irrepressible. The blackbirds whistled it in the hedges, the pigeons cooed it in the elms, it got into the din of the smithies and the tune of the church bells. And when the human beings listened to it, they secretly trembled, hearing in it a prophecy of their future doom.

Early in October, when the corn was cut and stacked and some of it was already threshed, a flight of pigeons came whirling through the air and alighted in the yard of Animal Farm in the wildest excitement. Jones and all his men, with half a dozen others from Foxwood and Pinchfield, had entered the five-barred gate and were coming up the cart-track that led to the farm. They were all carrying sticks, except Jones, who was marching ahead

contemptible [kənˈtɛmptəbl] *adj* 可鄙的，卑劣的；不屑一顧的
irrepressible [ɪrɪˈprɛsəbl] *adj* 壓抑不住的
doom [dum] *n* 厄運，毀滅

with a gun in his hands. Obviously they were going to attempt the re capture of the farm.

This had long been expected, and all preparations had been made. Snowball, who had studied an old book of Julius Caesar's campaigns which he had found in the farmhouse, was in charge of the defensive operations. He gave his orders quickly, and in a couple of minutes every animal was at his post.

As the human beings approached the farm buildings, Snowball launched his first attack. All the pigeons, to the number of thirty-five, flew to and fro over the men's heads and muted upon them from mid-air; and while the men were dealing with this, the geese, who had been hiding behind the hedge, rushed out and pecked viciously at the calves of their legs. However, this was only a light skirmishing manoeuvre, intended to create a little disorder, and the men easily drove the geese off with their sticks. Snowball now launched his second line of attack. Muriel, Benjamin, and all the sheep, with Snowball at the head of

defensive [dɪˈfɛnsɪv] *adj* 防禦的；保衛的
viciously [ˈvɪʃəslɪ] *adv* 充滿敵意地
skirmishing [ˈskɜ·mɪʃɪŋ] *n* （小）衝突；（小）爭執
manoeuvre [məˈnuvə·] *n* （軍事的）演習

them, rushed forward and prodded and butted the men from every side, while Benjamin turned around and lashed at them with his small hoofs. But once again the men, with their sticks and their hobnailed boots, were too strong for them; and suddenly, at a squeal from Snowball, which was the signal for retreat, all the animals turned and fled through the gateway into the yard.

The men gave a shout of triumph. They saw, as they imagined, their enemies in flight, and they rushed after them in disorder. This was just what Snowball had intended. As soon as they were well inside the yard, the three horses, the three cows, and the rest of the pigs, who had been lying in ambush in the cowshed, suddenly emerged in their rear, cutting them off. Snowball now gave the signal for the charge. He himself dashed straight for Jones. Jones saw him coming, raised his gun and fired. The pellets scored bloody streaks along Snowball's back, and a sheep dropped dead. Without halting for an instant, Snowball flung his fifteen stone against Jones's legs. Jones was hurled into a pile of dung and his gun flew out of his hands. But the most terrifying spectacle of all was Boxer, rearing up on his hind legs and striking out with his great iron-shod hoofs like a stallion. His very first blow took a

stable-lad from Foxwood on the skull and stretched him lifeless in the mud. At the sight, several men dropped their sticks and tried to run. Panic overtook them, and the next moment all the animals together were chasing them round and round the yard. They were gored, kicked, bitten, trampled on. There was not an animal on the farm that did not take vengeance on them after his own fashion. Even the cat suddenly leapt off a roof onto a cowman's shoulders and sank her claws in his neck, at which he yelled horribly. At a moment when the opening was clear, the men were glad enough to rush out of the yard and make a bolt for the main road. And so within five minutes of their invasion they were in ignominious retreat by the same way as they had come, with a flock of geese hissing after them and pecking at their calves all the way.

All the men were gone except one. Back in the yard Boxer was pawing with his hoof at the stable-lad who lay face down in the mud, trying to turn him over. The boy did not stir.

skull [skʌl] *n* 頭蓋骨；頭骨
vengeance [ˈvɛndʒəns] *n* 報復；報仇
invasion [ɪnˈveʒən] *n* 入侵，侵略
ignominious [ˌɪgnəˈmɪnɪəs] *adj* 可恥的

"He is dead," said Boxer sorrowfully. "I had no intention of doing that. I forgot that I was wearing iron shoes. Who will believe that I did not do this on purpose?"

"No sentimentality, comrade!" cried Snowball from whose wounds the blood was still dripping. "War is war. The only good human being is a dead one."

"I have no wish to take life, not even human life," repeated Boxer, and his eyes were full of tears.

"Where is Mollie?" exclaimed somebody.

Mollie in fact was missing. For a moment there was great alarm; it was feared that the men might have harmed her in some way, or even carried her off with them. In the end, however, she was found hiding in her stall with her head buried among the hay in the manger. She had taken to flight as soon as the gun went off. And when the others came back from looking for her, it was to find that the stable-lad, who in fact was only stunned, had already recovered and made off.

The animals had now reassembled in the wildest excitement, each recounting his own exploits in the battle

drip [drɪp] **v** 滴下
reassemble [riəˈsɛmbl] **v** 重新召集；再集合

at the top of his voice. An impromptu celebration of the victory was held immediately. The flag was run up and *Beasts of England* was sung a number of times, then the sheep who had been killed was given a solemn funeral, a hawthorn bush being planted on her grave. At the graveside Snowball made a little speech, emphasising the need for all animals to be ready to die for Animal Farm if need be.

The animals decided unanimously to create a military decoration, "Animal Hero, First Class," which was conferred there and then on Snowball and Boxer. It consisted of a brass medal (they were really some old horse-brasses which had been found in the harness-room), to be worn on Sundays and holidays. There was also "Animal Hero, Second Class," which was conferred posthumously on the dead sheep.

There was much discussion as to what the battle should be called. In the end, it was named the Battle of

impromptu [ɪmˈprɑmptju] *adj* 事先無準備的；即席的
solemn [ˈsɑləm] *adj* 莊重的；隆重的
unanimously [juˈnænəməslɪ] *adv* 無異議地；全體一致地
confer [kənˈfɝ] *v* 授予；賦予
posthumously [ˈpɑstʃəməslɪ] *adv* 於死後，於身後

the Cowshed, since that was where the ambush had been sprung. Mr. Jones's gun had been found lying in the mud, and it was known that there was a supply of cartridges in the farmhouse. It was decided to set the gun up at the foot of the Flagstaff, like a piece of artillery, and to fire it twice a year — once on October the twelfth, the anniversary of the Battle of the Cowshed, and once on Midsummer Day, the anniversary of the Rebellion.

anniversary [ˌænəˈvɜːsərɪ] **n** 週年紀念日

05 /

As winter drew on, Mollie became more and more troublesome. She was late for work every morning and excused herself by saying that she had overslept, and she complained of mysterious pains, although her appetite was excellent. On every kind of pretext she would run away from work and go to the drinking pool, where she would stand foolishly gazing at her own reflection in the water. But there were also rumours of something more serious. One day, as Mollie strolled blithely into the yard, flirting her long tail and chewing at a stalk of hay, Clover took her aside.

"Mollie," she said, "I have something very serious to say to you. This morning I saw you looking over the hedge that divides Animal Farm from Foxwood. One of Mr. Pilkington's men was standing on the other side of the hedge. And — I was a long way away, but I am almost certain I saw this — he was talking to you and you were allowing

pretext ['pritεkst] *n* 藉口；託辭
blithely ['blaɪðlɪ] *adv* 歡樂地；快活地；無掛慮地

him to stroke your nose. What does that mean, Mollie?"

"He didn't! I wasn't! It isn't true!" cried Mollie, beginning to prance about and paw the ground.

"Mollie! Look me in the face. Do you give me your word of honour that that man was not stroking your nose?"

"It isn't true!" repeated Mollie, but she could not look Clover in the face, and the next moment she took to her heels and galloped away into the field.

A thought struck Clover. Without saying anything to the others, she went to Mollie's stall and turned over the straw with her hoof. Hidden under the straw was a little pile of lump sugar and several bunches of ribbon of different colours.

Three days later Mollie disappeared. For some weeks nothing was known of her whereabouts, then the pigeons reported that they had seen her on the other side of Willingdon. She was between the shafts of a smart dogcart painted red and black, which was standing outside a public-house. A fat red-faced man in check breeches and gaiters, who looked like a publican, was stroking her nose and feeding her with sugar. Her coat was newly clipped and she wore a scarlet ribbon round her forelock. She

prance [præns] **v** （馬）騰躍

appeared to be enjoying herself, so the pigeons said. None of the animals ever mentioned Mollie again.

In January there came bitterly hard weather. The earth was like iron, and nothing could be done in the fields. Many meetings were held in the big barn, and the pigs occupied themselves with planning out the work of the coming season. It had come to be accepted that the pigs, who were manifestly cleverer than the other animals, should decide all questions of farm policy, though their decisions had to be ratified by a majority vote. This arrangement would have worked well enough if it had not been for the disputes between Snowball and Napoleon. These two disagreed at every point where disagreement was possible. If one of them suggested sowing a bigger acreage with barley, the other was certain to demand a bigger acreage of oats, and if one of them said that such and such a field was just right for cabbages, the other would declare that it was useless for anything except roots. Each had his own following, and there were some violent debates. At the Meetings Snowball often won over the majority by his

manifestly [ˈmænəˌfɛstlɪ] *adv* 顯然地，明白地
ratify [ˈrætəˌfaɪ] *v* 批准；認可
dispute [dɪˈspjut] *n* 爭論；爭執

brilliant speeches, but Napoleon was better at canvassing support for himself in between times. He was especially successful with the sheep. Of late the sheep had taken to bleating "Four legs good, two legs bad" both in and out of season, and they often interrupted the Meeting with this. It was noticed that they were especially liable to break into "Four legs good, two legs bad" at crucial moments in Snowball's speeches. Snowball had made a close study of some back numbers of the *Farmer and Stockbreeder* which he had found in the farmhouse, and was full of plans for innovations and improvements. He talked learnedly about field drains, silage, and basic slag, and had worked out a complicated scheme for all the animals to drop their dung directly in the fields, at a different spot every day, to save the labour of cartage. Napoleon produced no schemes of his own, but said quietly that Snowball's would come to nothing, and seemed to be biding his time. But of all their controversies, none was so bitter as the one that took place over the windmill.

liable ['laɪəbl] *adj* 易……的
bide [baɪd] *v* 等待，停留
controversy ['kɑntrə,vɝsɪ] *n* 爭論，辯論；爭議
windmill ['wɪnd,mɪl] *n* 風車

In the long pasture, not far from the farm buildings, there was a small knoll which was the highest point on the farm. After surveying the ground, Snowball declared that this was just the place for a windmill, which could be made to operate a dynamo and supply the farm with electrical power. This would light the stalls and warm them in winter, and would also run a circular saw, a chaff-cutter, a mangel-slicer, and an electric milking machine. The animals had never heard of anything of this kind before (for the farm was an old-fashioned one and had only the most primitive machinery), and they listened in astonishment while Snowball conjured up pictures of fantastic machines which would do their work for them while they grazed at their ease in the fields or improved their minds with reading and conversation.

Within a few weeks Snowball's plans for the windmill were fully worked out. The mechanical details came mostly from three books which had belonged to Mr. Jones — *One Thousand Useful Things to Do About the House*, *Every Man His Own Bricklayer*, and *Electricity for Beginners*. Snowball used as his study a shed which had once been used for

dynamo [ˈdaɪnəˌmo] **n** 發電機
conjure up [ˈkʌndʒɚ] [ʌp] 使呈現於腦際（或眼簾）；想起

incubators and had a smooth wooden floor, suitable for drawing on. He was closeted there for hours at a time. With his books held open by a stone, and with a piece of chalk gripped between the knuckles of his trotter, he would move rapidly to and fro, drawing in line after line and uttering little whimpers of excitement. Gradually the plans grew into a complicated mass of cranks and cog-wheels, covering more than half the floor, which the other animals found completely unintelligible but very impressive. All of them came to look at Snowball's drawings at least once a day. Even the hens and ducks came, and were at pains not to tread on the chalk marks. Only Napoleon held aloof. He had declared himself against the windmill from the start. One day, however, he arrived unexpectedly to examine the plans. He walked heavily round the shed, looked closely at every detail of the plans and snuffed at them once or twice, then stood for a little while contemplating them out of the corner of his eye; then suddenly he lifted his leg, urinated over the plans, and walked out without uttering a word.

The whole farm was deeply divided on the subject of

unintelligible [ˌʌnɪnˈtɛlədʒəbl̩] _adj_　難理解的，晦澀難懂的
aloof [əˈluf] _adv_　冷漠地；避開地
contemplate [ˈkɑntɛmˌplet] _v_　注視，凝視

the windmill. Snowball did not deny that to build it would be a difficult business. Stone would have to be carried and built up into walls, then the sails would have to be made and after that there would be need for dynamos and cables. (How these were to be procured, Snowball did not say.) But he maintained that it could all be done in a year. And thereafter, he declared, so much labour would be saved that the animals would only need to work three days a week. Napoleon, on the other hand, argued that the great need of the moment was to increase food production, and that if they wasted time on the windmill they would all starve to death. The animals formed themselves into two factions under the slogan, "Vote for Snowball and the three-day week" and "Vote for Napoleon and the full manger." Benjamin was the only animal who did not side with either faction. He refused to believe either that food would become more plentiful or that the windmill would save work. Windmill or no windmill, he said, life would go on as it had always gone on — that is, badly.

Apart from the disputes over the windmill, there was the question of the defence of the farm. It was fully

faction [ˈfækʃən] *n* 派別；小集團
plentiful [ˈplɛntɪfəl] *adj* 充足的；豐產的

realised that though the human beings had been defeated in the Battle of the Cowshed they might make another and more determined attempt to recapture the farm and reinstate Mr. Jones. They had all the more reason for doing so because the news of their defeat had spread across the countryside and made the animals on the neighbouring farms more restive than ever. As usual, Snowball and Napoleon were in disagreement. According to Napoleon, what the animals must do was to procure firearms and train themselves in the use of them. According to Snowball, they must send out more and more pigeons and stir up rebellion among the animals on the other farms. The one argued that if they could not defend themselves they were bound to be conquered, the other argued that if rebellions happened everywhere they would have no need to defend themselves. The animals listened first to Napoleon, then to Snowball, and could not make up their minds which was right; indeed, they always found themselves in agreement with the one who was speaking at the moment.

At last the day came when Snowball's plans were completed. At the Meeting on the following Sunday the

restive ['rɛstɪv] *adj* 倔強的；不聽話的
bound to [baʊnd] [tu] 一定會（做）

question of whether or not to begin work on the windmill was to be put to the vote. When the animals had assembled in the big barn, Snowball stood up and, though occasionally interrupted by bleating from the sheep, set forth his reasons for advocating the building of the windmill. Then Napoleon stood up to reply. He said very quietly that the windmill was nonsense and that he advised nobody to vote for it, and promptly sat down again; he had spoken for barely thirty seconds, and seemed almost indifferent as to the effect he produced. At this Snowball sprang to his feet, and shouting down the sheep, who had begun bleating again, broke into a passionate appeal in favour of the windmill. Until now the animals had been about equally divided in their sympathies, but in a moment Snowball's eloquence had carried them away. In glowing sentences he painted a picture of Animal Farm as it might be when sordid labour was lifted from the animals' backs. His imagination had now run far beyond chaff-cutters and turnip-slicers. Electricity, he said, could operate threshing machines, ploughs, harrows, rollers, and reapers and binders, besides supplying every stall with its

passionate [ˈpæʃənɪt] **adj** 激昂的；熱情的
eloquence [ˈɛləkwəns] **n** （語言等的）說服力
sordid [ˈsɔrdɪd] **adj** 可憐的；悲慘的

own electric light, hot and cold water, and an electric heater. By the time he had finished speaking, there was no doubt as to which way the vote would go. But just at this moment Napoleon stood up and, casting a peculiar sidelong look at Snowball, uttere d a high-pitched whimper of a kind no one had ever heard him utter before.

At this there was a terrible baying sound outside, and nine enormous dogs wearing brass-studded collars came bounding into the barn. They dashed straight for Snowball, who only sprang from his place just in time to escape their snapping jaws. In a moment he was out of the door and they were after him. Too amazed and frightened to speak, all the animals crowded through the door to watch the chase. Snowball was racing across the long pasture that led to the road. He was running as only a pig can run, but the dogs were close on his heels. Suddenly he slipped and it seemed certain that they had him. Then he was up again, running faster than ever, then the dogs were gaining on him again. One of them all but closed his jaws on Snowball's tail, but Snowball whisked it free just in time. Then he put on an extra spurt and, with a few inches to spare, slipped through a hole in the hedge and was seen no more.

bay [be] **v** （狗，獵犬）連續吠叫；咆哮

Silent and terrified, the animals crept back into the barn. In a moment the dogs came bounding back. At first no one had been able to imagine where these creatures came from, but the problem was soon solved: they were the puppies whom Napoleon had taken away from their mothers and reared privately. Though not yet full-grown, they were huge dogs, and as fierce-looking as wolves. They kept close to Napoleon. It was noticed that they wagged their tails to him in the same way as the other dogs had been used to do to Mr. Jones.

Napoleon, with the dogs following him, now mounted on to the raised portion of the floor where Major had previously stood to deliver his speech. He announced that from now on the Sunday-morning Meetings would come to an end. They were unnecessary, he said, and wasted time. In future all questions relating to the working of the farm would be settled by a special committee of pigs, presided over by himself. These would meet in private and afterwards communicate their decisions to the others. The animals would still assemble on Sunday mornings to salute the flag, sing *Beasts of*

fierce [fɪrs] *adj* 兇猛的；好鬥的
preside [prɪˈzaɪd] *v* 主持；指揮
salute [səˈlut] *v* 向……行禮，向……致敬

England, and receive their orders for the week; but there would be no more debates.

In spite of the shock that Snowball's expulsion had given them, the animals were dismayed by this announcement. Several of them would have protested if they could have found the right arguments. Even Boxer was vaguely troubled. He set his ears back, shook his forelock several times, and tried hard to marshal his thoughts; but in the end he could not think of anything to say. Some of the pigs themselves, however, were more articulate. Four young porkers in the front row uttered shrill squeals of disapproval, and all four of them sprang to their feet and began speaking at once. But suddenly the dogs sitting round Napoleon let out deep, menacing growls, and the pigs fell silent and sat down again. Then the sheep broke out into a tremendous bleating of "Four legs good, two legs bad!" which went on for nearly a quarter of an hour and put an end to any chance of discussion.

expulsion [ɪkˈspʌlʃən] *n* 驅逐
dismay [dɪsˈme] *v* 使驚慌，使沮喪
marshal [ˈmɑrʃəl] *v* 釐清；排列；整理
articulate [ɑrˈtɪkjəˌlet] *adj* 有說話能力的；善於表達的
menacing [ˈmɛnɪsɪŋ] *adj* 威脅的；險惡的

Afterwards Squealer was sent round the farm to explain the new arrangement to the others.

"Comrades," he said, "I trust that every animal here appreciates the sacrifice that Comrade Napoleon has made in taking this extra labour upon himself. Do not imagine, comrades, that leadership is a pleasure! On the contrary, it is a deep and heavy responsibility. No one believes more firmly than Comrade Napoleon that all animals are equal. He would be only too happy to let you make your decisions for yourselves. But sometimes you might make the wrong decisions, comrades, and then where should we be? Suppose you had decided to follow Snowball, with his moonshine of windmills — Snowball, who, as we now know, was no better than a criminal?"

"He fought bravely at the Battle of the Cowshed," said somebody.

"Bravery is not enough," said Squealer. "Loyalty and obedience are more important. And as to the Battle of the Cowshed, I believe the time will come when we shall find that Snowball's part in it was much exaggerated. Discipline,

moonshine [ˈmunˌʃaɪn] *n* 空話；蠢念
obedience [əˈbidjəns] *n* 服從，順從
exaggerated [ɪgˈzædʒəˌretɪd] *adj* 誇張的；言過其實的

comrades, iron discipline! That is the watchword for today. One false step, and our enemies would be upon us. Surely, comrades, you do not want Jones back?"

Once again this argument was unanswerable. Certainly the animals did not want Jones back; if the holding of debates on Sunday mornings was liable to bring him back, then the debates must stop. Boxer, who had now had time to think things over, voiced the general feeling by saying: "If Comrade Napoleon says it, it must be right." And from then on he adopted the maxim, "Napoleon is always right," in addition to his private motto of "I will work harder."

By this time the weather had broken and the spring ploughing had begun. The shed where Snowball had drawn his plans of the windmill had been shut up and it was assumed that the plans had been rubbed off the floor. Every Sunday morning at ten o'clock the animals assembled in the big barn to receive their orders for the week. The skull of old Major, now clean of flesh, had been disinterred from the orchard and set up on a stump at the foot of the flagstaff, beside the gun. After the hoisting of the flag, the animals were required to file past the skull in a reverent

maxim [ˈmæksɪm] **n** 格言，箴言；座右銘
reverent [ˈrɛvərənt] **adj** 恭敬的，虔誠的

manner before entering the barn. Nowadays they did not sit all together as they had done in the past. Napoleon, with Squealer and another pig named Minimus, who had a remarkable gift for composing songs and poems, sat on the front of the raised platform, with the nine young dogs forming a semicircle round them, and the other pigs sitting behind. The rest of the animals sat facing them in the main body of the barn. Napoleon read out the orders for the week in a gruff soldierly style, and after a single singing of *Beasts of England*, all the animals dispersed.

On the third Sunday after Snowball's expulsion, the animals were somewhat surprised to hear Napoleon announce that the windmill was to be built after all. He did not give any reason for having changed his mind, but merely warned the animals that this extra task would mean very hard work, it might even be necessary to reduce their rations. The plans, however, had all been prepared, down to the last detail. A special committee of pigs had been at work upon them for the past three weeks. The building of the windmill, with various other improvements, was expected to take two years.

That evening Squealer explained privately to the other

disperse [dɪˈspɝs] v 解散；疏散

animals that Napoleon had never in reality been opposed to the windmill. On the contrary, it was he who had advocated it in the beginning, and the plan which Snowball had drawn on the floor of the incubator shed had actually been stolen from among Napoleon's papers. The windmill was, in fact, Napoleon's own creation. Why, then, asked somebody, had he spoken so strongly against it? Here Squealer looked very sly. That, he said, was Comrade Napoleon's cunning. He had *seemed* to oppose the windmill, simply as a manoeuvre to get rid of Snowball, who was a dangerous character and a bad influence. Now that Snowball was out of the way, the plan could go forward without his interference. This, said Squealer, was something called tactics. He repeated a number of times, "Tactics, comrades, tactics!" skipping round and whisking his tail with a merry laugh. The animals were not certain what the word meant, but Squealer spoke so persuasively, and the three dogs who happened to be with him growled so threateningly, that they accepted his explanation without further questions.

cunning [ˈkʌnɪŋ] *n* 狡猾；靈巧
tactics [ˈtæktɪks] *n* 策略，手段
threateningly [ˈθrɛtənɪŋlɪ] *adv* 威脅地；脅迫地；危險地

06 ⁄

All that year the animals worked like slaves. But they were happy in their work; they grudged no effort or sacrifice, well aware that everything that they did was for the benefit of themselves and those of their kind who would come after them, and not for a pack of idle, thieving human beings.

Throughout the spring and summer they worked a sixty-hour week, and in August Napoleon announced that there would be work on Sunday afternoons as well. This work was strictly voluntary, but any animal who absented himself from it would have his rations reduced by half. Even so, it was found necessary to leave certain tasks undone. The harvest was a little less successful than in the previous year, and two fields which should have been sown with roots in the early summer were not sown because the ploughing

---

grudge [grʌdʒ] *v* 不情願做
strictly [ˈstrɪktlɪ] *adv* 完全地；僅僅
absent [ˈæbsṇt] *adj* 缺席的，不在場的

had not been completed early enough. It was possible to foresee that the coming winter would be a hard one.

The windmill presented unexpected difficulties. There was a good quarry of limestone on the farm, and plenty of sand and cement had been found in one of the outhouses, so that all the materials for building were at hand. But the problem the animals could not at first solve was how to break up the stone into pieces of suitable size. There seemed no way of doing this except with picks and crowbars, which no animal could use, because no animal could stand on his hind legs. Only after weeks of vain effort did the right idea occur to somebody — namely, to utilise the force of gravity. Huge boulders, far too big to be used as they were, were lying all over the bed of the quarry. The animals lashed ropes round these, and then all together, cows, horses, sheep, any animal that could lay hold of the rope — even the pigs sometimes joined in at critical moments — they dragged them with desperate slowness up the slope to the top of the quarry, where they were toppled over the edge,

foresee [fɔrˈsi] **v** 預見；預知
namely [ˈnemlɪ] **adv** 即，也就是說
utilise [ˈjutḷˌaɪz] **v** 利用
topple [ˈtɑpḷ] **v** 使倒塌

to shatter to pieces below. Transporting the stone when it was once broken was comparatively simple. The horses carried it off in cart-loads, the sheep dragged single blocks, even Muriel and Benjamin yoked themselves into an old governess-cart and did their share. By late summer a sufficient store of stone had accumulated, and then the building began, under the superintendence of the pigs.

But it was a slow, laborious process. Frequently it took a whole day of exhausting effort to drag a single boulder to the top of the quarry, and sometimes when it was pushed over the edge it failed to break. Nothing could have been achieved without Boxer, whose strength seemed equal to that of all the rest of the animals put together. When the boulder began to slip and the animals cried out in despair at finding themselves dragged down the hill, it was always Boxer who strained himself against the rope and brought the boulder to a stop. To see him toiling up the slope inch by inch, his breath coming fast, the tips of his hoofs clawing at the ground, and his great sides matted

shatter [ˈʃætə-] **v** 粉碎，砸碎

comparatively [kəmˈpærətɪvlɪ] **adv** 相對地

accumulate [əˈkjumjəˌlet] **v** 積成堆；累積

superintendence [ˌsuprɪnˈtɛndəns] **n** 指揮；監督

with sweat, filled everyone with admiration. Clover warned him sometimes to be careful not to overstrain himself, but Boxer would never listen to her. His two slogans, "I will work harder" and "Napoleon is always right," seemed to him a sufficient answer to all problems. He had made arrangements with the cockerel to call him three-quarters of an hour earlier in the mornings instead of half an hour. And in his spare moments, of which there were not many nowadays, he would go alone to the quarry, collect a load of broken stone, and drag it down to the site of the windmill unassisted.

The animals were not badly off throughout that summer, in spite of the hardness of their work. If they had no more food than they had had in Jones's day, at least they did not have less. The advantage of only having to feed themselves, and not having to support five extravagant human beings as well, was so great that it would have taken a lot of failures to outweigh it. And in many ways the animal method of doing things was more efficient and saved labour. Such jobs as weeding, for instance, could be done with a thoroughness impossible

spare [spɛr] _adj_ 空閒的
outweigh [aʊt'we] _v_ 比……更重要（或更有價值等）

to human beings. And again, since no animal now stole, it was unnecessary to fence off pasture from arable land, which saved a lot of labour on the upkeep of hedges and gates. Nevertheless, as the summer wore on, various unforeseen shortages began to make them selves felt. There was need of paraffin oil, nails, string, dog biscuits, and iron for the horses' shoes, none of which could be produced on the farm. Later there would also be need for seeds and artificial manures, besides various tools and, finally, the machinery for the windmill. How these were to be procured, no one was able to imagine.

One Sunday morning, when the animals assembled to receive their orders, Napoleon announced that he had decided upon a new policy. From now onwards Animal Farm would engage in trade with the neighbouring farms: not, of course, for any commercial purpose, but simply in order to obtain certain materials which were urgently necessary. The needs of the windmill must override everything else, he said. He was therefore making arrangements to sell a stack of hay and part of the current year's wheat crop, and later on, if more money were needed, it would have to be made up by the sale of eggs, for which

procure [proˈkjʊr] **v** 取得

there was always a market in Willingdon. The hens, said Napoleon, should welcome this sacrifice as their own special contribution towards the building of the windmill.

Once again the animals were conscious of a vague uneasiness. Never to have any dealings with human beings, never to engage in trade, never to make use of money — had not these been among the earliest resolutions passed at that first triumphant Meeting after Jones was expelled? All the animals remembered passing such resolutions: or at least they thought that they remembered it. The four young pigs who had protested when Napoleon abolished the Meetings raised their voices timidly, but they were promptly silenced by a tremendous growling from the dogs. Then, as usual, the sheep broke into "Four legs good, two legs bad!" and the momentary awkwardness was smoothed over. Finally Napoleon raised his trotter for silence and announced that he had already made all the arrangements. There would be no need for any of the animals to come in contact with human beings, which

uneasiness [ʌnˈizɪnɪs] **n** 擔心；不安
resolution [ˌrɛzəˈluʃən] **n** 決心；決定
timidly [ˈtɪmɪdlɪ] **adv** 膽小地
momentary [ˈmomənˌtɛrɪ] **adv** 短暫的；瞬間的

would clearly be most undesirable. He intended to take the whole burden upon his own shoulders. A Mr. Whymper, a solicitor living in Willingdon, had agreed to act as intermediary between Animal Farm and the outside world, and would visit the farm every Monday morning to receive his instructions. Napoleon ended his speech with his usual cry of "Long live Animal Farm!" and after the singing of Beasts of England the animals were dismissed.

Afterwards Squealer made a round of the farm and set the animals' minds at rest. He assured them that the resolution against engaging in trade and using money had never been passed, or even suggested. It was pure imagination, probably traceable in the beginning to lies circulated by Snowball. A few animals still felt faintly doubtful, but Squealer asked them shrewdly, "Are you certain that this is not something that you have dreamed, comrades? Have you any record of such a resolution? Is it

undesirable [ˌʌndɪˈzaɪrəbl] *adj* 令人不快的；討厭的
burden [ˈbɜdn̩] *n* 重擔；沉重的責任
solicitor [səˈlɪsɪtɚ] *n* 初級律師
intermediary [ˌɪntɚˈmidɪˌɛrɪ] *n* 中間人；仲裁者
faintly [ˈfentlɪ] *adv* 微弱地；模糊地
doubtful [ˈdaʊtfəl] *adj* 懷疑的，疑惑的
shrewdly [ˈʃrudlɪ] *adv* 精明幹練地

074

written down anywhere?" And since it was certainly true that nothing of the kind existed in writing, the animals were satisfied that they had been mistaken.

Every Monday Mr. Whymper visited the farm as had been arranged. He was a sly-looking little man with side whiskers, a solicitor in a very small way of business, but sharp enough to have realised earlier than anyone else that Animal Farm would need a broker and that the commissions would be worth having. The animals watched his coming and going with a kind of dread, and avoided him as much as possible. Nevertheless, the sight of Napoleon, on all fours, delivering orders to Whymper, who stood on two legs, roused their pride and partly reconciled them to the new arrangement. Their relations with the human race were now not quite the same as they had been before. The human beings did not hate Animal Farm any less now that it was prospering; indeed, they hated it more than ever. Every human being held it as an article of faith that the farm would go bankrupt sooner or later, and,

broker [ˈbrokɚ] **n** 經紀人
commission [kəˈmɪʃən] **n** （權限，任務等的）委任，委託
dread [drɛd] **n** 畏懼；擔心
reconcile [ˈrɛkənsaɪl] **v** 調解

above all, that the windmill would be a failure. They would meet in the public-houses and prove to one another by means of diagrams that the windmill was bound to fall down, or that if it did stand up, then that it would never work. And yet, against their will, they had developed a certain respect for the efficiency with which the animals were managing their own affairs. One symptom of this was that they had begun to call Animal Farm by its proper name and ceased to pretend that it was called the Manor Farm. They had also dropped their championship of Jones, who had given up hope of getting his farm back and gone to live in another part of the county. Except through Whymper, there was as yet no contact between Animal Farm and the outside world, but there were constant rumours that Napoleon was about to enter into a definite business agreement either with Mr. Pilkington of Foxwood or with Mr. Frederick of Pinchfield — but never, it was noticed, with both simultaneously.

It was about this time that the pigs suddenly moved into the farmhouse and took up their residence there. Again the animals seemed to remember that a resolution against this

championship [ˈtʃæmpɪənˌʃɪp] *n* 擁護，支持
simultaneously [saɪməlˈtenɪəslɪ] *adv* 同時地

had been passed in the early days, and again Squealer was able to convince them that this was not the case. It was absolutely necessary, he said, that the pigs, who were the brains of the farm, should have a quiet place to work in. It was also more suited to the dignity of the Leader (for of late he had taken to speaking of Napoleon under the title of "Leader") to live in a house than in a mere sty. Nevertheless, some of the animals were disturbed when they heard that the pigs not only took their meals in the kitchen and used the drawing-room as a recreation room, but also slept in the beds. Boxer passed it off as usual with "Napoleon is always right!", but Clover, who thought she remembered a definite ruling against beds, went to the end of the barn and tried to puzzle out the Seven Commandments which were inscribed there. Finding herself unable to read more than individual letters, she fetched Muriel.

"Muriel," she said, "read me the Fourth Commandment. Does it not say something about never sleeping in a bed?"

With some difficulty Muriel spelt it out.

mere [mɪr] *adj* 僅僅的，只不過的
sty [staɪ] *n* 豬欄；藏汙納垢之處
recreation [ˌrɛkrɪ'eʃən] *n* （身心的）休養
ruling ['rulɪŋ] *n* 規定；裁決

"It says, 'No animal shall sleep in a bed with sheets,'" she announced finally.

Curiously enough, Clover had not remembered that the Fourth Commandment mentioned sheets; but as it was there on the wall, it must have done so. And Squealer, who happened to be passing at this moment, attended by two or three dogs, was able to put the whole matter in its proper perspective.

"You have heard then, comrades," he said, "that we pigs now sleep in the beds of the farmhouse? And why not? You did not suppose, surely, that there was ever a ruling against beds? A bed merely means a place to sleep in. A pile of straw in a stall is a bed, properly regarded. The rule was against sheets, which are a human invention. We have removed the sheets from the farmhouse beds, and sleep between blankets. And very comfortable beds they are too! But not more comfortable than we need, I can tell you, comrades, with all the brainwork we have to do nowadays. You would not rob us of our repose, would you, comrades? You would not have us too tired to carry out our duties? Surely none of you wishes to see Jones back?"

perspective [pɚ'spɛktɪv] *n* 看法，觀點
repose [rɪ'poz] *n* 歇息

The animals reassured him on this point immediately, and no more was said about the pigs sleeping in the farmhouse beds. And when, some days afterwards, it was announced that from now on the pigs would get up an hour later in the mornings than the other animals, no complaint was made about that either.

By the autumn the animals were tired but happy. They had had a hard year, and after the sale of part of the hay and corn, the stores of food for the winter were none too plentiful, but the windmill compensated for everything. It was almost half built now. After the harvest there was a stretch of clear dry weather, and the animals toiled harder than ever, thinking it well worth while to plod to and fro all day with blocks of stone if by doing so they could raise the walls another foot. Boxer would even come out at nights and work for an hour or two on his own by the light of the harvest moon. In their spare moments the animals would walk round and round the half-finished mill, admiring the strength and perpendicularity of its walls and marvelling that they

---

compensate [ˈkɑmpənˌset] **v** 補上;補償
plod [plɑd] **v** 努力從事;埋頭苦幹
perpendicularity [ˌpɝpənˌdɪkjəˈlɛrətɪ] **n** 垂直;直立
marvel [ˈmɑrvl] **v** 對⋯⋯感到驚訝

should ever have been able to build anything so imposing. Only old Benjamin refused to grow enthusiastic about the windmill, though, as usual, he would utter nothing beyond the cryptic remark that donkeys live a long time.

November came, with raging south-west winds. Building had to stop because it was now too wet to mix the cement. Finally there came a night when the gale was so violent that the farm buildings rocked on their foundations and several tiles were blown off the roof of the barn. The hens woke up squawking with terror because they had all dreamed simultaneously of hearing a gun go off in the distance. In the morning the animals came out of their stalls to find that the flagstaff had been blown down and an elm tree at the foot of the orchard had been plucked up like a radish. They had just noticed this when a cry of despair broke from every animal's throat. A terrible sight had met their eyes. The windmill was in ruins.

With one accord they dashed down to the spot.

imposing [ɪmˈpozɪŋ] *adj* 壯觀的；氣勢宏偉的
enthusiastic [ɪnˌθjuzɪˈæstɪk] *adj* 熱情的；熱烈的
in ruins [ɪn] [ˈrʊɪnz] 成為廢墟
accord [əˈkɔrd] *n* 一致

Napoleon, who seldom moved out of a walk, raced ahead of them all. Yes, there it lay, the fruit of all their struggles, levelled to its foundations, the stones they had broken and carried so laboriously scattered all around. Unable at first to speak, they stood gazing mournfully at the litter of fallen stone Napoleon paced to and fro in silence, occasionally snuffing at the ground. His tail had grown rigid and twitched sharply from side to side, a sign in him of intense mental activity. Suddenly he halted as though his mind were made up.

"Comrades," he said quietly, "do you know who is responsible for this? Do you know the enemy who has come in the night and overthrown our windmill? SNOWBALL!" he suddenly roared in a voice of thunder. "Snowball has done this thing! In sheer malignity, thinking to set back our plans and avenge himself for his ignominious expulsion, this traitor has crept here under cover of night and destroyed our work of nearly a year. Comrades, here and now I pronounce the death sentence upon Snowball. 'Animal Hero, Second Class,' and half a

scatter [ˈskætɚ] **v** 使消散；使潰散
sheer [ʃɪr] **adj** 全然的
malignity [məˈlɪgnətɪ] **n** 惡毒行為；惡意

Animal Farm

bushel of apples to any animal who brings him to justice.
A full bushel to anyone who captures him alive!"

The animals were shocked beyond measure to learn
that even Snowball could be guilty of such an action.
There was a cry of indignation, and everyone began
thinking out ways of catching Snowball if he should ever
come back. Almost immediately the footprints of a pig
were discovered in the grass at a little distance from the
knoll. They could only be traced for a few yards, but
appeared to lead to a hole in the hedge. Napoleon snuffed
deeply at them and pronounced them to be Snowball's.
He gave it as his opinion that Snowball had probably
come from the direction of Foxwood Farm.

"No more delays, comrades!" cried Napoleon when the
footprints had been examined. "There is work to be done.
This very morning we begin rebuilding the windmill, and
we will build all through the winter, rain or shine. We will
teach this miserable traitor that he cannot undo our work so
easily. Remember, comrades, there must be no alteration in
our plans: they shall be carried out to the day. Forward,
comrades! Long live the windmill! Long live Animal Farm!"

indignation [ˌɪndɪgˈneʃən] *n* 憤怒；憤慨
alteration [ˌɔltəˈreʃən] *n* 變更，修改

07 ╱

It was a bitter winter. The stormy weather was followed by sleet and snow, and then by a hard frost which did not break till well into February. The animals carried on as best they could with the rebuilding of the windmill, well knowing that the outside world was watching them and that the envious human beings would rejoice and triumph if the mill were not finished on time.

Out of spite, the human beings pretended not to believe that it was Snowball who had destroyed the windmill: they said that it had fallen down because the walls were too thin. The animals knew that this was not the case. Still, it had been decided to build the walls three feet thick this time instead of eighteen inches as before, which meant collecting much larger quantities of stone. For a long time the quarry was full of snowdrifts and nothing could be

envious [ˈɛnvɪəs] *adj* 嫉妒的；羨慕的
rejoice [rɪˈdʒɔɪs] *v* 慶祝，歡樂
out of spite [aʊt] [ɑv] [spaɪt] 洩憤

done. Some progress was made in the dry frosty weather that followed, but it was cruel work, and the animals could not feel so hopeful about it as they had felt before. They were always cold, and usually hungry as well. Only Boxer and Clover never lost heart. Squealer made excellent speeches on the joy of service and the dignity of labour, but the other animals found more inspiration in Boxer's strength and his never-failing cry of "I will work harder!"

In January food fell short. The corn ration was drastically reduced, and it was announced that an extra potato ration would be issued to make up for it. Then it was discovered that the greater part of the potato crop had been frosted in the clamps, which had not been covered thickly enough. The potatoes had become soft and discoloured, and only a few were edible. For days at a time the animals had nothing to eat but chaff and mangels. Starvation seemed to stare them in the face.

It was vitally necessary to conceal this fact from the outside world. Emboldened by the collapse of the

drastically ['dræstɪk!ɪ] *adv* 大大地；激烈地
edible ['ɛdəbl] *adj* 可食的，食用的
starvation [stɑr'veʃən] *n* 飢餓
vitally ['vaɪtəlɪ] *adv* 極其，十分
embolden [ɪm'boldn̩] *v* 使大膽；使有勇氣

windmill, the human beings were inventing fresh lies about Animal Farm. Once again it was being put about that all the animals were dying of famine and disease, and that they were continually fighting among themselves and had resorted to cannibalism and infanticide. Napoleon was well aware of the bad results that might follow if the real facts of the food situation were known, and he decided to make use of Mr. Whymper to spread a contrary impression. Hitherto the animals had had little or no contact with Whymper on his weekly visits: now, however, a few selected animals, mostly sheep, were instructed to remark casually in his hearing that rations had been increased. In addition, Napoleon ordered the almost empty bins in the store-shed to be filled nearly to the brim with sand, which was then covered up with what remained of the grain and meal. On some suitable pretext Whymper was led through the store-shed and allowed to catch a glimpse of the bins. He was deceived, and continued to report to the outside world that there was no food shortage on Animal Farm.

famine [ˈfæmɪn] _n_ 饑荒
resort [rɪˈzɔrt] _v_ 訴諸，憑藉，求助
hitherto [hitherto] _adv_ 迄今；至此
deceive [deceive] _v_ 欺騙，蒙蔽

Nevertheless, towards the end of January it became obvious that it would be necessary to procure some more grain from somewhere. In these days Napoleon rarely appeared in public, but spent all his time in the farmhouse, which was guarded at each door by fierce-looking dogs. When he did emerge, it was in a ceremonial manner, with an escort of six dogs who closely surrounded him and growled if anyone came too near. Frequently he did not even appear on Sunday mornings, but issued his orders through one of the other pigs, usually Squealer.

One Sunday morning Squealer announced that the hens, who had just come in to lay again, must surrender their eggs. Napoleon had accepted, through Whymper, a contract for four hundred eggs a week. The price of these would pay for enough grain and meal to keep the farm going till summer came on and conditions were easier.

When the hens heard this, they raised a terrible outcry. They had been warned earlier that this sacrifice might be necessary, but had not believed that it would really happen. They were just getting their clutches ready

ceremonial [ˌsɛrəˈmonɪəl] *adj* 儀式的；正式的
surrender [səˈrɛndɚ] *v* 交出，放棄
outcry [ˈaʊtˌkraɪ] *n* 喊叫；強烈的抗議（或反對）

for the spring sitting, and they protested that to take the eggs away now was murder. For the first time since the expulsion of Jones, there was something resembling a rebellion. Led by three young Black Minorca pullets, the hens made a determined effort to thwart Napoleon's wishes. Their method was to fly up to the rafters and there lay their eggs, which smashed to pieces on the floor. Napoleon acted swiftly and ruthlessly. He ordered the hens' rations to be stopped, and decreed that any animal giving so much as a grain of corn to a hen should be punished by death. The dogs saw to it that these orders were carried out. For five days the hens held out, then they capitulated and went back to their nesting boxes. Nine hens had died in the meantime. Their bodies were buried in the orchard, and it was given out that they had died of coccidiosis. Whymper heard nothing of this affair, and the eggs were duly delivered, a grocer's van driving up to the farm once a week to take them away.

pullet [ˈpʊlɪt] *n* 小母雞
thwart [θwɔrt] *v* 反對，阻撓
ruthlessly [ˈruθlɪslɪ] *adv* 無情地；冷酷地；殘忍地
capitulate [kəˈpɪtʃəˌlet] *v* 投降；停止反抗
duly [ˈdjulɪ] *adv* 按時地；適當地

All this while no more had been seen of Snowball. He was rumoured to be hiding on one of the neighbouring farms, either Foxwood or Pinchfield. Napoleon was by this time on slightly better terms with the other farmers than before. It happened that there was in the yard a pile of timber which had been stacked there ten years earlier when a beech spinney was cleared. It was well seasoned, and Whymper had advised Napoleon to sell it; both Mr. Pilkington and Mr. Frederick were anxious to buy it. Napoleon was hesitating between the two, unable to make up his mind. It was noticed that whenever he seemed on the point of coming to an agreement with Frederick, Snowball was declared to be in hiding at Foxwood, while, when he inclined toward Pilkington, Snowball was said to be at Pinchfield.

Suddenly, early in the spring, an alarming thing was discovered. Snowball was secretly frequenting the farm by night! The animals were so disturbed that they could hardly sleep in their stalls. Every night, it was said, he came creeping

timber ['tɪmbə] **n** 木材，木料
seasoned ['siznd] **adj** 曬（風）乾的
incline ['ɪnklaɪn] **v** 心裡傾向，有意
creeping ['kripɪŋ] **adj** 偷偷摸摸的；鬼祟的

in under cover of darkness and performed all kinds of mischief. He stole the corn, he upset the milk-pails, he broke the eggs, he trampled the seedbeds, he gnawed the bark off the fruit trees. Whenever anything went wrong it became usual to attribute it to Snowball. If a window was broken or a drain was blocked up, someone was certain to say that Snowball had come in the night and done it, and when the key of the store-shed was lost, the whole farm was convinced that Snowball had thrown it down the well. Curiously enough, they went on believing this even after the mislaid key was found under a sack of meal. The cows declared unanimously that Snowball crept into their stalls and milked them in their sleep. The rats, which had been troublesome that winter, were also said to be in league with Snowball.

Napoleon decreed that there should be a full investigation into Snowball's activities. With his dogs in attendance he set out and made a careful tour of inspection of the farm buildings, the other animals following at a respectful distance. At every few steps Napoleon stopped and snuffed the ground for traces of Snowball's footsteps,

attribute [ˈætrəˌbjut] **v** 把……歸因於；把……歸咎於（**+to**）
decree [dɪˈkri] **v** 頒布；命令

which, he said, he could detect by the smell. He snuffed in every corner, in the barn, in the cow-shed, in the henhouses, in the vegetable garden, and found traces of Snowball almost everywhere. He would put his snout to the ground, give several deep sniffs, ad exclaim in a terrible voice, "Snowball! He has been here! I can smell him distinctly!" and at the word "Snowball" all the dogs let out blood-curdling growls and showed their side teeth.

The animals were thoroughly frightened. It seemed to them as though Snowball were some kind of invisible influence, pervading the air about them and menacing them with all kinds of dangers. In the evening Squealer called them together, and with an alarmed expression on his face told them that he had some serious news to report.

"Comrades!" cried Squealer, making little nervous skips, "a most terrible thing has been discovered. Snowball has sold himself to Frederick of Pinchfield Farm, who is even now plotting to attack us and take our farm away from us! Snowball is to act as his guide when the attack begins. But there is worse than that. We had thought that

detect [dɪˈtɛkt] **v** 發現，察覺；查出
pervade [pəˈved] **v** 彌漫於，滲透於；遍及於

Snowball's rebellion was caused simply by his vanity and ambition. But we were wrong, comrades. Do you know what the real reason was? Snowball was in league with Jones from the very start! He was Jones's secret agent all the time. It has all been proved by documents which he left behind him and which we have only just discovered. To my mind this explains a great deal, comrades. Did we not see for ourselves how he attempted — fortunately without success — to get us defeated and destroyed at the Battle of the Cowshed?"

The animals were stupefied. This was a wickedness far outdoing Snowball's destruction of the windmill. But it was some minutes before they could fully take it in. They all remembered, or thought they remembered, how they had seen Snowball charging ahead of them at the Battle of the Cowshed, how he had rallied and encouraged them at every turn, and how he had not paused for an instant even when the pellets from Jones's gun had wounded his back. At first it was a little difficult to see how this fitted in with his being on Jones's side. Even

vanity ['vænətɪ] *n* 虛榮（心）
stupefied ['stjupə,faɪd] *adj* 目瞪口呆的
rally ['rælɪ] *v* 團結，重整

Boxer, who seldom asked questions, was puzzled. He lay down, tucked his fore hoofs beneath him, shut his eyes, and with a hard effort managed to formulate his thoughts.

"I do not believe that," he said. "Snowball fought bravely at the Battle of the Cowshed. I saw him myself. Did we not give him 'Animal Hero, first Class,' immediately afterwards?"

"That was our mistake, comrade. For we know now — it is all written down in the secret documents that we have found — that in reality he was trying to lure us to our doom."

"But he was wounded," said Boxer. "We all saw him running with blood."

"That was part of the arrangement!" cried Squealer. "Jones's shot only grazed him. I could show you this in his own writing, if you were able to read it. The plot was for Snowball, at the critical moment, to give the signal for flight and leave the field to the enemy. And he very nearly succeeded — I will even say, comrades, he *would* have succeeded if it had not been for our heroic Leader, Comrade Napoleon. Do you not remember how, just at the moment when Jones and his men had got inside the yard, Snowball suddenly turned and fled, and many

lure [lʊr] *v* 引誘

animals followed him? And do you not remember, too, that it was just at that moment, when panic was spreading and all seemed lost, that Comrade Napoleon sprang forward with a cry of 'Death to Humanity!' and sank his teeth in Jones's leg? Surely you remember *that*, comrades?" exclaimed Squealer, frisking from side to side.

Now when Squealer described the scene so graphically, it seemed to the animals that they did remember it. At any rate, they remembered that at the critical moment of the battle Snowball had turned to flee. But Boxer was still a little uneasy.

"I do not believe that Snowball was a traitor at the beginning," he said finally. "What he has done since is different. But I believe that at the Battle of the Cowshed he was a good comrade."

"Our Leader, Comrade Napoleon," announced Squealer, speaking very slowly and firmly, "has stated categorically — categorically, comrade — that Snowball was Jones's agent from the very beginning — yes, and from long before the Rebellion was ever thought of."

graphically [ˈɡræfɪklɪ] *adv* 生動地，活靈活現地
at any rate [æt] [ˈɛnɪ] [rate] 至少；無論如何
categorically [ˌkætəˈɡɒrɪklɪ] *adv* 絕對地，直截了當地

"Ah, that is different!" said Boxer. "If Comrade Napoleon says it, it must be right."

"That is the true spirit, comrade!" cried Squealer, but it was noticed he cast a very ugly look at Boxer with his little twinkling eyes. He turned to go, then paused and added impressively: "I warn every animal on this farm to keep his eyes very wide open. For we have reason to think that some of Snowball's secret agents are lurking among us at this moment! "

Four days later, in the late afternoon, Napoleon ordered all the animals to assemble in the yard. When they were all gathered together, Napoleon emerged from the farmhouse, wearing both his medals (for he had recently awarded himself "Animal Hero, First Class," and "Animal Hero, Second Class"), with his nine huge dogs frisking round him and uttering growls that sent shivers down all the animals' spines. They all cowered silently in their places, seeming to know in advance that some terrible thing was about to happen.

Napoleon stood sternly surveying his audience; then he uttered a high-pitched whimper. Immediately the dogs

lurk [lɜk] **v** 潛伏，埋伏

sternly [ˈstɜnlɪ] **adv** 嚴厲地，堅決地

bounded forward, seized four of the pigs by the ear and dragged them, squealing with pain and terror, to Napoleon's feet. The pigs' ears were bleeding, the dogs had tasted blood, and for a few moments they appeared to go quite mad. To the amazement of everybody, three of them flung themselves upon Boxer. Boxer saw them coming and put out his great hoof, caught a dog in mid-air, and pinned him to the ground. The dog shrieked for mercy and the other two fled with their tails between their legs. Boxer looked at Napoleon to know whether he should crush the dog to death or let it go. Napoleon appeared to change countenance, and sharply ordered Boxer to let the dog go, whereat Boxer lifted his hoof, and the dog slunk away, bruised and howling.

Presently the tumult died down. The four pigs waited, trembling, with guilt written on every line of their countenances. Napoleon now called upon them to confess their crimes. They were the same four pigs as had protested when Napoleon abolished the Sunday Meetings. Without any further prompting they confessed that they had been secretly in touch with Snowball ever since his expulsion, that they had collaborated with him in destroying the

countenance [ˈkaʊntənəns] **n** 臉色；表情
collaborate [kəˈlæbəˌret] **v** 合作，勾結

windmill, and that they had entered into an agreement with him to hand over Animal Farm to Mr. Frederick. They added that Snowball had privately admitted to them that he had been Jones's secret agent for years past. When they had finished their confession, the dogs promptly tore their throats out, and in a terrible voice Napoleon demanded whether any other animal had anything to confess.

The three hens who had been the ringleaders in the attempted rebellion over the eggs now came forward and stated that Snowball had appeared to them in a dream and incited them to disobey Napoleon's orders. They, too, were slaughtered. Then a goose came forward and confessed to having secreted six ears of corn during the last year's harvest and eaten them in the night. Then a sheep confessed to having urinated in the drinking pool — urged to do this, so she said, by Snowball — and two other sheep confessed to having murdered an old ram, an especially devoted follower of Napoleon, by chasing him round and round a bonfire when he was suffering from a cough. They were all slain on the spot. And so the tale of confessions

confession [kənˈfɛʃən] _n_ 懺悔，供認
ringleader [ringleader] _n_ 首要分子；元兇
urge [ɝdʒ] _v_ 強烈要求

and executions went on, until there was a pile of corpses lying before Napoleon's feet and the air was heavy with the smell of blood, which had been unknown there since the expulsion of Jones.

When it was all over, the remaining animals, except for the pigs and dogs, crept away in a body. They were shaken and miserable. They did not know which was more shocking — the treachery of the animals who had leagued themselves with Snowball, or the cruel retribution they had just witnessed. In the old days there had often been scenes of bloodshed equally terrible, but it seemed to all of them that it was far worse now that it was happening among themselves. Since Jones had left the farm, until today, no animal had killed another animal. Not even a rat had been killed. They had made their way on to the little knoll where the half-finished windmill stood, and with one accord they all lay down as though huddling together for warmth — Clover, Muriel, Benjamin, the cows, the sheep, and a whole flock of geese and hens — everyone, indeed, except the cat, who had suddenly disappeared just before Napoleon ordered the animals to assemble. For some time nobody spoke. Only

treachery [ˈtrɛtʃərɪ] **n** 背叛，變節；背信
retribution [ˌrɛtrɪˈbjuʃən] **n** 報應；懲罰

Boxer remained on his feet. He fidgeted to and fro, swishing his long black tail against his sides and occasionally uttering a little whinny of surprise. Finally he said:

"I do not understand it. I would not have believed that such things could happen on our farm. It must be due to some fault in ourselves. The solution, as I see it, is to work harder. From now onwards I shall get up a full hour earlier in the mornings."

And he moved off at his lumbering trot and made for the quarry. Having got there, he collected two successive loads of stone and dragged them down to the windmill before retiring for the night.

The animals huddled about Clover, not speaking. The knoll where they were lying gave them a wide prospect across the countryside. Most of Animal Farm was within their view — the long pasture stretching down to the main road, the hayfield, the spinney, the drinking pool, the ploughed fields where the young wheat was thick and green, and the red roofs of the farm buildings with the smoke curling from the chimneys. It was a clear spring evening. The grass and

fidget ['fɪdʒɪt] *v* 坐立不安;煩躁
lumbering ['lʌmbərɪŋ] *adj* 笨重的
successive [sək'sɛsɪv] *adj* 連續的,相繼的

the bursting hedges were gilded by the level rays of the sun. Never had the farm — and with a kind of surprise they remembered that it was their own farm, every inch of it their own property — appeared to the animals so desirable a place. As Clover looked down the hillside her eyes filled with tears. If she could have spoken her thoughts, it would have been to say that this was not what they had aimed at when they had set themselves years ago to work for the overthrow of the human race. These scenes of terror and slaughter were not what they had looked forward to on that night when old Major first stirred them to rebellion. If she herself had had any picture of the future, it had been of a society of animals set free from hunger and the whip, all equal, each working according to his capacity, the strong protecting the weak, as she had protected the lost brood of ducklings with her foreleg on the night of Major's speech. Instead — she did not know why — they had come to a time when no one dared speak his mind, when fierce, growling dogs roamed everywhere, and when you had to watch your comrades torn to pieces after confessing to shocking crimes. There was no thought of rebellion or disobedience in her mind. She knew that, even as things were, they were

disobedience [ˌdɪsəˈbidɪəns] *n* 不服從，違反

far better off than they had been in the days of Jones, and that before all else it was needful to prevent the return of the human beings. Whatever happened she would remain faithful, work hard, carry out the orders that were given to her, and accept the leadership of Napoleon. But still, it was not for this that she and all the other animals had hoped and toiled. It was not for this that they had built the windmill and faced the bullets of Jones's gun. Such were her thoughts, though she lacked the words to express them.

At last, feeling this to be in some way a substitute for the words she was unable to find, she began to sing *Beasts of England*. The other animals sitting round her took it up, and they sang it three times over — very tunefully, but slowly and mournfully, in a way they had never sung it before.

They had just finished singing it for the third time when Squealer, attended by two dogs, approached them with the air of having something important to say. He announced that, by a special decree of Comrade Napoleon, *Beasts of England* had been abolished. From now onwards it was forbidden to sing it.

The animals were taken aback.

substitute [ˈsʌbstəˌtjut] *n* 代替人；代替物；代用品
aback [əˈbæk] *adv* 吃驚；猝不及防地

"Why?" cried Muriel.

"It's no longer needed, comrade," said Squealer stiffly. "*Beasts of England* was the song of the Rebellion. But the Rebellion is now completed. The execution of the traitors this afternoon was the final act. The enemy both external and internal has been defeated. In *Beasts of England* we expressed our longing for a better society in days to come. But that society has now been established. Clearly this song has no longer any purpose."

Frightened though they were, some of the animals might possibly have protested, but at this moment the sheep set up their usual bleating of "Four legs good, two legs bad," which went on for several minutes and put an end to the discussion.

So *Beasts of England* was heard no more. In its place Minimus, the poet, had composed another song which began:

Animal Farm, Animal Farm,
Never through me shalt thou come to harm!

and this was sung every Sunday morning after the hoisting of the flag. But somehow neither the words nor the tune ever seemed to the animals to come up to *Beasts of England.*

come up [come] [up] 比得上

08 /

A few days later, when the terror caused by the executions had died down, some of the animals remembered — or thought they remembered — that the Sixth Commandment decreed "No animal shall kill any other animal." And though no one cared to mention it in the hearing of the pigs or the dogs, it was felt that the killings which had taken place did not square with this. Clover asked Benjamin to read her the Sixth Commandment, and when Benjamin, as usual, said that he refused to meddle in such matters, she fetched Muriel. Muriel read the Commandment for her. It ran: "No animal shall kill any other animal *without cause*." Somehow or other, the last two words had slipped out of the animals' memory. But they saw now that the Commandment had not been violated; for clearly there was good reason for killing the traitors

square with [skwɛr] [skwɛr] （使）與……一致；符合
meddle [ˈmɛd!] ☑ 干涉；管閒事
slip [slɪp] ☑ 疏忽；被遺忘

who had leagued themselves with Snowball.

Throughout the year the animals worked even harder than they had worked in the previous year To rebuild the windmill, with walls twice as thick as before, and to finish it by the appointed date, together with the regular work of the farm, was a tremendous labour. There were times when it seemed to the animals that they worked longer hours and fed no better than they had done in Jones's day. On Sunday mornings Squealer, holding down a long strip of paper with his trotter, would read out to them lists of figures proving that the production of every class of foodstuff had increased by two hundred per cent, three hundred per cent, or five hundred per cent, as the case might be. The animals saw no reason to disbelieve him, especially as they could no longer remember very clearly what conditions had been like before the Rebellion. All the same, there were days when they felt that they would sooner have had less figures and more food.

All orders were now issued through Squealer or one of the other pigs. Napoleon himself was not seen in public as often as once in a fortnight. When he did appear, he was attended not only by his retinue of dogs but by a black

fortnight ['fɔrt,naɪt] *n* 兩星期

cockerel who marched in front of him and acted as a kind of trumpeter, letting out a loud "cock-a-doodle-doo" before Napoleon spoke. Even in the farmhouse, it was said, Napoleon inhabited separate apartments from the others. He took his meals alone, with two dogs to wait upon him, and always ate from the Crown Derby dinner service which had been in the glass cupboard in the drawing-room. It was also announced that the gun would be fired every year on Napoleon's birthday, as well as on the other two anniversaries.

Napoleon was now never spoken of simply as "Napoleon." He was always referred to in formal style as "our Leader, Comrade Napoleon," and the pigs liked to invent for him such titles as Father of All Animals, Terror of Mankind, Protector of the Sheep-fold, Ducklings' Friend, and the like. In his speeches, Squealer would talk with the tears rolling down his cheeks of Napoleon's wisdom, the goodness of his heart, and the deep love he bore to all animals everywhere, even and especially the unhappy animals who still lived in ignorance and slavery on other farms. It had become usual to give Napoleon the credit for every successful achievement and every stroke of good fortune. You would often hear one hen remark to

trumpeter [ˈtrʌmpɪtə] *n* 號手：吹鼓手

another, "Under the guidance of our Leader, Comrade Napoleon, I have laid five eggs in six days"; or two cows, enjoying a drink at the pool, would exclaim, "Thanks to the leadership of Comrade Napoleon, how excellent this water tastes!" The general feeling on the farm was well expressed in a poem entitled *Comrade Napoleon*, which was composed by Minimus and which ran as follows:

Friend of fatherless!
Fountain of happiness!
Lord of the swill-bucket! Oh, how my soul is on
Fire when I gaze at thy
Calm and commanding eye,
Like the sun in the sky,
Comrade Napoleon!

Thou are the giver of
All that thy creatures love,
Full belly twice a day, clean straw to roll upon;
Every beast great or small
Sleeps at peace in his stall,
Thou watchest over all,
Comrade Napoleon!

fountain ['faʊntɪn] *n* 噴泉，源泉

Had I a sucking-pig,
Ere he had grown as big
Even as a pint bottle or as a rolling-pin,
He should have learned to be
Faithful and true to thee,
Yes, his first squeak should be
"Comrade Napoleon!"

Napoleon approved of this poem and caused it to be inscribed on the wall of the big barn, at the opposite end from the Seven Commandments. It was surmounted by a portrait of Napoleon, in profile, executed by Squealer in white paint.

Meanwhile, through the agency of Whymper, Napoleon was engaged in complicated negotiations with Frederick and Pilkington. The pile of timber was still unsold. Of the two, Frederick was the more anxious to get hold of it, but he would not offer a reasonable price. At the same time there were renewed rumours that Frederick and his men were plotting to attack Animal Farm and to destroy the windmill, the building of which had aroused furious jealousy in him. Snowball was known to be still

portrait ['portret] *n* 肖像，描寫
arouse [ə'raʊz] *v* 喚起；引起

skulking on Pinchfield Farm. In the middle of the summer the animals were alarmed to hear that three hens had come forward and confessed that, inspired by Snowball, they had entered into a plot to murder Napoleon. They were executed immediately, and fresh precautions for Napoleon's safety were taken. Four dogs guarded his bed at night, one at each corner, and a young pig named Pinkeye was given the task of tasting all his food before he ate it, lest it should be poisoned.

At about the same time it was given out that Napoleon had arranged to sell the pile of timber to Mr. Pilkington; he was also going to enter into a regular agreement for the exchange of certain products between Animal Farm and Foxwood. The relations between Napoleon and Pilkington, though they were only conducted through Whymper, were now almost friendly. The animals distrusted Pilkington, as a human being, but greatly preferred him to Frederick, whom they both feared and hated. As the summer wore on, and the windmill neared completion, the rumours of an impending treacherous attack grew stronger and stronger.

skulk [skʌlk] **v** 躲藏；潛伏
precaution [prɪˈkɒʃən] **n** 預防措施
wore on [wor] [ɑn] 緩慢地進行（**wore** 為 **wear** 的動詞過去式）

Frederick, it was said, intended to bring against them twenty men all armed with guns, and he had already bribed the magistrates and police, so that if he could once get hold of the title-deeds of Animal Farm they would ask no questions. Moreover, terrible stories were leaking out from Pinchfield about the cruelties that Frederick practised upon his animals. He had flogged an old horse to death, he starved his cows, he had killed a dog by throwing it into the furnace, he amused himself in the evenings by making cocks fight with splinters of razor-blade tied to their spurs. The animals' blood boiled with rage when they heard of these things being done to their comrades, and sometimes they clamoured to be allowed to go out in a body and attack Pinchfield Farm, drive out the humans, and set the animals free. But Squealer counselled them to avoid rash actions and trust in Comrade Napoleon's strategy.

Nevertheless, feeling against Frederick continued to run high. One Sunday morning Napoleon appeared in the barn and explained that he had never at any time contemplated selling the pile of timber to Frederick; he considered it beneath his dignity, he said, to have dealings with scoundrels of that description. The pigeons who were still sent out to spread tidings of the Rebellion were forbidden to set foot anywhere on Foxwood, and were also ordered to drop their former slogan of "Death to Humanity" in favour of "Death to Frederick." In the late

summer yet another of Snowball's machinations was laid bare. The wheat crop was full of weeds, and it was discovered that on one of his nocturnal visits Snowball had mixed weed seeds with the seed corn. A gander who had been privy to the plot had confessed his guilt to Squealer and immediately committed suicide by swallowing deadly nightshade berries. The animals now also learned that Snowball had never — as many of them had believed hitherto — received the order of "Animal Hero, First Class." This was merely a legend which had been spread some time after the Battle of the Cowshed by Snowball himself. So far from being decorated, he had been censured for showing cowardice in the battle. Once again some of the animals heard this with a certain bewilderment, but Squealer was soon able to convince them that their memories had been at fault.

In the autumn, by a tremendous, exhausting effort — for the harvest had to be gathered at almost the same time — the windmill was finished. The machinery had still to be installed, and Whymper was negotiating the purchase

censure [ˈsɛnʃə] **v** 責備；譴責
bewilderment [bɪˈwɪldəmənt] **n** 困惑，迷亂
negotiate [nɪˈgoʃɪˌet] **v** 談判，協商，洽談

of it, but the structure was completed. In the teeth of every difficulty, in spite of inexperience, of primitive implements, of bad luck and of Snowball's treachery, the work had been finished punctually to the very day! Tired out but proud, the animals walked round and round their masterpiece, which appeared even more beautiful in their eyes than when it had been built the first time. Moreover, the walls were twice as thick as before. Nothing short of explosives would lay them low this time! And when they thought of how they had laboured, what discouragements they had overcome, and the enormous difference that would be made in their lives when the sails were turning and the dynamos running — when they thought of all this, their tiredness forsook them and they gambolled round and round the windmill, uttering cries of triumph. Napoleon himself, attended by his dogs and his cockerel, came down to inspect the completed work; he personally congratulated the animals on their achievement, and announced that the mill would be named Napoleon Mill.

Two days later the animals were called together for a special meeting in the barn. They were struck dumb with surprise when Napoleon announced that he had sold the pile

dumb [dʌm] *adj* （因吃驚等）說不出話的

of timber to Frederick. Tomorrow Frederick's wagons would arrive and begin carting it away. Throughout the whole period of his seeming friendship with Pilkington, Napoleon had really been in secret agreement with Frederick.

All relations with Foxwood had been broken off; insulting messages had been sent to Pilkington. The pigeons had been told to avoid Pinchfield Farm and to alter their slogan from "Death to Frederick" to "Death to Pilkington." At the same time Napoleon assured the animals that the stories of an impending attack on Animal Farm were completely untrue, and that the tales about Frederick's cruelty to his own animals had been greatly exaggerated. All these rumours had probably originated with Snowball and his agents. It now appeared that Snowball was not, after all, hiding on Pinchfield Farm, and in fact had never been there in his life: he was living — in considerable luxury, so it was said — at Foxwood, and had in reality been a pensioner of Pilkington for years past.

The pigs were in ecstasies over Napoleon's cunning. By seeming to be friendly with Pilkington he had forced

wagon [ˈwægən] *n* （四輪）運貨馬車
impending [ɪmˈpɛndɪŋ] *adj* 即將發生的；逼近的
ecstasy [ˈɛkstəsɪ] *n* 狂喜；出神；入迷

Animal Farm

Frederick to raise his price by twelve pounds. But the superior quality of Napoleon's mind, said Squealer, was shown in the fact that he trusted nobody, not even Frederick. Frederick had wanted to pay for the timber with something called a cheque, which, it seemed, was a piece of paper with a promise to pay written upon it. But Napoleon was too clever for him. He had demanded payment in real five-pound notes, which were to be handed over before the timber was removed. Already Frederick had paid up; and the sum he had paid was just enough to buy the machinery for the windmill.

Meanwhile the timber was being carted away at high speed. When it was all gone, another special meeting was held in the barn for the animals to inspect Frederick's bank-notes. Smiling beatifically, and wearing both his decorations, Napoleon reposed on a bed of straw on the platform, with the money at his side, neatly piled on a china dish from the farmhouse kitchen. The animals filed slowly past, and each gazed his fill. And Boxer put out his nose to sniff at the bank-notes, and the flimsy white things stirred and rustled in his breath.

cheque [ˈtʃɛk] *n* 支票（= check）
flimsy [ˈflɪmzɪ] *adj* 輕薄的

Three days later there was a terrible hullabaloo. Whymper, his face deadly pale, came racing up the path on his bicycle, flung it down in the yard and rushed straight into the farmhouse. The next moment a choking roar of rage sounded from Napoleon's apartments. The news of what had happened sped round the farm like wildfire. The banknotes were forgeries! Frederick had got the timber for nothing!

Napoleon called the animals together immediately and in a terrible voice pronounced the death sentence upon Frederick. When captured, he said, Frederick should be boiled alive. At the same time he warned them that after this treacherous deed the worst was to be expected. Frederick and his men might make their long-expected attack at any moment. Sentinels were placed at all the approaches to the farm. In addition, four pigeons were sent to Foxwood with a conciliatory message, which it was hoped might re-establish good relations with Pilkington.

The very next morning the attack came. The animals were at breakfast when the look-outs came racing in with

hullabaloo [ˌhʌləbəˈlu] *n* 喧囂；騷擾；吵鬧
forgery [ˈfɔrdʒərɪ] *n* 偽造物，贗品
treacherous [ˈtrɛtʃərəs] *adj* 背叛的；不忠的；奸詐的
conciliatory [kənˈsɪlɪəˌtorɪ] *adj* 安撫的；調和的

the news that Frederick and his followers had already come through the five-barred gate. Boldly enough the animals sallied forth to meet them, but this time they did not have the easy victory that they had had in the Battle of the Cowshed. There were fifteen men, with half a dozen guns between them, and they opened fire as soon as they got within fifty yards. The animals could not face the terrible explosions and the stinging pellets, and in spite of the efforts of Napoleon and Boxer to rally them, they were soon driven back. A number of them were already wounded. They took refuge in the farm buildings and peeped cautiously out from chinks and knot-holes. The whole of the big pasture, including the windmill, was in the hands of the enemy. For the moment even Napoleon seemed at a loss. He paced up and down without a word, his tail rigid and twitching. Wistful glances were sent in the direction of Foxwood. If Pilkington and his men would help them, the day might yet be won. But at this moment the four pigeons, who had been sent out on the day before, returned, one of them

sallied ['sæli] **v** 出擊；突圍
refuge ['rɛfjudʒ] **n** 躲避；避難；庇護
rigid ['rɪdʒɪd] **adj** 僵硬的；死板的
wistful ['wɪstfəl] **adj** 渴望的；嚮往的

bearing a scrap of paper from Pilkington. On it was pencilled the words: "Serves you right."

Meanwhile Frederick and his men had halted about the windmill. The animals watched them, and a murmur of dismay went round. Two of the men had produced a crowbar and a sledge hammer. They were going to knock the windmill down.

"Impossible!" cried Napoleon. "We have built the walls far too thick for that. They could not knock it down in a week. Courage, comrades!"

But Benjamin was watching the movements of the men intently. The two with the hammer and the crowbar were drilling a hole near the base of the windmill. Slowly, and with an air almost of amusement, Benjamin nodded his long muzzle.

"I thought so," he said. "Do you not see what they are doing? In another moment they are going to pack blasting powder into that hole."

Terrified, the animals waited. It was impossible now to venture out of the shelter of the buildings. After a few minutes the men were seen to be running in all directions.

intently [ɪnˈtɛntlɪ] *adv* 專心地，專注地
venture [ˈvɛntʃɚ] *v* 冒險；大膽行事

Then there was a deafening roar. The pigeons swirled into the air, and all the animals, except Napoleon, flung themselves flat on their bellies and hid their faces. When they got up again, a huge cloud of black smoke was hanging where the windmill had been. Slowly the breeze drifted it away. The windmill had ceased to exist!

At this sight the animals' courage returned to them. The fear and despair they had felt a moment earlier were drowned in their rage against this vile, contemptible act. A mighty cry for vengeance went up, and without waiting for further orders they charged forth in a body and made straight for the enemy. This time they did not heed the cruel pellets that swept over them like hail. It was a savage, bitter battle. The men fired again and again, and, when the animals got to close quarters, lashed out with their sticks and their heavy boots. A cow, three sheep, and two geese were killed, and nearly everyone was wounded. Even Napoleon, who was directing operations from the rear, had the tip of his tail chipped by a pellet. But the men did not go unscathed

vile [vaɪl] *adj* 卑鄙的，可恥的
hail [hel] *n* 冰雹
chip [tʃɪp] *v* 在……上造成缺口
unscathed [ʌnˈskeðd] *adj* 未受傷的；未受損失的

either. Three of them had their heads broken by blows from Boxer's hoofs; another was gored in the belly by a cow's horn; another had his trousers nearly torn off by Jessie and Bluebell. And when the nine dogs of Napoleon's own bodyguard, whom he had instructed to make a detour under cover of the hedge, suddenly appeared on the men's flank, baying ferociously, panic overtook them. They saw that they were in danger of being surrounded. Frederick shouted to his men to get out while the going was good, and the next moment the cowardly enemy was running for dear life. The animals chased them right down to the bottom of the field, and got in some last kicks at them as they forced their way through the thorn hedge.

They had won, but they were weary and bleeding. Slowly they began to limp back towards the farm. The sight of their dead comrades stretched upon the grass moved some of them to tears. And for a little while they halted in sorrowful silence at the place where the windmill had once stood. Yes, it was gone; almost the last trace of their labour was gone! Even the foundations were partially destroyed. And in rebuilding it they could not this time, as

ferociously [fəˈroʃəslɪ] *adv* 兇猛地
weary [ˈwɪrɪ] *adj* 疲倦的；厭倦的

before, make use of the fallen stones. This time the stones had vanished too. The force of the explosion had flung them to distances of hundreds of yards. It was as though the windmill had never been.

As they approached the farm Squealer, who had unaccountably been absent during the fighting, came skipping towards them, whisking his tail and beaming with satisfaction. And the animals heard, from the direction of the farm buildings, the solemn booming of a gun.

"What is that gun firing for?" said Boxer.

"To celebrate our victory!" cried Squealer.

"What victory?" said Boxer. His knees were bleeding, he had lost a shoe and split his hoof, and a dozen pellets had lodged themselves in his hind leg.

"What victory, comrade? Have we not driven the enemy off our soil — the sacred soil of Animal Farm?"

"But they have destroyed the windmill. And we had worked on it for two years!"

"What matter? We will build another windmill. We will build six windmills if we feel like it. You do not appreciate,

unaccountably [ˌʌnəˈkaʊntəblɪ] _adv_　莫名其妙：不可解釋地
sacred [ˈsekrɪd] _adj_　不可侵犯的：莊嚴的

comrade, the mighty thing that we have done. The enemy was in occupation of this very ground that we stand upon. And now — thanks to the leadership of Comrade Napoleon — we have won every inch of it back again!"

"Then we have won back what we had before," said Boxer.

"That is our victory," said Squealer.

They limped into the yard. The pellets under the skin of Boxer's leg smarted painfully. He saw ahead of him the heavy labour of rebuilding the windmill from the foundations, and already in imagination he braced himself for the task. But for the first time it occurred to him that he was eleven years old and that perhaps his great muscles were not quite what they had once been.

But when the animals saw the green flag flying, and heard the gun firing again — seven times it was fired in all — and heard the speech that Napoleon made, congratulating them on their conduct, it did seem to them after all that they had won a great victory. The animals slain in the battle were given a solemn funeral. Boxer and Clover pulled the wagon which served as a hearse, and

mighty ['maɪtɪ] *adj* 偉大的；強而有力的
slain [slen] *v* 殺死，殺害（**slay** 的動詞過去分詞）
hearse [hearse] *n* 靈車

Napoleon himself walked at the head of the procession. Two whole days were given over to celebrations. There were songs, speeches, and more firing of the gun, and a special gift of an apple was bestowed on every animal, with two ounces of corn for each bird and three biscuits for each dog. It was announced that the battle would be called the Battle of the Windmill, and that Napoleon had created a new decoration, the Order of the Green Banner, which he had conferred upon himself. In the general rejoicings the unfortunate affair of the banknotes was forgotten.

It was a few days later than this that the pigs came upon a case of whisky in the cellars of the farmhouse. It had been overlooked at the time when the house was first occupied. That night there came from the farmhouse the sound of loud singing, in which, to everyone's surprise, the strains of *Beasts of England* were mixed up. At about half past nine Napoleon, wearing an old bowler hat of Mr. Jones's, was distinctly seen to emerge from the back door, gallop rapidly round the yard, and disappear indoors again. But in the morning a deep silence hung over the farmhouse. Not a pig appeared to be stirring. It was nearly nine o'clock when Squealer made his appearance, walking

distinctly [dɪˈstɪŋktlɪ] *adv* 清晰地；無疑地

slowly and dejectedly, his eyes dull, his tail hanging limply behind him, and with every appearance of being seriously ill. He called the animals together and told them that he had a terrible piece of news to impart. Comrade Napoleon was dying!

A cry of lamentation went up. Straw was laid down outside the doors of the farmhouse, and the animals walked on tiptoe. With tears in their eyes they asked one another what they should do if their Leader were taken away from them. A rumour went round that Snowball had after all contrived to introduce poison into Napoleon's food. At eleven o'clock Squealer came out to make another announcement. As his last act upon earth, Comrade Napoleon had pronounced a solemn decree: the drinking of alcohol was to be punished by death.

By the evening, however, Napoleon appeared to be somewhat better, and the following morning Squealer was able to tell them that he was well on the way to recovery. By the evening of that day Napoleon was back at work,

dejectedly [dɪˈdʒɛktɪdlɪ] *adv* 沮喪地，灰心地
impart [ɪmˈpɑrt] *v* 告知；透露
lamentation [ˌlæmənˈteʃən] *n* 悲歎，哀悼；慟哭
contrive [kənˈtraɪv] *v* 策劃；圖謀

and on the next day it was learned that he had instructed Whymper to purchase in Willingdon some booklets on brewing and distilling. A week later Napoleon gave orders that the small paddock beyond the orchard, which it had previously been intended to set aside as a grazing-ground for animals who were past work, was to be ploughed up. It was given out that the pasture was exhausted and needed re-seeding; but it soon became known that Napoleon intended to sow it with barley.

About this time there occurred a strange incident which hardly anyone was able to understand. One night at about twelve o'clock there was a loud crash in the yard, and the animals rushed out of their stalls. It was a moonlit night. At the foot of the end wall of the big barn, where the Seven Commandments were written, there lay a ladder broken in two pieces. Squealer, temporarily stunned, was sprawling beside it, and near at hand there lay a lantern, a paint-brush, and an overturned pot of white paint. The dogs immediately made a ring round Squealer, and escorted him

booklet ['bʊklɪt] *n* 小冊子
sow [saʊ] *v* 播種於（土地等）（**+with**）
sprawl [sprɔl] *v* 伸開四肢躺（或坐）
escort ['ɛskɔrt] *v* 護衛，護送

back to the farmhouse as soon as he was able to walk. None of the animals could form any idea as to what this meant, except old Benjamin, who nodded his muzzle with a knowing air, and seemed to understand, but would say nothing.

But a few days later Muriel, reading over the Seven Commandments to herself, noticed that there was yet another of them which the animals had remembered wrong. They had thought the Fifth Commandment was "No animal shall drink alcohol," but there were two words that they had forgotten. Actually the Commandment read: "No animal shall drink alcohol *to excess*."

excess [excess] v 過量

09 /

Boxer's split hoof was a long time in healing. They had started the rebuilding of the windmill the day after the victory celebrations were ended. Boxer refused to take even a day off work, and made it a point of honour not to let it be seen that he was in pain. In the evenings he would admit privately to Clover that the hoof troubled him a great deal. Clover treated the hoof with poultices of herbs which she prepared by chewing them, and both she and Benjamin urged Boxer to work less hard. "A horse's lungs do not last for ever," she said to him. But Boxer would not listen. He had, he said, only one real ambition left — to see the windmill well under way before he reached the age for retirement.

At the beginning, when the laws of Animal Farm were first formulated, the retiring age had been fixed for horses and pigs at twelve, for cows at fourteen, for dogs at nine,

poultices [ˌʌnəˈkauntəbli] *n* 藥膏

for sheep at seven, and for hens and geese at five. Liberal old-age pensions had been agreed upon. As yet no animal had actually retired on pension, but of late the subject had been discussed more and more. Now that the small field beyond the orchard had been set aside for barley, it was rumoured that a corner of the large pasture was to be fenced off and turned into a grazing-ground for superannuated animals. For a horse, it was said, the pension would be five pounds of corn a day and, in winter, fifteen pounds of hay, with a carrot or possibly an apple on public holidays. Boxer's twelfth birthday was due in the late summer of the following year.

Meanwhile life was hard. The winter was as cold as the last one had been, and food was even shorter. Once again all rations were reduced, except those of the pigs and the dogs. A too rigid equality in rations, Squealer explained, would have been contrary to the principles of Animalism. In any case he had no difficulty in proving to the other animals that they were *not* in reality short of

liberal [ˈlɪbərəl] *adj* 慷慨的，大方的
pension [ˈpɑnsɪˌɑn] *n* 退休金；養老金
of late [ɑv] [let] 最近，近來
superannuated [ˈsupɚˈænjʊˌetɪd] *adj* 領取退休金而退休的

food, whatever the appearances might be. For the time being, certainly, it had been found necessary to make a readjustment of rations (Squealer always spoke of it as a "readjustment," never as a "reduction"), but in comparison with the days of Jones, the improvement was enormous. Reading out the figures in a shrill, rapid voice, he proved to them in detail that they had more oats, more hay, more turnips than they had had in Jones's day, that they worked shorter hours, that their drinking water was of better quality, that they lived longer, that a larger proportion of their young ones survived infancy, and that they had more straw in their stalls and suffered less from fleas. The animals believed every word of it. Truth to tell, Jones and all he stood for had almost faded out of their memories. They knew that life nowadays was harsh and bare, that they were often hungry and often cold, and that they were usually working when they were not asleep. But doubtless it had been worse in the old days. They were glad to believe so. Besides, in those days they had been slaves and now they were free, and that made all the difference, as

readjustment [ˌriəˈdʒʌstmənt] *n* 重新調整
enormous [ɪˈnɔrməs] *adj* 巨大的，龐大的
doubtless [ˈdaʊtlɪs] *adv* 無疑地，必定地

Squealer did not fail to point out.

There were many more mouths to feed now. In the autumn the four sows had all littered about simultaneously, producing thirty-one young pigs between them. The young pigs were piebald, and as Napoleon was the only boar on the farm, it was possible to guess at their parentage. It was announced that later, when bricks and timber had been purchased, a schoolroom would be built in the farmhouse garden. For the time being, the young pigs were given their instruction by Napoleon himself in the farmhouse kitchen. They took their exercise in the garden, and were discouraged from playing with the other young animals. About this time, too, it was laid down as a rule that when a pig and any other animal met on the path, the other animal must stand aside: and also that all pigs, of whatever degree, were to have the privilege of wearing green ribbons on their tails on Sundays.

The farm had had a fairly successful year, but was still short of money. There were the bricks, sand, and lime for the schoolroom to be purchased, and it would also be necessary to begin saving up again for the machinery for

piebald [ˈpaɪ‚bɔld] *adj* 斑紋的；雜色的
parentage [ˈpɛrəntɪdʒ] *n* 父母的身分

the windmill. Then there were lamp oil and candles for the house, sugar for Napoleon's own table (he forbade this to the other pigs, on the ground that it made them fat), and all the usual replacements such as tools, nails, string, coal, wire, scrap-iron, and dog biscuits. A stump of hay and part of the potato crop were sold off, and the contract for eggs was increased to six hundred a week, so that that year the hens barely hatched enough chicks to keep their numbers at the same level. Rations, reduced in December, were reduced again in February, and lanterns in the stalls were forbidden to save Oil. But the pigs seemed comfortable enough, and in fact were putting on weight if anything. One afternoon in late February a warm, rich, appetising scent, such as the animals had never smelt before, wafted itself across the yard from the little brew-house, which had been disused in Jones's time, and which stood beyond the kitchen. Someone said it was the smell of cooking barley. The animals sniffed the air hungrily and wondered whether a warm mash was being prepared for their supper. But no warm mash appeared,

forbade [fə-'bæd] _v_ 禁止；不許
appetising ['æpɪtaɪzɪŋ] _adj_ 引起食慾的
sniff [snɪf] _v_ 用力吸

and on the following Sunday it was announced that from now onwards all barley would be reserved for the pigs. The field beyond the orchard had already been sown with barley. And the news soon leaked out that every pig was now receiving a ration of a pint of beer daily, with half a gallon for Napoleon himself, which was always served to him in the Crown Derby soup tureen.

But if there were hardships to be borne, they were partly offset by the fact that life nowadays had a greater dignity than it had had before. There were more songs, more speeches, more processions. Napoleon had commanded that once a week there should be held something called a Spontaneous Demonstration, the object of which was to celebrate the struggles and triumphs of Animal Farm. At the appointed time the animals would leave their work and march round the precincts of the farm in military formation, with the pigs leading, then the horses, then the cows, then the sheep, and then the poultry. The dogs flanked the procession and at the head of all marched

tureen [tjʊˈrin] *n* 焙盤，蓋碗
procession [prəˈsɛʃən] *n* 遊行活動
spontaneous [spɑnˈtenɪəs] *adj* 自發的
flank [flæŋk] *v* 位於……的兩側

Napoleon's black cockerel. Boxer and Clover always carried between them a green banner marked with the hoof and the horn and the caption, "Long live Comrade Napoleon! " Afterwards there were recitations of poems composed in Napoleon's honour, and a speech by Squealer giving particulars of the latest increases in the production of foodstuffs, and on occasion a shot was fired from the gun. The sheep were the greatest devotees of the Spontaneous Demonstration, and if anyone complained (as a few animals sometimes did, when no pigs or dogs were near) that they wasted time and meant a lot of standing about in the cold, the sheep were sure to silence him with a tremendous bleating of "Four legs good, two legs bad!" But by and large the animals enjoyed these celebrations. They found it comforting to be reminded that, after all, they were truly their own masters and that the work they did was for their own benefit. So that, what with the songs, the processions, Squealer's lists of figures, the thunder of the gun, the crowing of the cockerel, and the fluttering of the flag, they were able to forget that their bellies were empty, at least part of the time.

caption [ˈkæpʃən] *n* 標語
recitation [ˌrɛsəˈteʃən] *n* 當眾吟誦

In April, Animal Farm was proclaimed a Republic, and it became necessary to elect a President. There was only one candidate, Napoleon, who was elected unanimously. On the same day it was given out that fresh documents had been discovered which revealed further details about Snowball's complicity with Jones. It now appeared that Snowball had not, as the animals had previously imagined, merely attempted to lose the Battle of the Cowshed by means of a stratagem, but had been openly fighting on Jones's side. In fact, it was he who had actually been the leader of the human forces, and had charged into battle with the words "Long live Humanity!" on his lips. The wounds on Snowball's back, which a few of the animals still remembered to have seen, had been inflicted by Napoleon's teeth.

In the middle of the summer Moses the raven suddenly reappeared on the farm, after an absence of several years. He was quite unchanged, still did no work,

proclaim [prə'klem] *v* 宣告；公布；聲明
complicity [kəm'plɪsətɪ] *n* 共謀；串通關係
stratagem ['strætədʒəm] *n* 策略；計謀；詭計
inflict [ɪn'flɪkt] *v* 使遭受（傷害等）

and talked in the same strain as ever about Sugarcandy Mountain. He would perch on a stump, flap his black wings, and talk by the hour to anyone who would listen. "Up there, comrades," he would say solemnly, pointing to the sky with his large beak — "up there, just on the other side of that dark cloud that you can see — there it lies, Sugarcandy Mountain, that happy country where we poor animals shall rest for ever from our labours!" He even claimed to have been there on one of his higher flights, and to have seen the everlasting fields of clover and the linseed cake and lump sugar growing on the hedges. Many of the animals believed him. Their lives now, they reasoned, were hungry and laborious; was it not right and just that a better world should exist somewhere else? A thing that was difficult to determine was the attitude of the pigs towards Moses. They all declared contemptuously that his stories about Sugarcandy Mountain were lies, and yet they allowed him to remain on the farm, not working, with an allowance of a gill of beer a day.

After his hoof had healed up, Boxer worked harder

strain [stren] **v** 盡力
beak [bik] **n** 鳥嘴
contemptuously [kənˈtɛmptʃʊəslɪ] **adv** 輕蔑地

than ever. Indeed, all the animals worked like slaves that year. Apart from the regular work of the farm, and the rebuilding of the windmill, there was the schoolhouse for the young pigs, which was started in March. Sometimes the long hours on insufficient food were hard to bear, but Boxer never faltered. In nothing that he said or did was there any sign that his strength was not what it had been. It was only his appearance that was a little altered; his hide was less shiny than it had used to be, and his great haunches seemed to have shrunken. The others said, "Boxer will pick up when the spring grass comes on"; but the spring came and Boxer grew no fatter. Sometimes on the slope leading to the top of the quarry, when he braced his muscles against the weight of some vast boulder, it seemed that nothing kept him on his feet except the will to continue. At such times his lips were seen to form the words, "I will work harder"; he had no voice left. Once again Clover and Benjamin warned him to take care of his health, but Boxer paid no attention. His twelfth birthday was approaching. He did not care what happened so long as a good store of

falter [ˈfɔltɚ] **v** 動搖，猶豫；畏縮

stone was accumulated before he went on pension.

Late one evening in the summer, a sudden rumour ran round the farm that something had happened to Boxer. He had gone out alone to drag a load of stone down to the windmill. And sure enough, the rumour was true. A few minutes later two pigeons came racing in with the news: "Boxer has fallen! He is lying on his side and can't get up!"

About half the animals on the farm rushed out to the knoll where the windmill stood. There lay Boxer, between the shafts of the cart, his neck stretched out, unable even to raise his head. His eyes were glazed, his sides matted with sweat. A thin stream of blood had trickled out of his mouth. Clover dropped to her knees at his side.

"Boxer!" she cried, "how are you?"

"It is my lung," said Boxer in a weak voice. "It does not matter. I think you will be able to finish the windmill without me. There is a pretty good store of stone accumulated. I had only another month to go in any case. To tell you the truth, I had been looking forward to my retirement. And perhaps, as Benjamin is growing old too, they will let him retire at the same time and be a companion to me."

accumulate [əˈkjumjəˌlet] **v** 累積，積聚

"We must get help at once," said Clover. "Run, somebody, and tell Squealer what has happened."

All the other animals immediately raced back to the farmhouse to give Squealer the news. Only Clover remained, and Benjamin, who lay down at Boxer's side, and, without speaking, kept the flies off him with his long tail. After about a quarter of an hour Squealer appeared, full of sympathy and concern. He said that Comrade Napoleon had learned with the very deepest distress of this misfortune to one of the most loyal workers on the farm, and was already making arrangements to send Boxer to be treated in the hospital at Willingdon. The animals felt a little uneasy at this. Except for Mollie and Snowball, no other animal had ever left the farm, and they did not like to think of their sick comrade in the hands of human beings. However, Squealer easily convinced them that the veterinary surgeon in Willingdon could treat Boxer's case more satisfactorily than could be done on the farm. And about half an hour later, when Boxer had somewhat recovered, he was with difficulty got on to his feet, and managed to limp back to his stall, where Clover and

veterinary [ˈvɛtərəˌnɛrɪ] *adj* 獸醫的
satisfactorily [ˌsætɪsˈfæktərɪlɪ] *adv* 令人滿意地

135

Benjamin had prepared a good bed of straw for him.

For the next two days Boxer remained in his stall. The pigs had sent out a large bottle of pink medicine which they had found in the medicine chest in the bathroom, and Clover administered it to Boxer twice a day after meals. In the evenings she lay in his stall and talked to him, while Benjamin kept the flies off him. Boxer professed not to be sorry for what had happened. If he made a good recovery, he might expect to live another three years, and he looked forward to the peaceful days that he would spend in the corner of the big pasture. It would be the first time that he had had leisure to study and improve his mind. He intended, he said, to devote the rest of his life to learning the remaining twenty-two letters of the alphabet.

However, Benjamin and Clover could only be with Boxer after working hours, and it was in the middle of the day when the van came to take him away. The animals were all at work weeding turnips under the supervision of a pig, when they were astonished to see Benjamin come galloping from the direction of the farm buildings, braying at the top of his voice. It was the first time that

alphabet [ˈælfəˌbɛt] *n* 字母

they had ever seen Benjamin excited — indeed, it was the first time that anyone had ever seen him gallop. "Quick, quick!" he shouted. "Come at once! They're taking Boxer away!" Without waiting for orders from the pig, the animals broke off work and raced back to the farm buildings. Sure enough, there in the yard was a large closed van, drawn by two horses, with lettering on its side and a sly-looking man in a low-crowned bowler hat sitting on the driver's seat. And Boxer's stall was empty.

The animals crowded round the van. "Good-bye, Boxer!" they chorused, "good-bye!"

"Fools! Fools!" shouted Benjamin, prancing round them and stamping the earth with his small hoofs. "Fools! Do you not see what is written on the side of that van?"

That gave the animals pause, and there was a hush. Muriel began to spell out the words. But Benjamin pushed her aside and in the midst of a deadly silence he read:

"'Alfred Simmonds, Horse Slaughterer and Glue Boiler, Willingdon. Dealer in Hides and Bone-Meal. Kennels Supplied.' Do you not understand what that means? They are taking Boxer to the knacker's!"

chorus [ˈkorəs] **v** 異口同聲
knacker [ˈnækə] **n** 屠宰場

A cry of horror burst from all the animals. At this
moment the man on the box whipped up his horses and
the van moved out of the yard at a smart trot. All the
animals followed, crying out at the tops of their voices.
Clover forced her way to the front. The van began to
gather speed. Clover tried to stir her stout limbs to a
gallop, and achieved a canter. "Boxer!" she cried. "Boxer!
Boxer! Boxer!" And just at this moment, as though he had
heard the uproar outside, Boxer's face, with the white
stripe down his nose, appeared at the small window at the
back of the van.

"Boxer!" cried Clover in a terrible voice. "Boxer! Get
out! Get out quickly! They're taking you to your death!"

All the animals took up the cry of "Get out, Boxer,
get out!" But the van was already gathering speed and
drawing away from them. It was uncertain whether Boxer
had understood what Clover had said. But a moment later
his face disappeared from the window and there was the
sound of a tremendous drumming of hoofs inside the
van. He was trying to kick his way out. The time had been
when a few kicks from Boxer's hoofs would have smashed

canter ['kæntə] *n* 慢跑

the van to matchwood. But alas! his strength had left him; and in a few moments the sound of drumming hoofs grew fainter and died away. In desperation the animals began appealing to the two horses which drew the van to stop. "Comrades, comrades!" they shouted. "Don't take your own brother to his death! " But the stupid brutes, too ignorant to realise what was happening, merely set back their ears and quickened their pace. Boxer's face did not reappear at the window. Too late, someone thought of racing ahead and shutting the five-barred gate; but in another moment the van was through it and rapidly disappearing down the road. Boxer was never seen again.

Three days later it was announced that he had died in the hospital at Willingdon, in spite of receiving every attention a horse could have. Squealer came to announce the news to the others. He had, he said, been present during Boxer's last hours.

"It was the most affecting sight I have ever seen!" said Squealer, lifting his trotter and wiping away a tear. "I

---

matchwood ['mætʃˌwʊd] *n* 碎木片

alas [ə'læs] *int* （表示悲痛、憐憫、遺憾、關切等）哎呀，唉

desperation [ˌdɛspə'reʃən] *n* 不顧一切，拼命

ignorant ['ɪgnərənt] *adj* 無知的

was at his bedside at the very last. And at the end, almost too weak to speak, he whispered in my ear that his sole sorrow was to have passed on before the windmill was finished. 'Forward, comrades!' he whispered. 'Forward in the name of the Rebellion. Long live Animal Farm! Long live Comrade Napoleon! Napoleon is always right.' Those were his very last words, comrades."

Here Squealer's demeanour suddenly changed. He fell silent for a moment, and his little eyes darted suspicious glances from side to side before he proceeded.

It had come to his knowledge, he said, that a foolish and wicked rumour had been circulated at the time of Boxer's removal. Some of the animals had noticed that the van which took Boxer away was marked "Horse Slaughterer," and had actually jumped to the conclusion that Boxer was being sent to the knacker's. It was almost unbelievable, said Squealer, that any animal could be so stupid. Surely, he cried indignantly, whisking his tail and skipping from side to side, surely they knew their beloved Leader, Comrade Napoleon, better than that? But the explanation was really very simple. The van had previously been the property of the knacker,

demeanour [dɪˈminə] **n** 行為，舉止
removal [rɪˈmuvl] **n** 移動

and had been bought by the veterinary surgeon, who had not yet painted the old name out. That was how the mistake had arisen.

The animals were enormously relieved to hear this. And when Squealer went on to give further graphic details of Boxer's death-bed, the admirable care he had received, and the expensive medicines for which Napoleon had paid without a thought as to the cost, their last doubts disappeared and the sorrow that they felt for their comrade's death was tempered by the thought that at least he had died happy.

Napoleon himself appeared at the meeting on the following Sunday morning and pronounced a short oration in Boxer's honour. It had not been possible, he said, to bring back their lamented comrade's remains for interment on the farm, but he had ordered a large wreath to be made from the laurels in the farmhouse garden and sent down to be placed on Boxer's grave. And in a few days' time the pigs intended to hold a memorial banquet in Boxer's honour. Napoleon ended his speech with a

tempered [ˈtɛmpəd] *adj* 緩和的
oration [oˈreʃən] *n* 演說，演講
lamented [ləˈmɛntɪd] *adj* 被悼念的
interment [ɪnˈtɜːmənt] *n* 埋葬

reminder of Boxer's two favourite maxims, "I will work harder" and "Comrade Napoleon is always right" — maxims, he said, which every animal would do well to adopt as his own.

On the day appointed for the banquet, a grocer's van drove up from Willingdon and delivered a large wooden crate at the farmhouse. That night there was the sound of uproarious singing, which was followed by what sounded like a violent quarrel and ended at about eleven o'clock with a tremendous crash of glass. No one stirred in the farmhouse before noon on the following day, and the word went round that from somewhere or other the pigs had acquired the money to buy themselves another case of whisky.

banquet [ˈbæŋkwɪt] *n* 宴會，宴請
crate [kret] *n* 板條箱
uproarious [ʌpˈrorɪəs] *adj* 喧鬧的；騷動的

10 /

Years passed. The seasons came and went, the short animal lives fled by. A time came when there was no one who remembered the old days before the Rebellion, except Clover, Benjamin, Moses the raven, and a number of the pigs.

Muriel was dead; Bluebell, Jessie, and Pincher were dead. Jones too was dead — he had died in an inebriates' home in another part of the country. Snowball was forgotten. Boxer was forgotten, except by the few who had known him. Clover was an old stout mare now, stiff in the joints and with a tendency to rheumy eyes. She was two years past the retiring age, but in fact no animal had ever actually retired. The talk of setting aside a corner of the pasture for superannuated animals had long since been dropped. Napoleon was now a mature boar of twenty-

inebriate [ɪnˈibrɪɪt] *n* 酒徒
joint [dʒɔɪnt] *n* 關節
rheumy [ˈrumɪ] *adj* 發炎產生分泌物的

four stone. Squealer was so fat that he could with difficulty see out of his eyes. Only old Benjamin was much the same as ever, except for being a little greyer about the muzzle, and, since Boxer's death, more morose and taciturn than ever.

There were many more creatures on the farm now, though the increase was not so great as had been expected in earlier years. Many animals had been born to whom the Rebellion was only a dim tradition, passed on by word of mouth, and others had been bought who had never heard mention of such a thing before their arrival. The farm possessed three horses now besides Clover. They were fine upstanding beasts, willing workers and good comrades, but very stupid. None of them proved able to learn the alphabet beyond the letter B. They accepted everything that they were told about the Rebellion and the principles of Animalism, especially from Clover, for whom they had an almost filial respect; but it was doubtful whether they understood very much of it.

morose [mə'ros] *adj* 陰鬱的；孤僻的
taciturn ['tæsə,tɜ-n] *adj* 沉默寡言的
dim [dɪm] *adj* 模糊的；不清楚的
filial ['fɪljəl] *adj* 子女的；孝順的

The farm was more prosperous now, and better organised: it had even been enlarged by two fields which had been bought from Mr. Pilkington. The windmill had been successfully completed at last, and the farm possessed a threshing machine and a hay elevator of its own, and various new buildings had been added to it. Whymper had bought himself a dogcart. The windmill, however, had not after all been used for generating electrical power. It was used for milling corn, and brought in a handsome money profit. The animals were hard at work building yet another windmill; when that one was finished, so it was said, the dynamos would be installed. But the luxuries of which Snowball had once taught the animals to dream, the stalls with electric light and hot and cold water, and the three-day week, were no longer talked about. Napoleon had denounced such ideas as contrary to the spirit of Animalism. The truest happiness, he said, lay in working hard and living frugally.

Somehow it seemed as though the farm had grown richer without making the animals themselves any richer —

prosperous [ˈprɑspərəs] *adj* 繁榮的，昌盛的
denounce [dɪˈnaʊns] *v* 指責，譴責（+as）
frugally [ˈfruɡlɪ] *adv* 節約地；儉樸地

except, of course, for the pigs and the dogs. Perhaps this was partly because there were so many pigs and so many dogs. It was not that these creatures did not work, after their fashion. There was, as Squealer was never tired of explaining, endless work in the supervision and organisation of the farm. Much of this work was of a kind that the other animals were too ignorant to understand. For example, Squealer told them that the pigs had to expend enormous labours every day upon mysterious things called "files," "reports," "minutes," and "memoranda." These were large sheets of paper which had to be closely covered with writing, and as soon as they were so covered, they were burnt in the furnace. This was of the highest importance for the welfare of the farm, Squealer said. But still, neither pigs nor dogs produced any food by their own labour; and there were very many of them, and their appetites were always good.

As for the others, their life, so far as they knew, was as it had always been. They were generally hungry, they slept on straw, they drank from the pool, they laboured in the fields; in winter they were troubled by the cold, and in

memoranda [ˌmɛməˈrændə] *n* 備忘録，記録（**memorandum** 的名詞複數）

summer by the flies. Sometimes the older ones among them racked their dim memories and tried to determine whether in the early days of the Rebellion, when Jones's expulsion was still recent, things had been better or worse than now. They could not remember. There was nothing with which they could compare their present lives: they had nothing to go upon except Squealer's lists of figures, which invariably demonstrated that everything was getting better and better. The animals found the problem insoluble; in any case, they had little time for speculating on such things now. Only old Benjamin professed to remember every detail of his long life and to know that things never had been, nor ever could be much better or much worse — hunger, hardship, and disappointment being, so he said, the unalterable law of life.

And yet the animals never gave up hope. More, they never lost, even for an instant, their sense of honour and privilege in being members of Animal Farm. They were still the only farm in the whole county — in all England! — owned and operated by animals. Not one of them, not

invariably [ɪnˈvɛrɪəblɪ] *adv* 不變地，總是
insoluble [ɪnˈsɑljəbl] *adj* 不能解決的；難以解釋的
profess [prəˈfɛs] *v* 表示；聲稱

even the youngest, not even the newcomers who had been brought from farms ten or twenty miles away, ever ceased to marvel at that. And when they heard the gun booming and saw the green flag fluttering at the masthead, their hearts swelled with imperishable pride, and the talk turned always towards the old heroic days, the expulsion of Jones, the writing of the Seven Commandments, the great battles in which the human invaders had been defeated. None of the old dreams had been abandoned. The Republic of the Animals which Major had foretold, when the green fields of England should be untrodden by human feet, was still believed in. Some day it was coming: it might not be soon, it might not be with in the lifetime of any animal now living, but still it was coming. Even the tune of *Beasts of England* was perhaps hummed secretly here and there: at any rate, it was a fact that every animal on the farm knew it, though no one would have dared to sing it aloud. It might be that their lives were hard and that not all of their hopes had been fulfilled; but they were conscious that they were not as other animals. If they went hungry, it was not from feeding tyrannical

imperishable [ɪmˈpɛrɪʃəbl̩] *adj* 不滅的；不朽的
hum [hʌm] *v* 哼曲子

human beings; if they worked hard, at least they worked for themselves. No creature among them went upon two legs. No creature called any other creature "Master." All animals were equal.

One day in early summer Squealer ordered the sheep to follow him, and led them out to a piece of waste ground at the other end of the farm, which had become overgrown with birch saplings. The sheep spent the whole day there browsing at the leaves under Squealer's supervision. In the evening he returned to the farmhouse himself, but, as it was warm weather, told the sheep to stay where they were. It ended by their remaining there for a whole week, during which time the other animals saw nothing of them. Squealer was with them for the greater part of every day. He was, he said, teaching them to sing a new song, for which privacy was needed.

It was just after the sheep had returned, on a pleasant evening when the animals had finished work and were making their way back to the farm buildings, that the terrified neighing of a horse sounded from the yard. Startled, the animals stopped in their tracks. It was

sapling [ˈsæplɪŋ] **n** 幼樹，樹苗
startled [ˈstɑrtld] **adj** 受驚嚇的

Clover's voice. She neighed again, and all the animals broke into a gallop and rushed into the yard. Then they saw what Clover had seen.

It was a pig walking on his hind legs.

Yes, it was Squealer. A little awkwardly, as though not quite used to supporting his considerable bulk in that position, but with perfect balance, he was strolling across the yard. And a moment later, out from the door of the farmhouse came a long file of pigs, all walking on their hind legs. Some did it better than others, one or two were even a trifle unsteady and looked as though they would have liked the support of a stick, but every one of them made his way right round the yard successfully. And finally there was a tremendous baying of dogs and a shrill crowing from the black cockerel, and out came Napoleon himself, majestically upright, casting haughty glances from side to side, and with his dogs gambolling round him.

He carried a whip in his trotter.

There was a deadly silence. Amazed, terrified,

neigh [ne] *v* （馬）嘶
stroll [strol] *v* 散步，漫步
trifle [ˈtraɪfl] *n* 少許；些許
haughty [ˈhɒtɪ] *adj* 高傲的，傲慢的

huddling together, the animals watched the long line of pigs march slowly round the yard. It was as though the world had turned upside-down. Then there came a moment when the first shock had worn off and when, in spite of everything — in spite of their terror of the dogs, and of the habit, developed through long years, of never complaining, never criticising, no matter what happened — they might have uttered some word of protest. But just at that moment, as though at a signal, all the sheep burst out into a tremendous bleating of —

"Four legs good, two legs *better*! Four legs good, two legs *better*! Four legs good, two legs *better*!"

It went on for five minutes without stopping. And by the time the sheep had quieted down, the chance to utter any protest had passed, for the pigs had marched back into the farmhouse.

Benjamin felt a nose nuzzling at his shoulder. He looked round. It was Clover. Her old eyes looked dimmer than ever. Without saying anything, she tugged gently at his mane and led him round to the end of the big barn, where the Seven Commandments were written. For a

huddle ['hʌdl] **v** 聚在一起
tug [tʌg] **v** 拉

minute or two they stood gazing at the tatted wall with its white lettering.

"My sight is failing," she said finally. "Even when I was young I could not have read what was written there. But it appears to me that that wall looks different. Are the Seven Commandments the same as they used to be, Benjamin?"

For once Benjamin consented to break his rule, and he read out to her what was written on the wall. There was nothing there now except a single Commandment. It ran:

ALL ANIMALS ARE EQUAL

BUT SOME ANIMALS ARE MORE EQUAL THAN OTHERS

After that it did not seem strange when next day the pigs who were supervising the work of the farm all carried whips in their trotters. It did not seem strange to learn that the pigs had bought themselves a wireless set, were arranging to install a telephone, and had taken out subscriptions to *John Bull*, *TitBits*, and the *Daily Mirror*. It did not seem strange when Napoleon was seen strolling in the farmhouse garden with a pipe in his mouth — no, not even when the pigs took Mr. Jones's clothes out of the wardrobes and put them on, Napoleon himself appearing in a black coat, ratcatcher breeches, and leather leggings, while his favourite sow appeared in the watered silk dress which Mrs. Jones had been used to wear on Sundays.

A week later, in the afternoon, a number of dogcarts drove up to the farm. A deputation of neighbouring farmers had been invited to make a tour of inspection. They were shown all over the farm, and expressed great admiration for everything they saw, especially the windmill. The animals were weeding the turnip field. They worked diligently, hardly raising their faces from the ground, and not knowing whether to be more frightened of the pigs or of the human visitors.

That evening loud laughter and bursts of singing came from the farmhouse. And suddenly, at the sound of the mingled voices, the animals were stricken with curiosity. What could be happening in there, now that for the first time animals and human beings were meeting on terms of equality? With one accord they began to creep as quietly as possible into the farmhouse garden.

At the gate they paused, half frightened to go on but Clover led the way in. They tiptoed up to the house, and such animals as were tall enough peered in at the dining-room window. There, round the long table, sat half a dozen farmers and half a dozen of the more eminent pigs,

deputation [ˌdɛpjəˈteʃən] *n* 考察團；代表團
eminent [ˈɛmənənt] *adj* （地位，學識等方面）出眾的，卓越的

Napoleon himself occupying the seat of honour at the head of the table. The pigs appeared completely at ease in their chairs The company had been enjoying a game of cards but had broken off for the moment, evidently in order to drink a toast. A large jug was circulating, and the mugs were being refilled with beer. No one noticed the wondering faces of the animals that gazed in at the window.

Mr. Pilkington, of Foxwood, had stood up, his mug in his hand. In a moment, he said, he would ask the present company to drink a toast. But before doing so, there were a few words that he felt it incumbent upon him to say.

It was a source of great satisfaction to him, he said — and, he was sure, to all others present — to feel that a long period of mistrust and misunderstanding had now come to an end. There had been a time — not that he, or any of the present company, had shared such sentiments — but there had been a time when the respected proprietors of Animal Farm had been regarded, he would not say with hostility, but perhaps with a certain measure of misgiving,

jug [dʒʌg] _n_ 水罐，甕，壺
incumbent [ɪnˈkʌmbənt] _adj_ 有責任的，義不容辭的
sentiment [ˈsɛntəmənt] _n_ 情緒；心情
proprietor [prəˈpraɪətə·] _n_ 所有人；業主，經營者

by their human neighbours. Unfortunate incidents had occurred, mistaken ideas had been current. It had been felt that the existence of a farm owned and operated by pigs was somehow abnormal and was liable to have an unsettling effect in the neighbourhood. Too many farmers had assumed, without due enquiry, that on such a farm a spirit of licence and indiscipline would prevail. They had been nervous about the effects upon their own animals, or even upon their human employees. But all such doubts were now dispelled. Today he and his friends had visited Animal Farm and inspected every inch of it with their own eyes, and what did they find? Not only the most up-to-date methods, but a discipline and an orderliness which should be an example to all farmers everywhere. He believed that he was right in saying that the lower animals on Animal Farm did more work and received less food than any animals in the county. Indeed, he and his fellow-visitors today had observed many features which they intended to introduce on their own farms immediately.

He would end his remarks, he said, by emphasising

.

enquiry [ɪnˈkwaɪrɪ] *n* 查證；詢問
prevail [prɪˈvel] *v* 盛行；普遍

once again the friendly feelings that subsisted, and ought to subsist, between Animal Farm and its neighbours. Between pigs and human beings there was not, and there need not be, any clash of interests whatever. Their struggles and their difficulties were one. Was not the labour problem the same everywhere? Here it became apparent that Mr. Pilkington was about to spring some carefully prepared witticism on the company, but for a moment he was too overcome by amusement to be able to utter it. After much choking, during which his various chins turned purple, he managed to get it out: "If you have your lower animals to contend with," he said, "we have our lower classes!" This *bon mot* set the table in a roar; and Mr. Pilkington once again congratulated the pigs on the low rations, the long working hours, and the general absence of pampering which he had observed on Animal Farm.

And now, he said finally, he would ask the company to rise to their feet and make certain that their glasses

subsist [səbˈsɪst] *v* 存在；繼續存在
witticism [ˈwɪtɪsɪzəm] *n* 妙語；名言
utter [ˈʌtə-] *v* 講出；表達
bon mot [bɒn] [ˈməʊ] 妙語

were full. "Gentlemen," concluded Mr. Pilkington, "gentlemen, I give you a toast: To the prosperity of Animal Farm!"

There was enthusiastic cheering and stamping of feet. Napoleon was so gratified that he left his place and came round the table to clink his mug against Mr. Pilkington's before emptying it. When the cheering had died down, Napoleon, who had remained on his feet, intimated that he too had a few words to say.

Like all of Napoleon's speeches, it was short and to the point. He too, he said, was happy that the period of misunderstanding was at an end. For a long time there had been rumours — circulated, he had reason to think, by some malignant enemy — that there was something subversive and even revolutionary in the outlook of himself and his colleagues. They had been credited with attempting to stir up rebellion among the animals on neighbouring farms. Nothing could be further from the truth! Their sole wish, now and in the past, was to live at peace and in normal business relations with their neighbours. This farm which

malignant [məˈlɪgnənt] *adj* 有惡意的，邪惡的
subversive [səbˈvɜ˞sɪv] *adj* 破壞性的
sole [sol] *adj* 唯一的；單獨的

he had the honour to control, he added, was a co-operative enterprise. The title-deeds, which were in his own possession, were owned by the pigs jointly.

He did not believe, he said, that any of the old suspicions still lingered, but certain changes had been made recently in the routine of the farm which should have the effect of promoting confidence stiff further. Hitherto the animals on the farm had had a rather foolish custom of addressing one another as "Comrade." This was to be suppressed. There had also been a very strange custom, whose origin was unknown, of marching every Sunday morning past a boar's skull which was nailed to a post in the garden. This, too, would be suppressed, and the skull had already been buried. His visitors might have observed, too, the green flag which flew from the masthead. If so, they would perhaps have noted that the white hoof and horn with which it had previously been marked had now been removed. It would be a plain green flag from now onwards.

He had only one criticism, he said, to make of Mr. Pilkington's excellent and neighbourly speech. Mr. Pilkington had referred throughout to "Animal Farm." He

suppressed [sə'prɛst] *adj* 抑制的

could not of course know — for he, Napoleon, was only now for the first time announcing it — that the name "Animal Farm" had been abolished. Henceforward the farm was to be known as "The Manor Farm" — which, he believed, was its correct and original name.

"Gentlemen," concluded Napoleon, "I will give you the same toast as before, but in a different form. Fill your glasses to the brim. Gentlemen, here is my toast: To the prosperity of The Manor Farm! "

There was the same hearty cheering as before, and the mugs were emptied to the dregs. But as the animals outside gazed at the scene, it seemed to them that some strange thing was happening. What was it that had altered in the faces of the pigs? Clover's old dim eyes flitted from one face to another. Some of them had five chins, some had four, some had three. But what was it that seemed to be melting and changing? Then, the applause having come to an end, the company took up their cards and continued the game that had been interrupted, and the animals crept silently away.

henceforward [ˈhɛnsˈfɔrwəd] *adv* 此後，今後
brim [brɪm] *n* （杯，碗等容器的）邊，緣
dregs [drɛgz] *n* 少量殘餘；少量

But they had not gone twenty yards when they stopped short. An uproar of voices was coming from the farmhouse. They rushed back and looked through the window again. Yes, a violent quarrel was in progress. There were shoutings, bangings on the table, sharp suspicious glances, furious denials. The source of the trouble appeared to be that Napoleon and Mr. Pilkington had each played an ace of spades simultaneously.

Twelve voices were shouting in anger, and they were all alike. No question, now, what had happened to the faces of the pigs. The creatures outside looked from pig to man, and from man to pig, and from pig to man again; but already it was impossible to say which was which.

furious [ˈfjʊərɪəs] *adj* 強烈的；狂怒的